Praise for *HALF BAD*

"Gripping."   —*Us Weekly*

"A bewitching new thriller."   —*The Wall Street Journal*

"This is an enthralling fantasy in the Harry Potter tradition, powered by Nathan's unique narrative voice."

—*Time* magazine (Best Books of 2014)

"Grit, loyalty and gentleness cast a spell more captivating than the warring witches and sinister sorcery of Sally Green's *Half Bad*."

—*Los Angeles Times*

"Green sets the stage for a rich mythology of characters to play with in her Half Bad trilogy . . . readers will want to revisit this world of witchcraft because, well, it's not half bad."   —*USA Today*

"Highly entertaining and dangerously addictive."   —*Time* magazine

"Genuinely engaging."   —*The New York Times Book Review*

"Green's *Half Bad* is much more than a book about witches. Her pageturner is a ruminative exploration of the nature of evil."

—*The Boston Globe*

"*Half Bad* by Sally Green isn't half bad—it's totally wonderful. The story is fast-moving, the action and dialogue keep the reader's interest, and the characters are believable and compelling."   —*The Examiner*

"Edgy, arresting and brilliantly written."

—Michael Grant, *New York Times* bestselling author of *Gone*

"[B]oth deeply unique and unsettling. This will haunt you."

—Marie Lu, *New York Times* bestselling author of
the Legend series and the Young Elites series

"Brilliant and utterly compelling—I loved it."

—Kate Atkinson, *New York Times* bestselling author of *Life After Life*

"A fast-paced, compelling story about the many shades of good and evil . . . will entice readers and leave them wanting more." —*BookPage*

★ "A grim and thrilling tale . . . an unforgettable protagonist."
—*Publishers Weekly*, starred review

★ "A horrifying, compelling trilogy that pushes the boundaries of what we believe to be good and evil . . . Nathan's survival is tenuous and marvelous—and only just beginning." —*Booklist*, starred review

"Interesting spin on the paranormal that runs adjacent to some important social issues, *Half Bad* leaves readers questioning if the division between good and evil is ever as simple as black and white." —*VOYA*

"Lovers of dark fantasy should enjoy this energetic, gripping volume."
—*SLJ*

"Rewards readers with a compelling story with plenty yet to resolve and a main character worth following in future installments." —*The Horn Book*

"Nathan's harrowing quest to build a father-son relationship will compel readers to the sequel." —*Kirkus Review*s

A *TIME* MAGAZINE BEST BOOK OF 2014
A SPRING 2014 KIDS' INDIE NEXT LIST PICK
A *BOOKLIST* TOP 10 SF/FANTASY/HORROR FOR YOUTH

Praise for *HALF WILD*
BOOK TWO IN THE HALF BAD TRILOGY

"Sparks of orginality will keep fans excited for the final chapter."
—*USA Today*

★ "Riveting . . . Features the same powerful language, well-developed characters, fascinating magic, and harrowing action sequences as its predecessor and will leave its readers anxiously awaiting the final volume."
—*Publishers Weekly*, starred review

★ "Once again, Green pushes the boundaries of definition; this time: What is wild? What is human or even civilized? The blood and gore, the willingness to endure and survive at any price, and the dichotomies between good and bad, love and hate, wild and civilized—all haunt the reader, climaxing in a tragic ending that portends the horror, violence, and possible relationships in the trilogy's final installment."
—*Booklist*, starred review

"Green delivers vibrant characters, and Nathan's relationships arc in thrilling highs and lows . . . A character-driven page-turner offering both emotional depth and gory thrills."
—*Kirkus Reviews*

"Strong writing and engaging plot . . . readers who enjoyed [*Half Bad*] will devour this sequel."
—*SLJ*

"Because this series has already been optioned for a movie, you better get on the books before the hype goes bananas."
—Bustle.com

HALF LOST

SALLY GREEN

speak

SPEAK
An imprint of Penguin Random House LLC
375 Hudson Street
New York, New York 10014

First published in the United States of America by Viking,
an imprint of Penguin Random House LLC, 2016
Published simultaneously in the UK by Penguin Books Ltd.
Published by Speak, an imprint of Penguin Random House LLC, 2017

THE LIBRARY OF CONGRESS HAS CATALOGED THE VIKING EDITION AS FOLLOWS:
Names: Green, Sally (Novelist), author.
Title: Half lost / Sally Green.
Description: New York : Viking Childrens Books, [2016] | Series: The half bad
trilogy ; 3 | Sequel to: Half wild
Identifiers: LCCN 2015042214 | ISBN 9780670017140 (hardback)
Subjects: | CYAC: Witches—Fiction. | Good and evil—Fiction. |
England—Fiction. | BISAC: JUVENILE FICTION / Fantasy & Magic. | JUVENILE
FICTION / Social Issues / Violence.
Classification: LCC PZ7.G826323 Ham 2016 | DDC [Fic]—dc23

Speak ISBN: 9780147511942

Printed in the United States of America

1 3 5 7 9 10 8 6 4 2

In memory of my father

Books by Sally Green

Half Bad

Half Wild

Half Lost

CONTENTS

PART TWO: *HALF FOUND*

PART THREE: *HALF LOST*

One and the same human being is, at various ages, under various circumstances, a totally different human being. At times he is close to being a devil, at times to sainthood. But his name doesn't change, and to that name we ascribe the whole lot, good and evil.

The Gulag Archipelago, Aleksandr Solzhenitsyn
Translated by Thomas P. Whitney

Wounded, Not Lost

"We should agree on some passwords."

"Yeah? Why?"

"Because one day you're going to go off on one of your trips and get killed, and then one of the Hunters with the Gift of disguise will pretend to be you, come back here to camp and kill me."

"More likely they'd find the camp, kill you, and wait for me to come innocently whistling home."

"That is also a possibility, though I can't imagine the whistling element."

"So, what's the password?"

"Not just one word but a phrase. I say a certain thing and you answer in the right way."

"Oh, right. So I say 'I'm whistling because I've killed ten Hunters' and you reply 'But I'd rather be climbing the Eiger.'"

"I was thinking of a question I might really ask."

"Like what?"

"You've been away a long time. Were you lost?"

"And what's my answer?"

"I was wounded, not lost."

"I don't think I'd ever say that."

"Still . . . You want to practice? Make sure you get it right?"

"No."

PART ONE

WHO TO TRUST

Stones

In the year that my father turned twenty-eight he killed thirty-two people. Celia used to make me learn facts about Marcus. That's one of them. It was the most he killed in any one year before the war between Soul's Council and the Alliance of Free Witches. I used to think that thirty-two was a lot.

In the year Marcus turned seventeen, the year of his Giving, he killed just four people. I'm still only seventeen. Before the Battle of Bialowieza—the day my father died, the day almost half of the Alliance died, the day now referred to as "BB" by anyone who dares refer to it at all—anyway, before that day I'd killed twenty-three people.

BB was months ago and now I've passed fifty kills.

I've killed fifty-two people to be precise.

It's important to be precise about these things. I don't include Pilot—she was dying anyway—and Sameen isn't in the count. What I did for her was a mercy. The Hunters killed Sameen. Shot her in the back as we fled from the battle. And Marcus? I definitely don't include him in the fifty-two. I didn't kill him. *She* killed him.

Annalise.

Her name makes me want to spew. Everything about

her makes me want to spew: her blonde hair, her blue eyes, her golden skin. Everything about her is disgusting, false. She said she loved me. And I said I loved her but *I* meant it. I did love her. What a stupid idiot! Falling for her, an O'Brien. She said I was her hero, her prince and, like the dumb, thick mug that I am, I wanted to believe her. I did believe her.

And now all I want is to kill her. To cut her open and rip screams out of her. But even that isn't enough; that won't come close to it. I'd have to make her know how hard it is to do what I did. I'd have to make her cut off her own hand and eat it, or cut out her own eyes and eat them, and still that'd be easier than what I did.

I've killed fifty-two people. But really all I want is to get my hands on her. I'd be happy with fifty-three. Just one more and I'll be satisfied.

"Just her."

But I've scoured every inch of the battlefield and the old camp. I've killed all the Hunters I've come across—some who were clearing up the mess after the battle, some who I've tracked since. But I've not seen her. Not a sign! Days and weeks following every track, every trail, every hint of a footprint and nothing leads me to her.

"Nothing."

I look up at the sound and listen. It's silent.

The noise was me, I think, talking to myself again.

"Shit!"

Annalise! She does this to me.

"Well, fuck her." I lift my head to look around me and shout at the treetops. "Fuck her!"

And then quietly to the stones I say, "I just want her dead. Obliterated. I want her soul to stop existing. I want her gone from this world. Forever. That's all. Then I'll stop."

I pick up a little stone and tell it, "Or maybe not. Maybe not."

Marcus wanted me to kill them all. Maybe I can do that. I think he knew I could or he wouldn't have said it.

I push my stones into a small pile. Fifty-two of them. It sounds a lot, fifty-two, but it's nothing really. Nothing to how many my father would have me kill. Nothing to how many have died because of Annalise. Over a hundred at BB. I've really got to up my game if I'm going to compete with her level of carnage. Because of her, the Alliance is virtually destroyed. Because of her, Marcus is dead—the one person who could have held the Hunters back when they attacked, the one person who could have defeated them. But instead, because of her, because she shot him, the Alliance was almost obliterated. And there's that niggling thought as well that all along she's been a spy for Soul. Soul is her uncle after all. Gabriel has never trusted Annalise and always said she could have been the one who told the Hunters where to find Mercury's apartment in Geneva. I never believed that but maybe he's right.

There's a movement in the trees and Gabriel appears. He's been collecting firewood. He's heard me shouting, I guess. And now he comes up, pretending as if he was coming back anyway, and drops the wood, and stands by my stones.

I've not told Gabriel what the stones are and he doesn't ask, but I think he knows. I pick one up. It's small, the size of my fingernail. They're only little but each one is quite individual. One for each person I've killed. I used to know who each stone represented—not names or anything like that; most of the Hunters are just Hunters—but I used the stones to help me remember incidents and fights and how they died. I've forgotten the individual fights now; they've all blurred into one never-ending pageant of blood, but I've got fifty-two little stones in my pile.

Gabriel's boots turn ninety degrees and stay still for a second or so before he says, "We need more wood. Are you coming to help?"

"In a bit."

His boots stay there for a few seconds more, then turn another forty-five degrees and stay there for four, five, six, seven seconds and then they make their way back into the trees.

I get out the white stone from my pocket. It's oval-shaped, pure white: quartz. Smooth but not shiny. It's Annalise's stone. I found it by a stream one day when I was searching for her. I thought it was a good sign. I was sure I'd find her trail that day. I didn't but I will, one day. When I kill her I won't add it to the pile but I'll throw it away. It'll be gone. Like her.

Maybe then the dreams will stop. I doubt it but you never know. I dream of Annalise a lot. Sometimes the dreams even start sort of nice but that doesn't last long. Sometimes she shoots my father and it's exactly like it was at BB. If I'm lucky I wake up before then, but sometimes it carries on and it's as if I'm living it all again.

I wish I'd dream of Gabriel. Those would be good dreams. I'd dream of us climbing together like we used to and we'd be friends, like the old days. We're friends now; we'll always be friends, but it's different. We don't talk much. Sometimes he talks about his family or things he did years ago, before all this, or he talks about climbing or a book he's read or . . . I don't know . . . stuff he likes. He's good at talking but I'm crap at listening.

The other day he was telling me some story about a climb he did in France. It was high above this river and very beautiful. I'm listening and imagining the woods he walked through to get there, and he describes the ravine and the river and then I'm not thinking about that at all but of Annalise being free. And I notice that a part of me says, *Listen to Gabriel! Listen to his story!* But another part of me wants to think about Annalise and it says, *While he's talking, Annalise is somewhere out there, free.* And my father's dead and I don't know where his body is, except, of course, some of it is in me because I ate his heart and that has to be the sickest thing ever, and here I am, this person, this kid who has eaten his father, and I'm sitting next to Gabriel, who's talking about a fucking climb and how he waded across the river to get to the start of it, and I'm thinking that I've eaten my own father and held him as he died and Annalise is wandering around free, and Gabriel is still talking about climbing, and how can that be normal and OK? And so I say to him as calmly as I can, "Gabriel, can you shut up about your fucking climb?" I say it really quietly because otherwise I'll scream.

And he pauses and then says, "Of course. And do you think you can say a sentence without swearing?" He's teasing, trying to keep it light, and I know he's doing that but somehow that pisses me off even more, so I tell him to fuck off. Only I don't just say the F-word but other words too and then I can hardly stop myself, well, I can't stop myself at all, and I'm swearing at him again and again and he tries to hold me, to take my arm and I push him away and tell him he should go or I'll hurt him and he goes then.

I calm down after he's walked away. And then I feel a huge wave of relief because I'm alone and I can breathe better when I'm alone. I'm OK for a bit and then when I'm properly calm I hate myself because I want him to touch my arm and I want to hear his story. I want him to talk to me and I want to be normal. But I'm not normal. I can't be normal. And it's all because of her.

We're sitting together looking at the fire. I've told myself that I've got to try harder and talk to Gabriel. Talk, like a normal person. And listen too. But I can't think of anything to say. Gabriel hasn't said much either. I think he's annoyed about the stones. I haven't told him about the two extra stones I added yesterday. I don't want to tell him about that . . . about them. I scrape round my tin bowl even though I've scraped round it already and there's nothing left. We've had cheese and soup from a packet; it was watery soup but better than nothing. I'm still hungry and I know Gabriel is too. He's looking dead thin. Gaunt, that's the word. Someone said I looked gaunt once. I remember I was really hungry then too.

I say, "We need meat."

"Yes, that would make a nice change."

"I'll put out some rabbit traps tomorrow."

"Do you want me to help?"

"No."

He says nothing but pokes at the fire.

"I'm faster on my own," I say.

"Yes, I know."

Gabriel pokes the fire again and I scrape out my bowl again.

It was Trev who said I was gaunt. I try to remember when but it's not coming back. I can remember him walking up the road in Liverpool, carrying a plastic bag. Then I remember the fain girl who was there too, and the Hunters who were chasing me, and it seems like a different world and a different lifetime.

I tell Gabriel, "There was this girl I met in Liverpool. A fain. She was tough. She had a brother and he had a gun . . . and dogs. Or maybe that wasn't her brother. No, it was someone else with the dogs. Her brother had a gun. She told me that, but I never saw him. Anyway, I went to Liverpool to meet Trev. He was a strange bloke. Tall and . . . I don't know . . . quiet and walked as if he was gliding along. White Witch. Good, though. He'd taken samples from my tattoo, the one on my ankle. Blood, skin, and bone. He was trying to work out what the tattoos did. Anyway, Hunters came and we ran off but I dropped the plastic bag that the samples were in and had to go back and this fain girl had found them. She gave them back to me and I burned them after."

Gabriel looks at me, as if he's waiting for the rest of the story. I'm not sure what the rest of the story is but then I remember.

"There were two Hunters. They nearly caught us, me and Trev. But the girl, the one with the brother, she was part of this fain gang. They caught the Hunters instead. I left. I don't know what they did to them." I look at Gabriel and say, "It never crossed my mind to kill the Hunters. Now it wouldn't cross my mind not to."

Gabriel says, "We're in a war now. It's different."

"Yeah. It sure is different." And then I add, "I was the gaunt one then, and now you are."

"Gaunt?"

And I realize I've not told him why I started the story and actually we're both gaunt and anyway I can't be bothered to explain, so I say, "It doesn't matter."

We sit looking at the fire. The only bit of brightness for miles. The sky's overcast. There's no moon. And I wonder where Trev is now, and his mate Jim. And then I remember it wasn't Trev who called me gaunt; it was Jim.

Gabriel says, "I went to see Greatorex."

"Yeah, I know." He came back with packets of soup and the cheese.

It's about an hour each way to Greatorex. Gabriel must have gone when I was counting the stones and then he collected the wood. I must have been counting for hours.

"Nothing much to report," he says. And I know that too.

The members of the Alliance who survived the battle are living in seven remote camps spread across Europe. We're with Greatorex's camp, a small group in Poland. Only we're not with them. I stay out of everyone's way. I have my own camp here. All the camps have numbers. Greatorex's is Camp Three. So I guess that makes mine Camp Three B or Camp Three and a Half. Anyway, Greatorex is in charge of the camp and communication with Camp One, Celia's camp, but there isn't much to communicate as far as I can tell. All Greatorex can do is train the young witches who have survived with her in the hope that someday the training can be used.

I watched the trainees last time I was at Camp Three. I like Greatorex but not the trainees. The trainees don't look at me, not when I'm looking at them. When I'm not looking I feel eyes all over me but whenever I glance at them suddenly they find the ground dead interesting.

I think it was like that for my father. No one wanted to

meet his eye either. But it didn't use to be like that for me. Before BB I was part of the team, the team of fighters, when me and Nesbitt were partnered up and Gabriel was with Sameen and we used to train with Greatorex and the others. We were a good team. We laughed and messed around and fought and ate and talked together. I miss that feeling; it's gone and I know it'll never come back. But still Greatorex is great with her team.

"She's good at training them," I say.

"Do you mean Greatorex?"

"That's who we're talking about, isn't it?" And I don't know why I snap at him.

"You should come into camp with me. Greatorex would like to see you."

"Yeah. Maybe." But we both know that means no.

It's been weeks since I've seen Greatorex, or anyone other than Gabriel. In fact, the last people I saw apart from Gabriel were those two Hunters and I killed them. Now I think about it, I generally kill the people that I meet. Greatorex should be grateful that I keep away.

"She wants to show off her trainees to you. They've improved a lot."

And I don't know what to say to that. What should I say? "Oh?" "Good." Or "Who the fuck cares 'cause it won't make any difference to anything?"

I really don't know what to say.

Then I think of something and I ask, "What day is it?"

Gabriel says, "You asked me that yesterday."

"And?"

"I don't know. I was going to ask Greatorex but I forgot." He turns to me, asking, "Does it matter?"

I shake my head. It doesn't matter at all what day it is except I'm trying to keep things clear in my head but each day seems like every other, and weeks have gone by but it could be months, and everything is merging in my memory. I need to concentrate and not lose track of things. I killed the two Hunters yesterday. Then I came back here, but already it feels like longer ago. I have to go back and check on the bodies. More Hunters will come looking for their pals. Maybe I'll get a chance to catch one, question them. Maybe they'll know something about Annalise. If she is a spy she'll have gone back to Soul; maybe the Hunters will have seen her.

I lie back and put my arm over my face.

I've not told Gabriel about the two Hunters because he'll tell Greatorex and she'll move the camp and I need to check on the Hunters before then. But first I need to sleep. Since Marcus died I've not slept much. I need sleep, then I can go and check on the Hunters. Or maybe leave it another day. Tomorrow I can scout to the south. Check if there's any sign of Annalise there, then come back here, then go to the Hunters' bodies. I need to get some more food as well. So, south and rabbit traps tomorrow, and dead Hunters and hopefully some live ones too the day after.

I realize I'm staring at my arm; I've still got my eyes open. I have to remember to close my eyes. I've got to sleep.

We're sitting close together, legs dangling over the outcrop. Leaves flutter down. Annalise's tanned leg is close to mine. She reaches out for a falling leaf, grabbing it and my sleeve at the same time. She turns back to me, holding the leaf in front of my face, getting my attention, and she taps my nose with the leaf. Her eyes sparkle, the silver glints twisting quickly. Her skin is smooth and velvety and I want to touch her. I try to lean forward but I can't move and I'm tied down on a bench and Wallend is standing over me, saying, "This may feel a little strange," and he puts the metal against my neck, and then I'm kneeling in the forest and my father is on the ground in front of me bleeding out from his stomach. I'm holding the Fairborn and feeling it vibrate in my hand as if it's alive and desperate to get on with the job. My right hand is holding Marcus's shoulder, feeling his jacket. And my father says, "You can do it." And we begin. The first cut is through his shirt and his flesh in one long stroke and then we cut across that, deeper. Then a third cut, deeper still, slicing through the ribs as if they're paper. The blood covers Marcus's skin and my hands, hot but cooling quickly. I put my fingers round his heart, and feel its beat as I lean forward. Bite. Blood spurts into my mouth. I'm gagging but I swallow. And I take another bite and look into my father's eyes and he's staring

I wake up coughing and puking and sweating. Gabriel shuffles over and holds me. And I hold on to him. And he doesn't say anything, just holds me, and that's good. We stay like that for a long time and eventually he says, "Can you tell me what happens in your dream?"

But I don't want to think about it. And no way am I going to talk about it. Gabriel knows what I did, what I had to do to take my father's Gifts. Gabriel saw me afterward, covered in blood, but at least he didn't see me do it. He thinks that if I talk about it I might feel better but talking about it isn't going to change a thing about what I did and all that will happen is he'll know how disgusting it was and—

"Nathan, talk to me, please."

And then he says, "It *was* a dream, wasn't it? You would tell me if you'd had another vision, wouldn't you?"

I push him away. I wish I hadn't told him I've started having visions.

Practice

•...✦

It's morning. I'm running back to my camp. I'm not feeling too bad now. I've done a long run: a few hours in the dark straight after I woke from the dream and Gabriel started pestering me about visions. Running helps me. When I run I can concentrate on the forest, the trees, the ground, and I can think better. And I can practice my Gifts.

I go invisible. I'm best at that now, but I've had to work at it. I have to think of being transparent, of being air. Breathe in and let myself become like air. And once I'm invisible I can stay like that if I concentrate on my breathing.

I can shoot out lightning from my hands too. For that I need to clap my hands together, as if I'm striking stones together to create a spark. The first time that's all it was, but now I can make long bolts of lightning that stretch for ten meters.

Sending flames from my mouth is the one I've learned most recently. I have to flick my tongue against the roof of my mouth and let out a breath. It's not a deadly weapon and I can't do flames while I'm thinking about air and being invisible. But it's still a good Gift to have.

I practice my new Gifts every day, and every day I try

to find the other Gifts my father had. He could move objects by the power of thought, change his appearance like Gabriel can, make plants grow or die, heal others, contort metal objects, and make cuts. All great Gifts but the best one was that he could stop time. I'm sure that I have all those Gifts too now. It makes sense that if I've got one from him then I've got them all, but I've not been able to find out how to access all of them. I saw how my father stopped time before he died and I've worked on that more than on the others but nothing's happened. That's the Gift I want most. What I'd do with that Gift! But I haven't been able to find that. Of course the Gift I don't want, the Gift of visions of the future, is the one that comes anyway, whether I like it or not.

Having visions is more of a curse than a Gift. Visions screwed up my life. Screwed up my relationship with my father, screwed up everything. I wonder how my life would have been different if he hadn't had the vision that I'd kill him. I mean, it ended up coming true even though he avoided me for the first seventeen years of my life. So all that meant was that I spent my childhood without him, not knowing him, a prisoner of White Witches. Then when I escaped, when we were finally united, within months the vision came true. Without the vision I don't think my father would have left me with Gran; he'd have wanted me with him. So, seventeen years of separation because of a vision. And weirder than that is the fact that I don't think I could have done what I did if I didn't know about the vision, if my father hadn't told me he'd seen that I would eat his heart and take his Gifts.

Visions aren't like dreams. For a start they only happen when I'm awake, and they come like a cloud moving overhead, bringing a chill feeling and turning things duller, and, even though I know what's going to happen and that the vision is coming and I don't want it, I've got about as much chance of stopping it as I have of stopping a cloud from blocking out the sun.

And, of course, once you've seen a vision you can't unsee it, can't forget it.

I've had my vision six or seven times now and there's a bit more detail each time. In it I'm standing on the edge of a wood, trees behind me and a rolling meadow in front, and the sun is low in the sky. The light is golden and it's all beautiful and peaceful and I turn to see Gabriel standing in the trees. He waves at me to come to him and I look back at the meadow one final time and then turn back to Gabriel and then I'm flying backward through the air.

That's all I saw the first time I had the vision, and I told Gabriel about it. But since then I've seen more. There's a dark figure walking away through the trees. And Gabriel has a gun in his hand. I fly backward through the air and it feels like I'm flying but then I land on my back, looking at sky and treetops, and the pain in my stomach hits me and I know I've been shot and then it goes black. And that's the end of the vision.

I reckon it lasts about two minutes, tops, and I end up sweating and my stomach burning and cramping for real. I know the vision is important, otherwise I wouldn't be having it, and, let's face it, being shot is never a good thing, but I don't understand it. Why is Gabriel beckoning me toward someone who is going to shoot me? And then comes the worst question of all, the one I try not to think about. Is it Gabriel who shoots me? But I know he wouldn't ever do that—I know he loves me—so that shows you how fucked up visions are. You start believing them instead of what you know.

I arrive back in camp and drop down by the fire. I'm not sure why I've come back. I was going to run to the south and set traps for rabbits, but it's only now I'm back at camp I remember that.

"You've been gone a long time. Were you lost?" Gabriel says, coming over to me.

Him and his bloody passwords.

I say, "You've got it wrong. You're supposed to say, 'You've been *away* a long time,' and I've only been away a few hours so the whole thing is stupid."

"I'm trying to keep to the spirit of it rather than word for word."

"If I was a Hunter you'd be dead now anyway."

"And you're doing your best to make that seem preferable."

I swear at him.

He shuffles his feet, scuffing the dirt up a little. I get out the Fairborn and my sharpening stone and set to work.

Gabriel crouches beside me and says, "Are you doing that for a reason?"

"Thought I'd take a look around. Check on stuff."

"I thought you were going to set rabbit traps today."

I look at him. "I'm feeling lucky. Might find some Hunters too."

I know I said I'd do rabbits today and check on the Hunters tomorrow but I've changed my mind. I want to get back to the Hunters and see if more have turned up.

"We need food. You said you'd do the traps."

"I'll do them too."

"Yes? Really? Or will you go off for days and leave me not knowing if you're alive or dead?"

I carry on with the knife.

Gabriel reaches out to touch my arm. "Talk to me, Nathan. Please."

I stop sharpening the knife and turn to look him in the eyes. "I told you. I'll do both."

Gabriel shakes his head at me. "Why won't you tell me what's going on?"

"You know what's going on, Gabriel. I'm trying to find the witch that killed my father. Though somehow she's disappeared. The good thing is that, in my search for her, I'm finding Hunters. There's a lot of them around. It's a big country but I'm finding them and killing them."

"Do you really think you can kill them all?"

It's a genuine question, but I think it's more to test my sanity rather than my ability.

I smile at him and try to look as mad as possible. "My father seemed to think I could."

Gabriel shakes his head and turns away from me, saying, "Sometimes I think you've got a death wish."

Sometimes I wonder that too, but it's when I'm fighting that I'm absolutely sure I don't. It's then that I'm sure I'm desperate to stay alive.

Gabriel continues. "You risk your life with each attack. They *can* kill you, Nathan."

"I go invisible. They don't know I'm there until it's too late."

"You can still get hit. With bullets flying all over the place it's a miracle that hasn't happened. You nearly died from a Hunter bullet in Geneva. The poison nearly killed you. A wound—"

"I'm careful. And I'm better than them. Lots better."

"They can become invisible too. They can still—"

"I told you I'm careful."

Gabriel frowns. "It's not just about you. Your attacks bring more Hunters our way, lead them closer to us and to Greatorex, bringing more danger for everyone."

"Greatorex and her gang are training for that day, though as I recall the last two times we moved camp there was no confrontation and it's just me who's done any killing, just me who's got blood on his hands. It's as if that lot only want to train and hide away and—"

"You know that's not true."

"And it's not true for me either."

I run my finger along the Fairborn's blade, drawing blood. I suck my finger and then heal the cut before I put the sharpening stone in my backpack and the Fairborn in its sheath.

"Nathan, another few Hunters dead won't change the war. It won't change anything."

"Tell that to them as I slice their guts open."

"You know as well as I do that most of them are kids. They're manipulated into believing in Soul's cause. The war isn't against them; it's against Soul. He runs the Council of White Witches; he employs Wallend to come up with his perverted magic. They are the people you should be fighting. They are the ones who started the war, and it's only by killing them that it'll end."

"Well, I'll get round to them soon enough. Think of these attacks as practice. When I've mastered all my father's Gifts, then I'll be ready to go against Soul."

"And in the meantime you *practice* by killing kids."

I go invisible, take the Fairborn from its sheath, and reappear with the tip of the knife at Gabriel's throat.

"They're Hunters, Gabriel. They're working with Soul to hunt and kill us, but I intend to hunt and kill them. All of them if I have to. Young or old. New recruits or hardened veterans. They joined up. They made their choice and I'm making mine."

Gabriel swipes at my arm, knocking the Fairborn away.

"Don't point that thing at me. I'm not your enemy, Nathan."

I swear at him.

"Is that all you're good for?" Gabriel takes a step back onto the pile of fifty-two stones. "Swearing and killing?" He looks down at them, saying, "How many stones do you want in that pile, Nathan? You want a mountain of them?" Gabriel kicks at the stones with the side of his foot. "Will it make you feel better? Will it help you sleep at night?"

"Knowing there are a few less Hunters makes me feel better than knowing there are a few more. And as for helping me sleep at night, let's face it, it can't make things any worse." I make sure I throw in every swear word I can come up with as well.

I pick up my backpack and Gabriel reaches out to hold my arm but I shake him off and head out of the camp at a fast jog. I don't look back.

A Basic Trap

This time while I'm running I think of Annalise. I imagine I'm chasing after her, close on her tail. I can run for hours without stopping anyway but when I'm thinking of her time passes even faster. But I can't think of Annalise too much. I've got to be strict with myself: I've got to concentrate on hunting Hunters. Gabriel's right about one thing: it is dangerous and however good I am they could still get lucky. To keep luck on my side I have to keep improving. I've got to get even better, even faster, even stronger. I've got to work out where I'm weak. Celia taught me that. *Learn from your mistakes but expect your enemies to learn from theirs.* So every time I attack a group of Hunters I'm learning, improving the control of my new Gifts.

I have to keep practicing and I do that now as I run: going invisible; sending lightning from my left hand and then from my right; sending a plume of fire from my mouth. Up to now the only Gift from my father that I've used in a fight with the Hunters is invisibility, but even so, last time I was grazed by a bullet—I've not told Gabriel that. It took a few hours for me to drive the poison out where the bullet broke my skin. But I learned from the experience so Celia would be pleased. I was too slow. I stayed in the same place half a second too long. That won't happen again. And now I'm ready to try using lightning while I'm invisible so I don't have to get in close. It will give my position away so I must shoot it out and keep moving. I send out a flash from my left hand, then dive and roll to the right, sending out another flash from my right hand as I go.

Then I do it again. Faster and stronger.

And again.

I keep moving until it's dark and then I camp by a stream, which means I stop and lie down. I'm hungry. I puked up the soup and cheese from last night and haven't had anything else since. But before I can think about food I need to do one more thing: try stopping time again. I go over it in my head, remembering Marcus and how he moved his hands in a circle, rubbing his palms together. I try the same technique and I think of slowing things around me, think of everything coming to a stop. The forest is still and I hold my breath, wondering if I've done it. But I know I haven't; the quality of stillness when time stops is different. I wish I could ask my father how to access this Gift. I wish I could ask him so many things. More than anything I wish we'd had more time together.

The gold ring my father gave me is on my finger and I put it to my lips and kiss it. The time we did have together, though brief, was amazing. I learned by copying my father. I transformed into an eagle and we flew to-

down in the autumn, and now that it's winter the area feels open and light but colder somehow too. The bodies of the Hunters are gone.

I don't go into the clearing yet. I make my way round it, sticking to the edge, keeping trees between me and the open, just in case. I carry on round the clearing and find nothing. I'm sure I'm alone here. Fairly sure. Ninety-five percent sure.

Now I move slowly forward, keeping low and quiet, to where the bodies were. There are a lot of footprints, and not from the dead Hunters before they died but from live ones I think, and the marks lead north out of the clearing. They've taken the bodies. Looking at the tracks I think more than two Hunters and less than eight were here, which means four or six as they only ever work in pairs. But really I don't read tracks well, so it's a guess. And I'm certainly not good enough to say how old the tracks are, but the Hunters have only been dead three days so I think their bodies were taken recently. Very recently.

I try to follow the trail but I lose it and have to go back on myself and try again. This time I spot another footprint lying over one of the boot prints. This is different: something like a trainer, definitely not a Hunter's boot. My heart rate jumps.

Annalise?

That's a stupid idea. Why would she be here? The chances of it being her are minuscule.

But, still, minuscule is more than zero.

I follow the Hunter tracks, scanning further into the forest and after a short distance I see the trainer prints again. I follow them but it's a slow process. I can't do it quickly in case I miss something, and there's no obvious path. Unlikely as it seems, I wish I had Nesbitt with me. He's the best tracker the Alliance has, but he's never around when I need him.

I follow the trail through the forest and through the afternoon, until the sun is low in the sky. It's too dark to see footprints now, but I don't need to. From the top of a gentle slope looking down into the next valley I see something better: a thin line of smoke coming through the treetops.

They must be relaxed to light a fire.

Or it's a trap.

Celia's voice in my head says, *Hunters wouldn't give themselves away so close to where they'd lost two of their own.*

I'm not sure how many of them there are. And they can go invisible, thanks to Wallend and his magic. They used their invisibility at BB, and many Hunters I've caught since had the ability. But I've got it too. And I want to get into the camp. There's someone with them. I'm convinced of that. And it may be Annalise. There's probably no more than six of them. Six I can take.

Six plus Annalise. If they've found her they'll take her back as a prisoner. Or maybe not. Maybe she'd be a hero to them: she shot Marcus, and perhaps Gabriel's right and she was a spy for them all along. Perhaps it was her who told the

Hunters about the apartment in Geneva and the cut that led to Mercury's cottage.

I need to take a closer look.

I'm weaving slowly and silently down the valley through the trees. The ground is bare in places but in others the trees thin and brambles block my path. It's dark by the time I work my way through, and the distant hissing in my head from mobile phones is louder, so I go invisible and move silently on.

Then I see the first Hunter, a guard. I watch her for a minute or two. She stays in her position looking out to the forest.

If there are six Hunters, I'm guessing two will be on guard while the other Hunters are resting, eating, or perhaps already sleeping.

I move back and circle round to find the other guard. She's at the edge of a small clearing. Two guards, as I thought. I'm making my way round to the first guard again when I pick up the hissing sound of a mobile phone. A third guard! But I can't see her. She's invisible.

So, three guards. I've not been right round the camp so I do that now and, guess what, I pick up another hissing sound, another invisible guard. Four.

I go past her and back to the first Hunter, one of the visible ones. I find a place to watch from and let myself become visible. After an hour or so, I hear footsteps—a fifth Hunter, coming up behind the first. This one is older. She walks up to the first Hunter and says a few words. The younger woman nods and goes back into the camp. I can't see flames or smoke from the fire but I reckon it's only thirty meters or so further on. The older Hunter looks relaxed but not lazy, like she's done this a thousand times before. It's the middle of the night and she's probably dog tired but she casts her gaze around, seems to look at me, and my heart races, adrenaline kicking in. Has she spotted me?

I stay still. I don't think she's seen me. I've done nothing to give myself away. I've been sitting here well back, well hidden, though not invisible. I need to stay put. Any movement will alert her. Even going invisible now may change a shadow or a shape.

My breathing seems loud and I force it to calm.

Wait.

And she looks away. She's continuing to scan the area slowly and carefully but she hasn't seen me. It was chance that she looked my way.

I need to work out what to do. There's four guards. Four guards means at least six Hunters in total but probably more. They know someone killed their two friends. From my tracks they'll know the killer was alone, that he killed with a knife. Will they know it's me? I'm sure Celia would be smacking her forehead at this point, telling me, *Of course they know it was you!*

And that means they'll be hoping I will come back. So this is a trap. And again in my head I can see Celia saying, *Are you stupid?! Two visible, two invisible. They want you to think they're a smaller party than they are.*

It's a pretty basic trap, but it's a trap for sure. The one thing I think they haven't realized about me is that I can sense their mobile phones.

What *do* they know about me? They know I've eaten my father's heart; they have his body so they'll have worked that out. So they know I've got his Gifts. They know what his Gifts were but they won't know which ones I've mastered yet. They probably know I won't have mastered them all. They probably think I will, given time, so catching me sooner is better than later. Obviously they'd rather kill than catch me. This is definitely a trap.

And the other person in there? Could it be Annalise? They might know I want her. They might think I'll want to rescue her. They might have caught her after the battle.

If it's a trap, I should leave. But if that *is* Annalise . . .

I've searched for her for months. I can't miss this chance.

So my options . . .

Option one: leave. Go back and tell Greatorex and get her little team out here to put their training to good use for once. They'd take two days to get here if we went at it hard. It's a possibility. But then there's also a possibility that the Hunters will have left and Annalise, if it's her, will have gone too. And Greatorex might not agree to come at all. She'll probably say it's not worth the risk and move camp instead.

Option two: scout out the camp but don't attack. Check if it's Annalise in there. This is a good option. I can stay invisible long enough to get past the guards and into the camp and out again if I have to. If it's not Annalise I can go and get Greatorex. Or just go. If it is Annalise . . .

Option three: attack. I've never attacked more than four Hunters in a group. They'll be able to go invisible but they don't like to do that in close fighting, in case they shoot each other. I can always kill a few and escape. If there are too many I can run, let them hunt me and pick them off one by one. There was only ever that one fast girl who could keep up with me. But if this is a trap then these Hunters will probably have been chosen because they have powerful Gifts that can be used against me, and I've no way of knowing what they are. The Gift I fear most is the one Celia has: the deafening, high-pitched noise. It incapacitates me, makes me vulnerable, and I'm not sure I could stay invisible if I got hit by something like that.

So: attacking is madness; scouting is risky; leaving is the sensible option.

That's that then. Decision made. I attack.

Option Three

I may be mad but I'm not suicidal: my attack has to be in the darkest, coldest part of the night, guerrilla style rather than all-out battle mode. I wait a few hours, but my hands are stiff, almost numb, which isn't good, and I move back through the trees and run for ten minutes, getting myself warmed up, getting myself in the zone. I know what I have to do: remove the guards one by one, silently but quickly. Difficult, because two of them are invisible, but then who wants easy? Once I've finished with the guards, I can go into the camp and deal with whoever's in there. I have to move fast but calmly. *Be professional and keep thinking*, Celia would say. *Kill them quick*, I say.

Back at my spot in the trees I look down at the first guard. She's the old hand; she'll be a good fighter. I mustn't give her a chance to fight.

I take a deep breath, think of cool air, check I'm invisible, and then walk down to her, careful not to make any sound. Close now. The Fairborn in my hand. The Hunter is right in front of me, staring through me. I take one more step and slice across her throat, grabbing her body with my free hand. She tries to hit me, her lips moving, but instead of words blood comes out of her mouth.

I lower her to the ground as carefully as I would a sleeping baby, listening all the time. I can't hear anything, so I run to the trees and on to the next guard, the first invisible one, slowing as I hear the hiss of her mobile. It's loud but it gives me no sense of where she really is. I stop and listen for another noise, anything: her breath, a movement. But I get nothing, only the loud hiss of her phone.

I edge forward. It's dark but now I see the trampled bracken and her footprints. I take another small step, arms outstretched, and the Fairborn helps me now. It senses her. It wants her blood.

I let it lead my hand. The Fairborn is straining and I know I'm only millimeters away from her. So I let the Fairborn loose, thrust fast into the air at chest level. The knife's so sharp that her jacket, skin, even bone, hardly slow it and I feel warm blood on my fingers, and my right hand finds the Hunter's mouth as she grunts loud and I pull the Fairborn down, ripping material and flesh. Hot, slippery guts spill over my left hand. The Hunter is visible now, writhing on the ground, and I'm kneeling over her, holding her jaw closed, muffling her whimper. She's another young woman, maybe in her mid-twenties.

I wipe my hand on her clothes, and I clean the Fairborn too, risking going visible for a second or two, but I have to move much faster now. That was too slow and she made a noise—not a big one but enough to alert the other guards, if they're good. I can't risk the guards waking the others.

I have to get into the camp.

I go as fast and quiet as I can. The fire is low but bright and I can make out the shapes of three people lying near it. Further away, by a large tree, is another Hunter and near her, chained to the tree, is a hooded prisoner, a female prisoner, petite and slim. I need to concentrate. So, four Hunters here, two left keeping guard, and the prisoner.

I slit the throat of the nearest sleeping Hunter but she kicks and jerks and I have to move to the next one fast. I don't need to worry about being silent now. I need to be quick; the sleepers are waking but still don't know what's happening. The next Hunter is getting up but I push her down and stab her throat and take a step toward the third, but the second one isn't giving in without a fight and she gets hold of my leg, clinging on, bleeding out. Somehow she has her gun in her hand and shoots. I'm still invisible but off balance and the bullet misses me and I kick her in the face and roll away.

That's four Hunters dead, four still alive and it's chaos now. The Hunter by the prisoner has gone invisible but is shouting for the guards. The Hunter by the campfire has got her gun. Fairborn in sheath, I send lightning out from both hands, one in the direction of each Hunter. Smoke and a scream comes from the one by the fire and I leap at her, falling on to her, and the Fairborn back in my hand knows where to drive itself: into her stomach and then ripping upward. She screams again and the Fairborn slashes across and the Hunter goes silent. Then there's shooting and I push away from the dead Hunter and roll away still further.

That's five down. I crouch. The sixth Hunter, who was by the prisoner, is now invisible and moving. She's shooting all over the place but I can't get an exact position on her. I throw myself flat to the ground and wait.

The shooting stops. My hands are slick with blood but the Fairborn is happy. I feel its vibration, its desire to do more work. There's still three Hunters alive. And the prisoner. I look over to her. She's still there, now lying curled up on the ground. Then I realize I'm not invisible any more. *Fuck! Concentrate! Breathe. Think air!* I check my hand and I'm invisible again. I was lucky they didn't see me but it's dark and I'm flat on the ground and anyway I'm invisible again.

Then a shout—"Lady two!"—and whoever said it is moving fast to my right. It's code for something, something that they've planned. I need to get out!

I run to my left as fast and silent as I can but only get three paces before my muscles cramp up: first my legs and then my arms and my stomach. I drop to my knees. Head on the ground. Trying to breathe quietly. Wanting to vomit. It's some kind of magic. Bad, but not as bad as Celia's noise. I can fight it if I heal.

I get a buzz from the healing and then run for the trees. I've almost reached them when the cramp hits me again. I'm on my knees and the shooting starts again and I roll over and over and send lightning out of my hands. And I hit a tree trunk and I heal again and get to my feet and the shooting is mad and there's shouting and I dive to the side and throw lightning bolts, as many as I can, as far as I can. I'm buzzing from healing and somehow that seems to help me and I'm pissed off and terrified too. And I run around the clearing, sending lightning and flames and there's a scream and more shots, but no more cramping. That has stopped.

I scan the clearing and the edge of the trees. I'm still, my breath coming hard, panicked. I have to calm it. Have to stay invisible too. I think I got the one who can do the cramp thing, but only because she's not doing it any more. Then I see her, surprisingly close, lying half hidden by a tree, her arm outstretched to me, her eyes open.

So that means there's two Hunters left.

I hear a sound to my right. I send lightning there. The biggest bolt I can make. And I run a few steps through the trees. The shooting starts again. I drop to the ground and lie flat.

It goes quiet.

I wait.

And wait.

If they're dead they're visible. I raise my head to look.

Nothing . . . or maybe something. Smoke. And then I see the seventh Hunter. She's not dead but kneeling on the ground, blackened. Her jacket smoking. Her right arm limp at her side and her left hand holding her gun loosely. She's looking around. Dazed.

And then the final Hunter becomes visible behind her. Somehow I got her too, even though she's further away. I can't see her face. She's lying on the ground.

I have to concentrate hard on staying invisible—*breathe slowly, think air*—and then I move to look more closely at the girl on the ground. Her face is burned and blackened. Her eyes open. She's definitely not faking it. I allow myself to become visible.

The kneeling Hunter is breathing hard. I step toward her so she can see me and she tries to raise her gun. The Fairborn slits her throat. More blood on my hand. Another body lying on the ground.

The prisoner is still curled up on the ground. Ankles chained to the tree. Hands zip-tied in front. A canvas hood covers her head, tied round her neck where strands of her blonde hair stick out.

I'm shaking. I take a breath and another and some more.

My hands are sticky with blood. I grip the Fairborn tighter and grab the prisoner by the shoulder. She jolts back but is silent. I cut at the string that ties the hood, careless of the point of the Fairborn as it nicks her neck. That's the least of what Annalise deserves. I pull off the hood.

Blonde hair tumbles out and half covers her face. Annalise's hair?

It's hard to see in the dark.

She shakes her head back. She's gagged but her eyes are staring at me. Blue eyes full of fear, full of silver. White Witch eyes.

My hands are shaking harder now, shaking with rage and fury, and the Fairborn is buzzing in my grip and I drive it into the ground and walk away.

The Prisoner

The fire, a rucksack, a sleeping bag: I kick them all and curse them all. I stop short of kicking a dead body but I curse it and everything else that lies on the ground in this crappy camp. By the time I've worked my way back to the prisoner, I don't know if I've worked myself up or down but I'm still mad. I don't know who she is but she's not Annalise.

The girl stares at me. Some of the fear has gone from her eyes and she tries to talk, but she's gagged and I'm not in the mood for messing with that. I turn my back on her and find a water canister to wash my hands and clean the Fairborn. All the time I do it, I swear. The swearing helps, a little.

I go through the camp looking for anything that may be useful: useful to me and useful to Greatorex. There's plenty of stuff but no paperwork, plans, or orders. I put a blanket, water, food, knives, guns, and ammo into a rucksack. I also find rope, zip ties, and keys, I guess, to the prisoner's chains. There's a medical kit too. I don't need one but some in the Alliance don't heal as well or as quickly as me.

When I try to lift the rucksack I can hardly move it. I take out four of the guns, the blanket, the medical kit; I tip out most of the water but keep the canister, all the ammo and food. There's some clothes on the ground by one of the sleeping bags. I take a fleece and a jacket and turn back to the prisoner. She's sitting up now. Watching me. I drop the jacket and fleece by her feet, crouch in front of her, and pull off her gag.

"Thanks. Thanks. I thought . . . I thought they'd kill me."

I drop the keys at her feet and tell her, "Unlock your ankles."

"Yes, yes. Thanks." She starts to do it and then stops, saying, "Can you cut off the zip tie?"

"Unlock the chain. We're leaving."

While she does that I think of something else I've got to do. I check all the bodies for tattoos. The Alliance first spotted that the Hunters had these months ago, just before BB. They seem to mean that the Hunters can go invisible. It's some perverted magic that Wallend has made. And yes—all of these Hunters have tattoos. Small black circles on their chests, above their hearts.

When I go back to the prisoner she's standing, stomping her legs. I cut the zip tie round her wrists. Her wrists are raw. It looks like she's only in a thin jumper. She must be freezing.

"Thanks," she says.

"Do you have one of those tattoos?" I ask, pointing at the nearest Hunter's chest.

"No."

I stare at her.

"What? You want to check?"

I wait.

She swears under her breath but then pulls her jumper up to her neck.

She's skinny, muscular, and pale. But she doesn't have a tattoo.

"I'm not one of them. I was trying to join the Alliance," she says, pulling her clothes back down.

"We need to get going. Put those on." I point to the jacket and fleece on the ground. "Keep warm."

She does as I say. The jacket is massive on her.

I take a new zip tie from the rucksack and tie it round her wrists, behind her back. Her hands are like ice.

She doesn't say anything at first but then turns to look at me and says really quietly, "Why are you doing this? I'm on your side. I was their prisoner."

"Says you."

She takes a step back from me and says, "OK, OK, I get that you don't know who I am, but look at me. I can't hurt you."

"Says you."

I wonder what Gift she has. As a final thought, I grab the rope, the gag, and the hood, and stuff them in her jacket pocket.

"You won't need those," she says, her voice panicked.

I search the camp once more. It's getting light now, but there's nothing new to see. I swing the rucksack on and walk back to the girl. "OK," I say. "Let's go."

"Where are we going?"

"That way," I say, and shove her forward. She stumbles but then starts walking ahead of me.

"Faster," I tell her.

And she speeds up. Her body is tense and I can see she's struggling because her hands are tied. Well, that's just too bad.

After half an hour, she slows and I have to push her on. She says, "You're with the Alliance, aren't you? Is that where we're going? I was trying to join them, but the Hunters found me."

"They'll find you again if you don't speed up."

"Can't you untie my hands?"

"I can gag you, if you think that'll help."

She's quiet then and she speeds up.

An hour or so later she slows again and however much I urge, curse, and push her she looks done in. So we stop. I give her all the water and feed her a chocolate bar, which she bites so greedily I'm in danger of losing a finger.

Her mouth full of chocolate, she says, "They hardly gave me anything to eat!"

I let her rest for ten minutes then say, "Get up. We need to keep moving."

"I'm not sure I can."

I reckon she needs the right motivation so I try a different tactic.

"I'm leaving. I'm going to the Alliance base. You can come with me and go at my speed or you can stay here and the Hunters will pick you up again soon enough." And I set off.

Sure enough, I hear her running and stumbling to keep up. I don't go too fast, I've worked out her pace now, but I do circle round and check our trail in case she's deliberately leaving any tracks or signs. But she's not.

A few hours later, she drops behind again. After a few minutes, I lose sight of her. I stop and wait but she doesn't appear.

Shit.

Do I go back?

I go back.

She's not that far behind, kneeling on the ground. She looks up at me when I approach, tears running down her cheeks, and says, "I'm too tired."

"Tough. We need to keep going."

She tries to get to her feet but her knees buckle and with her hands tied she can't balance.

Shit!

I go to her and haul her up. She's as light as a feather.

"There's a small stream up ahead. We can get water and rest there." I cut her zip tie and tell her, "Anything. Any trouble, any . . . anything and I slit your throat."

She nods lots and says, "Thank you."

I've no idea how far it is to the stream. I know I passed two on the way and followed the course of one for a short distance. So off we go again, slow but now she's on her feet she's OK.

Eventually we reach the stream. The water flows slowly but it's clean. I fill the canister and watch the girl glug the water down. I find another chocolate bar and give it to her.

She eats this one more slowly. When she's finished it she says, "I'm Donna."

"Hi, Donna. I'm Freddie."

She actually smiles a little at that. I guess she knows I'm no Freddie, but does she know who I really am?

I get to my feet, saying, "Time to go, Donna."

"I thought we were staying here for the night."

"It's not dark for a few hours. We keep going."

As it gets dark, I tell Donna, "This is a good spot. We'll camp here."

She doesn't reply but folds up on herself and sits on the ground. We've walked a long way but nothing to what Hunters can cover in a day. I'm sure Donna's fit enough but she does look really thin and weak.

It's cold and she needs to save her energy for walking, not for keeping warm, so I make a fire and cook a couple of the dehydrated meals I took from the Hunters. She eats both. I'm not sure about tying her wrists again but I do. She doesn't even complain, just lies down and falls asleep. I put some more wood on the fire and go to check if we're being followed.

I run back the way we came, stopping frequently to listen for movement or for the hiss of mobile phones. I go fast in the dark. I can't see that well, but I can sense my way.

I run halfway back to the Hunter camp but I hear and see nothing. If it was a trap, what would I do if I was Jessica, my half-sister, leader of the Hunters, when I found out it hadn't worked?

When she hears about that camp, Jessica will know I can kill eight Hunters on my own. So she's going to want to follow us with more than eight. She'll know we'll go to an Alliance camp so she'll want a lot more than eight. It might take her a while, a day maybe, to get enough Hunters in the right area. We've not left very obvious tracks, but they're Hunters—they'll work it out. We've probably got a day's start on them, a day and a half with luck. But that's not much. I've got to get Donna to Camp Three and then Greatorex will have to either be ready for a fight or move. Greatorex will want to move.

I get back while it's still dark and start the fire again. Donna's asleep. The forest is quiet. I lie down and close my eyes. I really need an hour or two of sleep.

I'm in a forest with Annalise. She's running ahead of me and I'm chasing her, but it's a game. She's laughing and dodging and at first I'm pretending I can't catch her but then when I do try to grab her she's too quick and I'm snatching at air and she's laughing again, laughing at me. And I get madder and try harder to grab her but she skips out of my reach and smiles and laughs and I get madder and I'm so angry and I have the Fairborn in my hand and I'm cursing her and still she laughs and then she stops and stands in front of me and says, "You're my prince. You saved me." But I'm so angry I stab her and slash her and the Fairborn cuts her and my arm is aching with the effort I put into it.

I wake up and open my eyes. It's early morning. My arm is stiff and sore.

I turn my head and see Donna is watching me.

"Bad dream?" she asks.

"Is there any other kind?"

She gives a quick smile and looks down and very quietly says, "No."

We set off. Donna seems stronger today. I guess she can't have slept much if she was a terrified prisoner of the Hunters. But whatever she is—wannabe freedom fighter, spy, or just some sad teenage White Witch with parents who've joined up with Soul—I really don't care. Greatorex can work it out.

We make good progress all day, keeping up a steady pace, stopping frequently but only for a few minutes at a time. At one stop I give Donna the last chocolate bar and she takes it, breaks it in half, and offers me half back.

I tell her, "You have it."

"Thanks."

"I'm not being nice. I'm being practical. We won't be eating until tonight and you need the calories."

She does one of her little smiles and says, "OK."

Then she says, "The Hunters who caught me were horrible . . . scary. They put the hood on me and gagged me and then it was like they forgot I was there. And . . . they talked about things. They talked about how they were setting a trap for this witch called Nathan. He's famous. He's the son of Marcus. Half Black Witch and half White Witch. They said he'd killed lots of Hunters. But famous or not, they said, he wouldn't stand a chance against them. Apparently two of them were some special elite. The trap was that they'd make it look like there were only four Hunters, so he'd think he had a good chance against them. But they could all go invisible and one of them had this weird Gift that makes you double up in pain and another one could blind you. So they were going to catch him and then take us both back to the Council and have us executed." She glances at me and then looks away. "Anyway, that Nathan guy sounds really nasty but he's working for the Alliance so I'm glad he didn't fall for the trap and I'm really grateful that it's you who found me and rescued me, Freddie."

I have to rub my face to cover my smile. "Yeah."

"Anyway, I know that you don't trust me, and that's fine. It's understandable. But that doesn't mean I'm not grateful."

"Did they say if any other Hunters were nearby?"

"No. Well, I mean they didn't say there were or there weren't. They talked about 'base' and getting information to base and things like that but I'm not sure how close it was."

"We need to go. Wherever it is, it's too close."

We set off again. It's early afternoon but very gloomy.

The rain starts and quickly turns to sleet. The trees are protecting us from the worst of the weather but it's muddy and wet and cold. If I didn't have Donna with me I'd be back with Gabriel by now, but we'll be lucky to make it by tomorrow night. And it's impossible not to leave tracks in this mud.

When it gets dark, I find a place to camp. The rain has petered out but everywhere is wet. The least wet and muddy place is under a large tree. We sit there and shelter for a while, but Donna starts to shiver.

"We need wood for a fire. Come on." I pull her to her feet.

"I'm too tired. Can't I wait here?"

"No. You need to help and you need to keep moving until we get the fire going."

We wander off together and Donna does help, soon getting an armful. But I tell her, "Most of that's too wet."

"It's better than nothing," she replies, looking at my empty arms. "I'll take it back."

I let her go and carry on searching. The rain starts again, heavier than ever, and I realize it's impossible. There's no dry wood.

I go back to the shelter of the big tree. Donna is bent over the rucksack, her arm inside it. Some of the contents are tipped out. There's a gun by Donna's side. I run at her, sending a flash of lightning to hit the ground close to her. She cowers down.

"What are you doing?" I shout.

"I was looking for food! I'm starving."

I'm breathing hard. She looks up at me. "I'm just hungry. This is all dehydrated stuff. I thought there might be some energy bars or chocolate or something."

I swear at her and grab her wrists, zip-tying them behind her back. "Don't ever go in my stuff again."

I pack the rucksack back up, cleaning the mud off things as best I can. The ammo is all packed at the bottom. None of the guns are loaded. Was Donna going through looking for a loaded gun? Looking for ammo? Or was she really looking for food?

I get the least damp wood I can find and light the fire with flames from my mouth. Donna cowers further from me. The fire is poor. I make up the dehydrated meals with lukewarm water. They're disgusting but I eat one and feed Donna another.

She hardly speaks, just says sorry a few times. I don't speak to her, but tie her to a tree and head back to check for anyone following our trail. Nothing. I go back to the fire and keep watch all night. It rains on and off. When it starts to get light I make one more meal up, boiling the water as best I can. Beef stew for breakfast. I cut Donna's zip tie off and share the food with her.

"Thanks." She steals a glance at me. "I won't do anything stupid again. Sorry."

"Shut up."

"Freddie, I really—"

"I said shut up."

She's silent and I look over at her and see she's started crying again. So I kick the fire out, pack up, and drag her to her feet and off we go again. It's cold and damp and moving is the only thing to keep the chill out of our bones. But at least Donna keeps going at a reasonable pace and she's not talking.

It's late afternoon when we get back to Camp Three and a Half. There's no sign of Gabriel and it looks like he hasn't been here for a few days: the fire is cold and my fifty-two stones are scattered in the mud where Gabriel kicked them. He must be at Camp Three with Greatorex. He'll wait there and hope I go to him. That's his way of getting me to go and see Greatorex. Well, as it happens, that's what I'm going to do anyway.

Donna has sat down on the ground by the dead fire and I tell her, "Ten minutes and then we leave."

"I thought we were stopping here for the night."

"You thought wrong."

"I'm tired."

"Join the club."

"Are we nearly there yet?" She smiles a little and glances up at me, I think realizing she sounds like a little kid.

"We'll be at the Alliance camp soon."

"Really?" Donna perks up but then looks at me suspiciously. "An hour soon or a day soon?"

"At my pace, an hour. At yours, it could be three days."

Her shoulders droop a little but she says, "Thanks,

Freddie. For bringing me, I mean. I know you could have left me."

I drink some water and pass it to her, saying, "Shut up and drink."

She sips the water and says, "Freddie, I—"

"Can you stop calling me fucking Freddie?"

She smiles briefly. "Sure. It really doesn't suit you. You're definitely not a Freddie." She sips the water again, then adds quietly and cautiously, "But even if you chose a better name I think I'd know who you are. You really are famous, you know. I was being honest. I'm glad I've met you and I am really grateful . . . Nathan."

"Yeah."

She shakes her head. "You're famous for being the son of Marcus. Famous for being a Half Code. Famous for being bad . . . evil. Downright nasty."

"Are you trying to piss me off?"

"I'm trying to talk to you." And she adds a small smile.

"Well, I'm not into talking. But, yes, I'm mostly nasty. Sometimes I'm evil. And sometimes I do bad things. Your job is to make sure I don't want to do them to you. So I suggest you shut up and get moving."

"You prefer being nasty, don't you? It's easier for you."

"My father would have slit your throat back at the camp. The Hunters would take you back to the White Witches and torture and kill you."

"So now you're saying you're the *good* guy?"

"And don't you forget it."

"I won't. I agree; you rescued me and I'm grateful. But being nasty suits you."

"I've still got the gag, don't forget. I think that suited you."

She actually laughs at that and says, "See, that's just what I mean. You love being nasty."

"Save your breath for your wheezing. Let's go."

I pull her to her feet again and we're off.

Back at Camp

It's dark and raining when we approach Camp Three. There's a guard ahead and as I approach I shout, "It's me, Nathan. Password's 'Orion's Belt.'"

A shot rings out and hits a tree close to my left.

I push Donna to the ground and roll to my right. I go invisible and run at the guard, knocking the gun upward and out of her hands, and then I push her to the ground. She starts to get up and I hit her in the face with the butt of the gun so that she falls back, blood pouring from her nose.

I'm panting hard and no longer invisible. The girl looks up at me. She's one of the trainees.

Greatorex runs up, gun pointing at me but shouting at her guards. "Report!"

Another trainee appears from my right, a third from my left. All with guns pointing at me. I keep my gun pointed at the girl on the ground who now, despite her broken nose, shouts, "Wrong password! Wrong password!"

Greatorex advances on me, gun still aimed at my head. She says, "What's the password?"

"I don't know. You've changed it and no one's told me."

"So why attack my guard?"

"She shot at me!"

"Unless you can prove to me you're really Nathan, I'll have to shoot you."

"You want me to go invisible, throw lightning, breathe flames, and kill the lot of you? Will that be *proof* enough?"

Gabriel runs up now, taking in the situation, and asks, "What's happening?"

Greatorex tells him. "This *person* says he's Nathan. But he might be an impostor."

"Fuck off, Greatorex." I can't believe she's serious but her gun is still on me.

Gabriel says, "He swears like Nathan, but any uneducated idiot can do that."

I swear at him now, not sure if he's joking or not. "Just tell her it's me, Gabriel."

He comes to me, puts a hand on my chest and looks into my eyes, saying, "But is it you?" Then he leans closer to me, his body against mine, and he moves his mouth to my ear and I feel his breath as he whispers, "You've been away a long time. Were you lost?"

I turn to him, my lips brushing his hair as I mumble, "I got fucking wounded, bloody lost, and climbed the shitting Eiger."

"Close, but not exactly—"

"I'm sticking to the spirit of it rather than word for word."

Gabriel turns to Greatorex, saying, "It's him. But still feel free to shoot him."

"Tempting," Greatorex replies, but she lowers her gun.

The girl at my feet tries to get up but I push her down with my boot. "You can keep still; you could have killed me."

Greatorex steps up and says, "It's you who got the password wrong, Nathan. She was doing her job."

I shove the gun into Greatorex's hands and say, "Well, tell her to point this at her over there." I turn to indicate Donna, who is walking toward us with a nervous smile on her face, her hands tied behind her back. "She was in a Hunter camp. She was tied up and she says she wants to join the Alliance, but she could be an infiltrator or a spy. Anyway, you deal with her. I want some food and some sleep."

"Wait! You've been in a Hunter camp? Where?"

"Two days away."

"They'll track you."

"They're all dead, but, yes, more will come."

Greatorex doesn't swear, though I'm sure she wants to. She barks a few orders to her trainees to check my trail and then goes to talk to Donna while I walk with Gabriel into the camp.

I need to relax but as we enter the camp I tense up again. This camp is all organized rows of tents with trainees standing by them, guns in hand, staring at me. I slow and Gabriel moves close to me and says, "They heard gunfire. They're bound to be nervous."

"I was the one being shot at. How do you think I feel?"

"Let's sit by the fire." Gabriel virtually pulls me to the ground and sits with me, saying, "It's OK. You're just wound up."

I sit and stare at the fire and Gabriel is close to me, our arms touching. I say to him quietly, "I thought it was Annalise in the Hunter camp. But it wasn't her. It was Donna." I glance at the other trainees, who are in a huddle, a few of them still looking over at me.

"You're shaking, Nathan."

"I'm hungry. Knackered." And that's part of it for sure.

"Shall I find you some food?"

"In a bit." And we stay staring at the fire for a while before Gabriel goes to look for some food. When he comes back it's more packet soup but it tastes OK and it's warm. I've stopped shaking.

Gabriel says, "Try to sleep. I'll stay here." And I lie down and stare at the fire some more.

The camp is being broken up around me. Trainees bustle about and I'm sitting on the ground eating porridge, or at least I think that's what the almost-solid gray mass of lumps is that I've scraped out of a dented saucepan.

"We're moving out soon," Gabriel says, joining me. It's barely past dawn but I know Greatorex will think we're dilly-dallying.

I hold the pan out to him and say, "Want some? It's disgusting."

He shakes his head. "I had some earlier."

"Where've you been?" I try to sound curious, not child-ish. But he said he'd stay with me, and yet when I woke he wasn't there, though Greatorex was.

"Greatorex asked me to talk to Donna."

"And you asked Greatorex to do what in return?" I have a sick feeling he asked her to sit with me, to watch over me like a child.

He doesn't reply at first, only keeps eye contact. "I told her you have bad dreams and to kick you if you started screaming and crying."

I swear at him but he leans closer to me and says, "I just asked her to get me if you woke up."

I throw the saucepan into the fire—all very mature. I did have a dream, not a really bad wake-up-blubbering one, but he wasn't to know that.

"Are you going to tell me what happened when you left our camp, after you drew your knife on me?"

"I shouldn't have done that."

"No."

"I was . . . I'd found two Hunters a couple of days be-fore. I killed them." And I tell him everything about that and the trap and finding Donna. I don't tell him much about the fight, no details; he'll know it was bad.

Gabriel says, "Greatorex wanted me to see if I can work Donna out."

"And?"

"She seems genuine enough. Do you think she's a spy?"

I shrug. "You were the one who told me they don't go around with big signs over their heads."

"Yes, I did say that, didn't I? Very wise."

"So what did Donna say, O wise one?"

"That she ran away from England a few weeks ago, when things got bad. Her mother was arrested. Her dad died years ago. She made her way to France and then here."

"That's it?"

"That's the short version. She's quite chatty. Didn't hold back. She talked about you quite a bit too. She likes you."

"I saved her life . . . rescued her from the clutches of evil."

We sit in silence again and then Gabriel says, "She said there were eight of them. Some kind of elite Hunters, two with strong Gifts."

"Not that strong, evidently."

Gabriel sounds sad and worried when he says, "You could have been killed."

"I could have been killed walking back into camp last night."

But I know he's right. The one with the Gift for projecting pain was a problem. I think her Gift was weak or maybe she couldn't control it in the heat of battle but there'll be more like her to come. I think I got lucky and the other one with the Gift for making you blind must have been one of the guards I killed at the start.

Greatorex shouts, "We're leaving in two minutes. Get your packs ready."

Gabriel starts to get up but I need to tell him something. "They were all women. Some of them were still sleeping when I killed them. One tried to flee and I slit her throat. Some I killed by ripping their guts open and two burned to death from the lightning I hit them with."

Gabriel sits back closer to me, his hand on my leg. "We're in a war."

"So I'm a war hero, not a psychopathic murderer?"

"You're not a psychopath and you're not a murderer. You're not bad. You're not remotely evil. You're someone caught up in a bloody war and it's eating you up—and that just proves how sane you are."

Against Anyone Normal They'd Be Lethal

Greatorex leads us out of the camp. There must be about twenty of us. Everyone is helping carry a load. Even Donna has a large rucksack on her back, though I notice her hands are zip-tied in front of her. We troop out in a line. The idea is to go through a cut, which has already been set up, and once through it we close it behind us, leaving this camp with no cuts, no links to any of the other camps. As Greatorex says, "It's served its purpose."

I like Greatorex. Some people would blame me and say, "We'd not have to move if it wasn't for Nathan," but Greatorex doesn't see it like that. She knows that things will always be changing and moving is part of her job.

I drop to the back and then stop and listen for Hunters. It would be like them to attack while we're vulnerable, concentrating on other things. But I hear nothing. I put my load down and run back to check along my trail for a few minutes. I know Greatorex has had her people check and recheck it too, but it can't do any harm to have a final look.

Nothing.

I retrieve my load and catch up with the group as they disappear through the cut. Greatorex waits until we're all through and goes last. Few people can make cuts. Only one person can do it for the Alliance now. Marcus had the ability but I've no idea how to access that Gift. Anyway, closing cuts doesn't require a Gift or even any magic, just a small explosion.

When we're through, Greatorex unpins a hand grenade and Gabriel and I hold her left arm as she slides her right hand and the grenade into the cut. The cut pulls her but we dig our heels in and pull her back as she lets the grenade slide out of her hand. It will explode when it's still inside the cut; within a few seconds the cut loses its magic and fades to nothing.

We check and the cut is gone.

Within hours the new Camp Three is set up and everything is organized and as if we've been here for days. Greatorex and Celia had the location already decided. Greatorex is professional and calm but I can sense the trainees are on edge and, unlike her, they seem to blame me. It's something about the way they huddle together and sneak looks at me. Greatorex senses it too, I think. She keeps them busy with chores: setting up tents, scouting the surrounding area, cooking. Then in the late afternoon she decides on a bit of training: fighting.

Me and Gabriel watch the hand-to-hand fighting class. Donna is watching too, sitting opposite us, her hands still zip-tied together.

Greatorex takes a break and comes to stand with us to

view her pupils. I ask her, "What's happening with Donna?"

"She says she wants to join the Alliance but, since BB, Celia's given strict instructions that anyone wanting to join has to be questioned under a truth potion."

"And what are the results?"

"We don't have any potion. I've sent word back to Camp One that we need some, but until then she's a prisoner."

"But what does your gut instinct tell you? Is she genuine or a spy?"

"I like her. She's got a positive attitude. She's intelligent, quick, and not at all cocky. She likes you, though, which does make me wonder about her judgment."

"Very funny."

"Actually, I think she has good judgment. She sticks up for you."

I wonder to whom she sticks up for me.

Greatorex nods toward the trainees, saying, "They're looking better, don't you think?"

"Yeah, better. But they're still slow and soft."

"I think they could take you now in a straight fight."

I shake my head.

"Try them? It'll be good for them. Four of my best against you. Just don't kill anyone."

"If those four win against me I'll kill myself."

Greatorex smiles. "OK then. Those four and me against you."

Greatorex is a good fighter, almost as good as Celia. I

shake my head and say, "I don't want to hurt you, Greatorex."

"I'll heal. So will you. Not scared of a few trainees and an ex-Hunter, are you?" Greatorex is thin and delicate-looking, but also fast, tough, and lethal, and very smart.

I look to Gabriel, saying, "What do you think?"

"I hope they kick your butt."

"Pick your team then," I say to Greatorex.

She rubs her hands and calls out, "Sophie, Scott, Adele, Kirsty."

They walk over to her. I recognize Kirsty as she's huge, slow, and strong. Scott is toned and fast, as is Sophie. Adele must have come from one of the other Alliance camps as I've not seen her before. Greatorex gives them a pep talk, basically saying that she'll attack me first and they have to back her up with everything they've got while I'm busy with her. When she's finished her little speech I say to her so that they can all hear, "You haven't told them what to do once I kill you."

Greatorex smiles and says, "When you're begging for mercy I'll remind you of that." The trainees nod and try to look tough.

I move to the middle, encouraging them to come behind me, which they think will help them. They'll think getting behind me is the way to beat me, but I'll be moving too fast. My main problem is going to be not hurting anyone too badly.

"No Gifts," Greatorex says to me. "No going invisible."

We've trained together like that and it is just too easy for me.

"No guns, no knives," I reply. "And no truncheons." I know her tricks.

"Course not—what do you think we are?" she says, holding her arms out as if to show she's unarmed.

I beckon her forward and the others move round.

Celia has taught me great technique, and she's taught it to Greatorex too, but I'm stronger, bigger, and faster than she is. If I can knock her out quickly the other trainees will drop like flies. I hope none of them run. I'm tougher on the ones that run.

Greatorex moves back and I move forward and then suddenly the trainees rush at me all together. Greatorex's pep talk must all have been a ruse; they have planned this. I knock Scott out with a blow to the face and Adele with my elbow to her face a split second later, but then my kidneys explode with pain and I drop and heal at the same time. I try to roll away but I'm stopped by someone landing on my legs and Greatorex kicks my face.

I taste blood, a bit of tooth loose in my mouth, and then I'm healed and grabbing at Greatorex but she's moved out of the way, so I twist to hammer-blow the girl grappling with my legs. There's more kicking to my back and I twist to grab that leg and snap it to the side. I know I've broken it from the sound and the scream. Then I'm on my feet and there's just Greatorex and the biggest girl, Kirsty, left—though Adele is getting back up. I feint to Kirsty, but then jump and kick at Greatorex. She's quick, though, and dodges to the side so I barely catch the side of her face. Kirsty comes at me from behind, which is a good move, and wraps her arms round me, which isn't—I snap my head back to break her nose. She still doesn't let me go, so I do it again and at the same time heel her in the shin. She drops. Then I turn to Adele as she's up now and coming at me, so I punch her face again but this time, as my fist flies forward, I see her face change color and then there's an excruciating pain in my hand as it slams into her metallic jaw. I must've broken a few fingers. I drop back and heal. Adele is smirking and her face changes back from shiny gray to her normal pale skin.

"What happened to the no-Gifts rule?" I shout.

Adele shrugs.

I shrug back, saying, "Let's see what happens if I send lightning to you."

Greatorex runs between us shouting, "No! No Gifts. Adele is still learning to control hers. She—"

I kick at Greatorex, connecting with the side of her head and sending her sprawling. "No rule against talking about using them, is there?"

That leaves me and Adele. I spin and kick out at Adele and she turns gray again. My foot feels like it's kicked a car. I heal and feint a punch to see if she turns gray. She does and then she tries to hit me but she's too slow and I grab her arm and throw her to the ground on her stomach, pulling her head back. I see now that her skin is like metal, but after a few seconds the color fades and she's vulnerable. So I put her in a stranglehold and her face changes color again but this time it's red. Her Gift isn't working now.

She bangs on the ground to indicate she's surrendering and I stand, telling her, "Stay down." But she starts to get up and I see she's really mad. I've not noticed before but her eyes are those of a Black Witch, and she's definitely angry enough for one. She lashes out at me, turning gray, but again it only lasts for a few seconds and when she's back to normal I punch her in the face, hard. She wobbles and then goes down on her backside, blood running from her nose.

"If you could control that Gift it would be pretty handy," I tell her.

I turn to look around me. Greatorex is standing now, holding her hands up in defeat. She says, "OK. You win, Nathan. No more." She looks at the groaning bodies on the ground, saying, "Though I still think they've improved."

"Yeah, against anyone normal they'd be lethal."

The voice comes from the trees and I look over and Nesbitt is there, grinning at me.

Blood Lust

The beautiful blonde Black Witch lights her cigarette and then throws the lighter to me. It's good to have a cigarette now and again, especially one of hers. The smoke I inhale is deliciously thick, with the flavor of blueberries, and I blow out a long plume of heavy violet smoke and watch it hover above my head and fade to nothing. I didn't use to trust Van enough to smoke her stuff, but these are no stronger than tobacco and taste better.

Van says, "I believe you attacked a group of Hunters, Nathan."

"They're the enemy. Isn't that what we're supposed to do?"

"You're supposed to follow orders. There were no orders to attack."

"I stumbled across them. Seemed like a good opportunity. I didn't have time to get permission."

"You know you wouldn't have got permission if you'd sought it."

We're sitting in the center of the new Camp Three with Nesbitt, Gabriel, and Greatorex. Van's an expert at potions and I assume she's here to mix up a truth potion for Donna, though so far there's been no mention of that and the conversation is more on me.

Van continues. "You risk your life and the lives of others for a few Hunters. Your attacks do little but satisfy your lust for blood."

"Nothing'll satisfy that," Nesbitt mutters from behind.

"I took a risk and it paid off."

"We'd rather you didn't take the risk."

"We all risk being killed at any time. We might all be dead by this time tomorrow. If I choose to attack some of them, that's up to me."

Van shakes her head and looks to Gabriel. He says, "Nathan takes calculated risks and wouldn't endanger anyone else." And somehow it feels worse that he's covering for me when I know he doesn't approve of my attacks.

"Well, calculated or not," continues Van, "if they carry on, the likelihood is that you will get killed, Nathan. And we need you for a bigger purpose."

"Yeah?" I say. So maybe this is the real point of her visit.

"The longer the war goes on, the stronger Soul gets. He is drawing more White Witch councils from Europe under his influence. We're still trying to recruit from all sections of the witch community, but after our defeat at Bialowieza— well, it's hard." She glances at me and draws heavily on her cigarette before blowing out a stream of lilac smoke. "And there's another factor holding people back. They don't see the point in joining the fight when they believe you'll kill Soul in any case. Rumors are circulating that some witches have had visions of you doing that. Personally, I'm not sure if they're visions or desperate hopes. But everyone knows that you took your father's Gifts."

"So it's all down to me? Is that what you believe too, Van?"

"If you do have your father's Gifts and can control them, then you are stronger than Soul."

"Soul alone," I say. "Not Soul and hundreds of Hunters."

"Soul knows you're the last real threat to him," says Nesbitt. "That's why he's sending messages out about the amnesty. Not that anyone believes he'd stick to his promises."

"What amnesty?" I ask.

Nesbitt grins. "You haven't heard? Anyone would think you've been living under a stone, mate."

Van says, "Two weeks ago, Soul announced an amnesty for everyone in the Alliance and that all Alliance prisoners will be released—if we hand you over to him."

"It's a tempting offer," Nesbitt adds. "But I've told everyone that if they give you up I'll never speak to them again. That seems to have deterred them so far."

There was a time, years ago, when Celia wouldn't have thought twice about killing me or letting me die, but now I know she'd never do that. There was also a time when Nesbitt's comment would have annoyed me. Now I blow smoke rings.

One of the trainees mutters something about the conditions the prisoners are kept in. I realize then that all the trainees are standing round, listening in. I wonder how many of them would like to hand me over in exchange for an amnesty.

Nesbitt has heard the comment too and he looks over at the trainees and then says loud enough for all to hear, "Course you *could* give yourself up to Soul, Nathan. I know you'd love to help the prisoners, alleviate their suffering."

I grind my cigarette butt into the ground, saying, "It wouldn't alleviate anything." Maybe the prisoners would be released, but I doubt it, and the fact of Soul being in power would mean others would suffer. He'll never stop persecuting Black Witches or anyone who objects to his hold on power.

I can imagine the prisoners in the cells below the Council building, some in the same cell where I was held once, before I was tattooed. I was left in complete darkness, chained to the wall. I feel for any Black Witches among the prisoners—they'll suffer most being kept inside at night—but I know that giving myself up won't stop Soul's cruelty.

Van stands and says, "Walk with me, Nathan. I don't think we need an audience for this."

I get up and she takes my arm in hers and we stroll away from camp. Gabriel and Nesbitt follow close behind.

"Soul wants you, Nathan. But I believe he'd rather have you alive than dead. The Council kept you in a cage and trained you to kill your father. As a plan, that was twisted enough, but I think Soul is even more ambitious now. I think he wants to turn you into his private assassin, to kill whomever he wishes."

"Are people having visions about that too?"

"Not as far as I know. But it fits with his plan to control witches around the world. He'd love you to be his henchman. I've never met Soul, of course, but Celia knows him and you have met him too, I understand. Would he want that?"

My gut instinct says yes. I tell Van, "He wanted to give me three gifts on my seventeenth birthday. I always thought that was odd. Like he was making it personal."

"Yes, I think it is personal to him. I don't think he needs you but he wants you. Partly ego, partly"—she shrugs—"obsession. You got away from him and he wants you back. But most of all he wants power. And he thinks having you will symbolize his strength."

"Good job he hasn't got me then."

"Exactly. But, unlike Soul, the Alliance is weak and vulnerable. Celia is working hard to keep morale up and training the few recruits we have, but for the time being our first priority is to keep safe. Keep our heads down. Not attack the Hunters. And not risk losing you. We need you, Nathan. If you die, the Alliance will be broken. You can't risk your life going after small groups of Hunters; that isn't the way to defeat Soul." Van stops and stares at me. "Though I sense that isn't your top priority at the moment."

I shrug.

She persists. "You're searching for Annalise?"

"What do you think? Because of her my father is dead. Because of her half the Alliance is dead."

"What will you do if you find her?" Van asks.

I snort a laugh. "You mean, will I kill her quick or slow? I'm favoring quick at the moment but I'll have to see."

Van takes a deep breath and pulls her cigarette case out of her jacket, offers me one and takes one herself. We smoke in silence for a minute before she asks, "Are you able to use any of the Gifts your father had?"

"You know, it's bad manners to ask a White Witch about their Gifts and I am half White, Van."

She blows smoke in my face and says, "And I seem to lose my manners completely around you, Nathan."

For some reason that makes me smile. "I'm working on them. My Gifts, I mean, not my manners."

She looks like she's suppressing a grin and says, "With what results?"

"I can go invisible—that's working the best—and I can kill with lightning. I can breathe fire." And to demonstrate I blow out a small smoke ring without the help of a cigarette.

"And controlling time?"

"I'm working on it but it's hard. But, you know, the smoke rings aren't that easy either."

That actually does make her smile and then she blows a huge smoke ring and series of smaller ones to me.

I'm still not sure where this is all leading. "Do you believe the visions of me killing Soul, Van?"

"I don't need to believe in visions when I've got something better, something tangible that will enable you to kill Soul and will allow the Alliance to win." She pauses for a long drag on her cigarette and then continues. "Even with all your father's Gifts, you'll still be vulnerable. His own death must show you that. More important than mastering his Gifts, you need protection. You need something that will make you invulnerable, something that will keep you safe. You need the Vardian amulet."

"OK. I admit I've no idea what that is."

"It's an ancient and very powerful item. Believed to date back to the earliest days of witchcraft. All amulets protect those who hold them, but this one was something unique. It was created by a Black Witch called Vardia. Times were different then and Blacks and Whites lived together." Van smiles, almost as if she can't believe it herself. "Vardia fell in love with a powerful man, Linus, a prince, some say, but he was also a White Witch. He had little magical power, though, and he wanted Vardia's protection. He told her he loved her and she created the amulet to protect him. He won many battles with the amulet pressed against his skin over his heart. He fought those stronger than himself but he was never hurt. He became more and more powerful. Linus was grateful to Vardia but he didn't truly love her and knew he never could. Eventually he grew tired of his deception and told Vardia the truth: that he didn't love her. He sent her away. But, despite his betrayal, Vardia still loved him and so, before she left, in desperation she ripped the amulet in two and gave Linus half, keeping half herself, saying that when he wanted her protection she would return, that he'd be safe when they and the amulet were reunited. But Linus never asked her to return and he was killed in the next battle he fought."

Of course I have once seen half an amulet. It wasn't a metal or jeweled ornament as I would have expected but a piece of worn, old parchment with strange writing on it laid out in a series of circles—well, semicircles because the parchment was ripped in half.

"The half of the amulet that Gabriel gave you?" I say. "That's one of the pieces?"

"Yes."

"But not much use without the other half."

"No. However, many years ago I learned who had the other half and since then I've been searching for that person. A witch called Ledger."

"And now you've found him? Her?"

"Yes."

"And have you got the other half of the amulet?"

"It's not quite as simple as that. But I do believe the way to beat Soul is by using the amulet. If you have it you'll be protected as Linus was. You'll be indestructible."

"If the amulet is ripped in half, how do you know it'll work? How do you even know these pieces are part of the Vardian amulet? It might all be a stupid old story anyway."

Van's blue eyes seem to explode with sapphire sparks as she says, "There are no guarantees, but I think Ledger will know how to make it work. She's a powerful witch. Possibly the most powerful ever."

"More powerful than my father?"

Van takes my arm again and says, "Ledger is very different from your father. She's unusual for a Black Witch and most people haven't even heard of her. She's extremely private, though I was honored to meet her a few days ago. She has many Gifts and a vast knowledge of magic. She may be able to help you access your father's Gifts as well as find how to make the amulet work."

"But why would she help me? And I can't imagine she's going to hand her half of the amulet over for nothing, if at all."

"She might be persuaded. I told her about you and she was extremely interested in meeting you."

I look at Van. She's as cool and sophisticated as always. The scars from her battle with Mercury are all but faded. She's not in one of the pastel-colored suits she used to wear but dark casual trousers, jumper, and winter jacket. And she's as hard to read as ever. I trust her, but I know she always has her own agenda.

"Why would Ledger want to meet me?"

"You'll have to go and see her to find out."

"You say I'm taking risks; if she's so powerful, how do you know she won't just take Gabriel's half of the amulet and kill me?"

Van smiles faintly. "I don't think murder is her style. And anyway I already gave it to her."

"*What?*"

"It was a sign of good faith. Ledger will know how to make the amulet whole. She said she will do it for the right person. We simply have to hope that you are that person, Nathan."

Dreading You

Van goes back to camp with Nesbitt, and me and Gabriel go for a run. I ask him, "Are you bothered about Van giving away your half of the amulet?"

"Of course not. I gave it to her in exchange for helping me, for saving my life. It's hers to do with as she wants. And I told you back then, Nathan, I'm not interested in those things anymore. I never was particularly to start with."

"And do you think I should go for the amulet?"

"I'm thinking about that."

So am I. Ledger sounds interesting and so does the amulet but if I'm doing that I'm not looking for Annalise. But I'm beginning to realize—or rather I'm having to face up to what I've known for weeks now—that Annalise has escaped from here. She could be anywhere by now.

We run for a couple of hours and then head back into camp. Greatorex, Van, and Nesbitt are sitting with Donna and we go over to join them. Nesbitt is supporting Donna, who looks like she's going to pass out.

On the ground is one of Van's small stone bowls with dregs of liquid in it. Truth potion, I guess.

Van looks at me and then back to Donna and asks, "Why do you want to join the Alliance?"

"I can do good if I join." Donna's voice is slurred, like she's drunk.

"What sort of good?"

"Kill the bad guys."

"Who are the bad guys?"

"The evil ones, the bad guys."

"But who? Name one."

"Bad guys." Donna looks like she's going to sleep.

Van persists. "Are the Hunters bad?"

"They kill the Alliance."

"Yes, but are the Hunters bad?"

"They tied me up and starved me and gagged me." Donna seems to focus on me for a second or two and says, "He killed them."

"Do you know the name of this person?" Van points at me.

"Nathan. Also known as Freddie."

Van raises her eyebrows and looks at me. "Freddie?"

I nod.

"Is Nathan a bad guy?"

"He killed the Hunters."

"So does that make him good or bad?"

"Everyone says he's bad."

"What do *you* say?"

"He let me have all the chocolate."

Van blows her cheeks out. She looks tired. "Are you a spy?"

"No."

"Are you an assassin?"

"I'd like to kill the bad guys."

"Who are the bad guys?"

"The evil ones, the bad guys."

I get the feeling this is not the first time the questioning has gone round in circles and I leave them to it.

Later I ask Van how it went. She shakes her head. "Difficult. To work best, any potion has to be tailored specifically to the individual. The one I used was a general truth potion, but even so everything she said should have been the truth."

"So? What's the verdict?"

"I don't like the fact that her answers were always the same. They were honest but not open. But it's hard to judge. I'll need to make a potion specifically for her."

Van offers me a cigarette and I accept it. I inhale the smoke and breathe out. I'm surprised that the cigarettes seem to be ordinary fain ones.

"American," Van says, as if reading my thoughts.

"I don't suppose you've got any of that other potion, the one that helped me sleep."

Van hesitates but asks, "Bad dreams?"

I shrug. "They're just dreams." I wonder if I should tell her about my vision. Maybe another time.

"I've got this." She reaches into her jacket and takes out a few small pieces of paper. Or, rather, pieces of paper folded over several times to make them small. She selects three. "It's strong. Only one a night or you'll never wake up." She holds them over my outstretched palm. "You wouldn't be tempted to take all of them at once, would you, Nathan?"

I look into the blue of her eyes. I tell her, "Most days I'm tempted."

I don't tell her that the thought that stops me is of Annalise being out there somewhere, alive and free, and if she was alive and I was dead then the injustice of it would consume me in flames. Only when she's dead will I give up.

I've pretty much decided to go to see Ledger, but Greatorex wants me, Nesbitt, and Gabriel to help secure the camp first. Greatorex is establishing a new routine of daily checks in the immediate vicinity and weekly checks in a wider area. Each Alliance camp is connected to the others by a cut, with one escape cut leading somewhere far away. Greatorex says, "The network of cuts that link them allows us to keep the camps small and less visible, but the cuts themselves may be a problem. There's at least one Hunter who can sense where they are."

I nod. "My father thought it might be best to fill the world with cuts. Overload the Hunters with information."

"Nice idea, but at the moment we'll keep hiding and moving frequently."

A few of the trainees are sent out close to the camp for the daily check, and I go further out with Nesbitt and Gabriel, looking for any signs of Hunter activity.

It's good to get out of the camp for a few days. Me, Nesbitt, and Gabriel agree on an area to cover each day, splitting up in the morning and meeting again in the evening. We take three days to make a wide circuit of Camp Three and find nothing alarming; on the contrary, it looks like a good place.

And every day I practice my Gifts. Invisibility, flames, and lightning are all getting stronger and more controllable and I even think at one point that I'm on the verge of stopping time. Only I'm not stopping time. That isn't what my father did. He stopped the world, or slowed it down so much that it seemed to stop. And I do what I saw my father do, rub my palms together in a circle, and as I do that I think of the world turning and then I put the palms of my hands on my head, and as I do that I think of the world stopping but me carrying on moving. And I look up and see all is still around me. I turn to Gabriel and he's still, watching me. And then it starts again. Gabriel blinks.

"Did you notice anything?" I ask him.

"Something funny happened with your head," he replies. "One second you were looking away, then you were looking right at me."

I grin at him. "I think I've done my first ever stopping of time."

"Do it again?"

And I try and it doesn't work, but I know that I just need to keep practicing.

The final night before we head back to camp we're lying by the fire. Nesbitt's snoring is quiet, but I can't sleep with it so I sit up and poke at the embers.

Gabriel hasn't said much all evening; he lights a cigarette, which he must have got from Van, drags on it, and passes it to me. He says, "Your control over your Gifts has improved. Still not as strong as your father, but definitely better."

I puff a smoke ring and then blow a narrow flame through the middle of it.

Gabriel says, "Nice trick."

I breathe out another smoke ring and try an even more delicate stream of flame through its middle.

"I'm not so sure you need any help from Ledger to improve your Gifts. I mean, she may be able to give you a few pointers, but really all you need is time and practice."

"Uh-huh." I huff out a large ring of flame. "I can do that and still go after the amulet."

"And the amulet might work, but on the other hand it might not."

"Are you trying to say I shouldn't go?"

"I'm trying to say that maybe we should think of other options."

"Such as?"

He stubs the cigarette out on the ground and then turns to look at me. "Leaving completely. Leaving the war. Leaving it all."

"Like the other Black Witches have done? You tired of it too?"

"Of course I'm tired of it! I'm tired of the cold. Tired of being hungry. Tired of being afraid. Being out here these last few days has reminded me of what we used to be like. It used to be fun. You, in your own individual way, used to be fun."

"It's war, that's what you said."

"Yes, it's war and I'm tired of it. And . . . I'm getting tired of you, Nathan. I never thought I'd say that, but it's true. I'm tired of your revenge, your anger, your hate. The war is killing you. Not your body but your mind, your soul. You've changed. I feel I'm losing you. Or you're losing yourself. You don't need Ledger or the amulet. You don't need to kill Annalise. You don't need any of it. What you need is to get away from it. Get back into nature like we have done these last few days, before the war turns you into something else . . . something bad."

"I thought you didn't believe in all the good versus evil stuff. I thought you said there was no good or bad in it."

"That was about using your Gift. There isn't anything good or bad in the animal you."

"I've killed people when he took over, when the animal took over."

"You killed for food or to survive. You didn't murder people in their sleep."

I shake my head. "No. If I kill as an animal, I eat people, Gabriel. And I'll tell you something—eating people isn't good. None of it's good. If I kill as an animal or a person, the end result is the same: there's another dead body at my feet."

"As an animal you don't kill through hate."

"Hunters are my enemies. Do you want me to love them to death?"

Gabriel shakes his head. "I said before all this started that the Alliance would only be interested in how many you could kill, and you'd kill a lot. I stand by that. They want you to get the amulet and kill Soul for them. And they'll let you kill many others along the way."

"You want Soul to carry on?"

"No. But I'm more concerned for you than him."

"If I get the amulet and it works I'll be invulnerable."

"That's what I'm worried about. Another thing I said was that I thought Annalise would see the Black Witch side of you, see the killing you do, see how you change, and she'd come to dread you. I stand by that too. Though I admit I wasn't that bothered about it. I never liked her, never trusted her, never understood your attraction to her. And I admit I wanted her to see that side of you. I wanted her to realize that you weren't right for each other. But . . . what makes you Nathan—what makes you so special—is that you are both White Witch and Black Witch, both dark and full of light. That's what I love about you. What I've always loved. And I love you still, Nathan, and I know I always will. But you're changing. And now . . . now what I fear is that you'll get the amulet and you'll hone the Gifts you took from your father. You'll be invulnerable and you'll kill more people, many, many more people. I fear you won't be able to stop and you'll lose yourself completely. And then I'll come to dread you too."

Spit

.•·🍂

I sit up and watch the fire, thinking about what Gabriel said to me. Of course I don't want him to dread me but I remember my vision and him beckoning me over, the gun in his hand. Would he ever shoot me? I can't believe that. Even if he dreaded me, he wouldn't do that. And as for all the stuff about losing myself—I feel like for years I didn't really know who I was, but now that I know I'm more and more like my father, I feel clearer about that, good about that. To do what I need to do, to kill Soul and Wallend and bring an end to their reign of terror, I have to be as tough and ruthless as Marcus was.

The next day we have one last slow scout around and then work our way back to Camp Three, arriving as it's getting dark. Nesbitt immediately goes to look for Van, but Greatorex tells us that she has left because she was needed at Camp One.

I ask her, "Has something happened?"

"You need a haircut," a different voice interrupts before Greatorex can reply.

I turn to find Celia looking me up and down. I haven't seen her for months and I inspect her too. She's looking tired and thinner but otherwise as neat and ugly as ever.

She says, "Good to see you're still with him, Gabriel."

We sit by the campfire and Celia asks about my Gifts and I tell her I think I might be able to stop time soon. I expect some criticism for attacking the Hunter camp but she's more interested than irritated and seems pleased that I managed to overcome eight of them. "But, of course, eight is nothing. Eighty is how many you will have to beat if you want to get to Soul."

I expect her to go on about the amulet but she doesn't mention it.

I ask, "And if I do go up against Soul, how many Alliance soldiers will there be to back me up?"

"In truth, not as many as I'd like. But Soul rules by fear. If we can defeat him, many of those too scared to stand up and fight him now will come over to our side. Then I do believe that we have a chance of working together, Whites, Blacks, Half Bloods. It won't be easy and there will always be troublemakers, but if all are considered equal and treated equally under the law then we'll have a fair society, a better society for us all."

I still struggle to believe Celia is saying this. The woman who kept me chained in a cage now does seem to genuinely believe in a world where Black and White Witches can live together peacefully. And here I am, a Half Code sitting between her, a White Witch, and Gabriel, a Black Witch.

But the conversation is strange. All this talk of Blacks

and Whites and no mention of the amulet, which I thought she'd be desperate for me to get. I wonder what's up, or if she's hiding something.

It suddenly occurs to me that I haven't asked about Arran, and I'm shocked that I haven't thought of my brother until now. I haven't seen him since the days after BB. He was with Celia then, helping with healing as best he could, though there was hardly anyone to heal. Most were dead. I brace myself to ask about him, wondering if this is what Celia is hiding, but she seems to guess what I'm thinking and says, "Arran's well. He's a good healer, a good person to have in the Alliance. He's a reasonable voice. Although he's quiet, Blacks and Whites listen to him."

So back to the issue of Black Witches and White Witches again.

Celia leaves us to go to her tent for the night and I wonder again why she's really come to Camp Three. Is it to see me? To see Greatorex? Is there a problem with the Alliance? And why has Van disappeared just when she was going to tell me how to find Ledger?

The next morning I go with Gabriel to watch the trainees sparring. Nesbitt joins in. He loves the chance to wrestle with women. Gabriel and I offer helpful advice to the trainees, and one of them eventually manages to kick Nesbitt in the balls.

Donna is there too, sitting opposite us like last time, and I see the zip ties are still on.

I say to Gabriel, "Donna's going to spend the rest of her life with her hands tied."

"Nesbitt told me that Van had started to make up a special truth potion for her but hadn't finished it before she had to go to Camp One. So, yes, she'll be like that for a while."

"I think I was right not to trust her: her answers under the simple truth potion were odd." But then as I look at the trainees I realize I like Donna more than them and I say, only partly joking, "Mind you, I wouldn't trust any of them as far as I could throw them."

Nesbitt flops on the ground near us, his eyes still glued on the trainees, and says, "Who do you want to throw?"

Gabriel looks him over. "Nesbitt, do you know that if you add up the ages of all the trainees and multiply that by the number of times you manhandled them, the resulting number would still only be half the age they think you are?"

Nesbitt laughs and says, "Yes, but have you noticed how few blokes there are around here? There are at least two girls to every fella, and some of these girls are bound to be—"

"Desperate?"

"Interested in a more mature person."

"What!"

"And, though I say so myself, I'm keeping myself in order these days." He slaps his stomach and I have to admit that where there used to be a little bit of flab there is now nothing but muscle. But then no one here is flabby; our diets aren't exactly rich. "OK, I'm a little older but—"

"A little!" Gabriel and I reply in unison.

"Ageist, that's what you fellas are!"

"There is one woman here who I've heard admiring you, Nesbitt," Gabriel says. "White Witch. Blonde."

"So many blondes here," Nesbitt says with a whimper.

"Intelligent too. And super fit," Gabriel continues.

Nesbitt surveys the trainees. "Hmm? Which one?"

Gabriel doesn't reply and Nesbitt looks to him. "Well? Come on, mate, share."

"She arrived in camp last night."

"*Celia?*" Nesbitt pulls a face and then laughs.

Just then Adele comes over and says, "Celia wants a word with you, Nesbitt."

"Ha! It might be that *she's* after *me*, fellas." Nesbitt gets to his feet, brushing himself down. "Well, desperate times and all that."

"And she wants to speak to you too," Adele adds, and I glance up at her but realize she's talking to Gabriel, not me.

Adele leads Gabriel and Nesbitt back to Celia. Greatorex must be there too as she's not with the trainees. I wonder when I'll be summoned.

It's less than an hour before Adele comes back and asks me to go with her. Celia is sitting near the fire, Greatorex sitting to her right, Nesbitt and Gabriel standing to her left. They're all watching me as I approach. Nesbitt seems nervous and is muttering something in Gabriel's ear.

Gabriel comes toward me as I approach. He looks so serious I feel instantly on alert. I've no idea what this is about but it isn't good, whatever it is.

I stop. Gabriel is facing me, half blocking my way to Celia, his shoulder close to mine. He's near me, not holding me back but touching my arm with his body.

"What's happening?" I ask him.

"Celia will explain, but please, Nathan, try to keep calm."

Celia says, "Sit down, Nathan. We need to talk."

"I can talk standing up."

Celia stands too, as does Greatorex. "There have been some developments that I need to tell you about. There are some Black Witches at Camp One who aren't happy. Gus and a few others are causing some trouble."

I've met Gus on a couple of occasions, one being when my father cut his ear off for attacking me. I'm not surprised he's causing trouble.

"That's why I asked Van to go back," Celia continues. "She's a well-respected Black Witch. Well respected by both Blacks and Whites. She'll calm things down."

"Are you going to get to the point?" I ask.

"The unrest is because of a prisoner we have there."

"A prisoner?"

And I feel like I can't catch my breath, like I already know what's coming next, but I daren't think it in case I'm wrong and there are no clues on Celia's face and even when she says "Annalise" I daren't quite believe it in case I heard wrong so I say, "Annalise?"

Celia says, "Yes, she's our prisoner. She's at Camp One."

And I need a second to get my head together. I know this isn't straightforward, and the way they are all being with me is like they don't trust me, but they have her. She hasn't got away. I find I'm saying, "I need to go there, to Camp One."

"We'll come to that in a minute. First, you need to understand the situation, Nathan." Celia hesitates and then goes on. "We caught Annalise a few days after BB. She—"

"What? But then . . . you've had her for weeks? Months?"

"It's three months."

"And no one's bothered to tell me?"

"I'm telling you now."

Celia's voice is low and quiet. Mine is not as I say, "I've been scouring the fucking country for her!"

"Yes, I know."

I swear again.

"And who else knew you had her?" I ask, glaring around. Nesbitt at least doesn't look away so I know he didn't know, and Gabriel, still close to me, meets my eyes too, but with a look that says everything.

"You knew?" I ask him. "You knew and didn't tell me?"

"I'd heard a rumor. I had an idea what might have happened and—"

"You didn't think to share that rumor with me? Didn't think to tell me what idea you had?" I swear at him and turn away. "So all the time I was out searching for her, with you telling me not to risk my life attacking Hunters, you could have stopped me at any time by telling me about your 'idea'?"

"I didn't know you were going to attack the Hunters."

But I can't listen to him. I can't make sense of it. I don't know why he wouldn't tell me about Annalise. He knew it was driving me insane. "You knew about her and told me nothing!"

"I was trying—"

"You told me nothing." I lean forward to shout in his face. "Nothing!"

"I was—"

"I trusted you," I hiss at him.

Now Gabriel leans in to me, close to my face, and hisses back, "No, you don't trust me—not anymore. You don't tell me what you're doing or what you've done. You disappear for days and don't tell me where you've been, who you've killed. You tell me the minimum when you have to. When it suits you."

I can't believe he's blaming me. He's hidden Annalise and he's blaming me! I spit at Gabriel. The spit lands on his cheek.

Gabriel stares at me. I've never seen him angry before. And Nesbitt is getting in between us, pushing Gabriel away from me and saying to him, "He's just being Nathan. You've got to love him for it really."

Celia shouts, "Nathan, you need to calm down."

I turn from Gabriel to Celia, and swear at her and then I

take a breath and say, "I take it everyone else knew?"

"Greatorex knew and had orders not to tell you, to keep you out of Camp One, which turned out to be easy, as you hardly even spent time at Camp Three."

"And why are you telling me now?"

"Like I said last night, the Alliance has to ensure all witches are treated equally, that the rule of law prevails. This is war but we must still have rules and we must all follow them. Annalise is our prisoner. She'd like to leave the war. She doesn't support Soul and never will, but she doesn't believe war is the answer."

"I don't give a shit what she believes. What I want to know is what you're going to do with her."

"We're going to put her before the new court that is being set up: a court of Black and White Witches who can make a judgment. She shot Marcus, a Black Witch and a valued member of the Alliance. And, as a result of her actions, the Alliance suffered a terrible defeat. There are a number of Black Witches, led by Gus, who want to see Annalise punished. And the Alliance wants—needs—to be seen to be acting fairly, to be treating all witches equally, whether they are Black or White. That is how we can show the Alliance to be different from the Council of White Witches. But also a fair trial for Annalise means she can put her case."

"And what is her case?"

"That she acted in the heat of the moment. She insists that she was only trying to help her brother."

And now I'm not feeling anger but disgust at Annalise, her lies. I tell Celia, "Connor was already dead when she shot Marcus."

"This will be proven in the trial then. There will be truth potions for all witnesses to take. Trust me, Nathan. The truth will come out."

"Then trust me when I say this is the truth: my father killed Connor O'Brien, a Hunter, who was reaching for a gun. Annalise shot Marcus when Connor was already dead, then she ran off and left us to deal with the consequences. Because of her my father is dead. Because my father is dead there was no one to stop the Hunters and a hundred Alliance members died. All their deaths are on her hands."

"Your testimony will be heard, Nathan. It's right that it should be." Celia pauses and then adds, "And it's also right that you allow the court to deal with Annalise. That you don't seek your own revenge."

"If they let her go I'll seek what I like."

"Well, then the courts will have to deal with you too."

"Let them try."

Celia says, "I take it you know what her Gift is?"

I've given it a lot of thought and I have my suspicions. After Annalise shot Marcus, a huge gun battle started. Gabriel pulled me to the ground to protect me and when I looked up again Annalise had gone. At first I thought she'd run off and hidden in the trees, but I think I've always known that she disappeared, literally.

"She can become invisible," Celia confirms.

"How appropriate that she's got the same Gift as her esteemed father and glorious brother. How perfect. Now we know that she's just like them."

"Yes, that's Gus's argument, but some would say you're just like your father."

"I can be proud of that."

"Be careful, though, Nathan. There are many White Witches in the Alliance, many more White than Black, and, while they have no love for Annalise's family, she has the advantage of being seen as weak and insignificant, despite her Gift. You are neither of those things. They see that you are like your father. They know what you did to take his Gifts from him."

"What I had to do!"

"It isn't good if they fear you, Nathan. And many White Witches fear what you are or may become. They feel sympathy for Annalise acting out of love and devotion to a misguided brother, but you they see as a murderous Black Witch, son of Marcus, eater of hearts. You killed Marcus. Some are saying that it is you who should be put on trial."

"I wanted to save him! It was hopeless. He was dying. I didn't want to do it!"

"Calm down, Nathan," Celia says, her voice low and quiet.

I swear at her.

"There are some White Witches, supporters of Annalise,

who think the best way to defend her is to focus on you. They say the law must be applied equally."

"You want to arrest me? Is that it? For eating my father's heart after she shot him?"

"You can't be treated differently. I have to take you to answer the charges too. You can explain. I don't think it will—"

"You going to put me in a fucking cage?"

And I know they'd love that, all the Whites would love to see me in chains. And there is no way, *no way*, I'll ever let them do that to me again. And before I know it there's lightning shooting out from my hands, hitting the ground to either side of Celia's feet, and then I breathe a ball of fire and Celia is already stepping back from me as the flames burst between us.

And then her noise fills my head and it's agony and I hate it and I'm on my knees.

She stops it quickly, though.

"I don't want to hurt you, Nathan. I don't want to use my Gift on you, but I will have to if you don't calm down."

I look up at her and get back on my feet. I hate her noise so much and all I know is I'm going to stop her, stop everything. She's never going to use her noise on me again.

Never.

I rub the palms of my hands together and feel the world moving, and I move my hands faster and faster and then stop. I hold my hands close to my head and think of stillness.

There are no noises at all now. All is quiet. All is still.

Celia is standing in front of me, her face calm, concentrated. Gabriel is staring at me, still angry. Nesbitt is poised on one leg as if he was backing away and Greatorex has her gun pointed at me. And further back from that group are all the trainees. They must have heard the shouting and come to watch and listen. Most look afraid; one looks gleeful. Donna is there too, her hands still tied, looking serious.

And I walk away from them. I don't know how long time will be stopped for. I don't care. There is no way they'll get me in a cage.

I walk away and behind me I hear shouting. Time has started up again. I run.

Drugs

I'm sitting in the forest. It's getting late. I'm not sure what to do. I haven't hurt anyone. But I could have. I was close to it. And I spat in Gabriel's face. How could I have done that?

It's almost dark when I hear footsteps. They stop, then they get louder, clumsier. He's making sure I know he's coming, and when the footsteps get nearer they stop again and a voice calls out, "That was some fancy magic you did back there, mate."

I don't answer and after a minute Nesbitt comes and squats next to me.

"No one could work it out at first. It was like you'd vanished into thin air. Gab said you must've done the trick with stopping time."

"Yeah."

"Nice!"

"Yeah."

"So, anyway, a few of us thought we'd see if we could find you. And . . . so . . . here I am. Mind you, it wasn't hard 'cause as usual you left a trail a mile wide."

"I'm not trying to hide. I just needed to think."

"Yeah, well, that's understandable." Nesbitt manages to

stay still and silent for half a minute and then says, "They won't put you in a cage. Celia won't let them. She said that."

I'm not sure what to believe, though I don't think Celia would lie to me.

Nesbitt adds, "Van won't let them do it either. Nor me, and definitely not lover boy. And I don't think Greatorex would be too happy about it. You've got more friends than you think."

I wonder if that's true. If I have friends how come I always feel alone?

"Is Gabriel still mad at me?"

Nesbitt hesitates and then says, "On a scale of one to ten, I'd say he's at nine and a half."

"So, it could be worse then."

"He'll calm down." Nesbitt nudges me and says, "The best thing about arguments is the making-up after. I see a big reconciliation ahead for you two: you apologize and he takes you into his arms and—"

"Nesbitt, shut up."

We sit in silence for a bit and then I ask him, "So, what's the plan?"

"The plan is that I use my charm and charisma to persuade you to calm down and come back to camp. Then when Celia is sure that you aren't going to kill Annalise with a bolt of lightning or whatever . . . then we go to Camp One, where you give evidence in the trial of the century. Annalise's, I mean. You're not going on trial, at least not yet. Celia says best case it'll never come to that. Course that means that worst case it will. But if Annalise is found guilty you won't have a case to answer. Celia says she'll make it clear to everyone that you have come voluntarily to give evidence. She says I have to emphasize that you haven't been arrested and that so far there are no charges against you."

"She better not try to arrest me. I'm not going on trial. Not ever. Not for anything and definitely not for killing my father. I don't have to explain myself to them. And I'm never going back in a cage, never going in a cell, never going behind a locked door."

"OK. Well, that's pretty clear." After a minute Nesbitt adds, "To be honest, mate, I think they'd struggle to arrest you, and even if they managed to get you in a cell I think you've got enough Gifts now to get out pretty easy, so I wouldn't worry about it." And he nudges me with his elbow. "Mind you, if you were struggling, I could bake a cake and do the old trick of smuggling a file in to you. Or Gab could disguise himself as the big fat sweaty jailer and steal the keys and—"

"Nesbitt, shut up."

"I was just saying—"

"When I was fourteen they put a collar on me. If I went too far from the cage, the collar would open and let out acid. They'd do that again."

Nesbitt is quiet for a moment, then says, "No wonder you're so messed up."

"Thanks."

"Anyway, I don't think even that's really going to be a problem for you. You managed to walk away from a load of seriously Gifted witches. I mean, Celia was doing her noise thing and you vanished. Greatorex and the trainees—"

"Nesbitt, can you shut up? Just for a minute?"

He manages to stay quiet for almost a minute before saying, "You got any food? I haven't eaten a thing since that disgusting porridge."

I don't have any food but we light a fire and sit looking at it and poking it and Nesbitt chats on into the night. When he falls asleep, I go over it all again. I can't let Annalise get away with it. Because of her, Marcus is dead. I said I'd kill her and maybe that's what I have to do. But I'd like to see her on trial. I'd like to see her questioned. I'd like to see her in a cage, wondering if she'll ever get out. So I will go and give evidence. Let's see if the Alliance can make a fair trial work. If not, well, I can decide what to do later.

I take out the packets of potion that Van gave me. Perhaps she knew I'd need them when I heard about Annalise. Probably. I'm not tempted to take all three. I want to see Annalise. I want her to see me too. I want to spit in her face. And then I think of Gabriel again. How could I have done that to him?

I open one of the packets and inside lies a smudge of fine yellow powder. I lick a few grains from the tip of my finger but only taste a faint suggestion of mint, so I pour the contents to the back of my throat and the mint flavor fills my mouth and then changes to become a dry bitterness and I wish I'd got some water, but then I realize I don't need to bother and my body feels like it's floating away into the darkness.

The blackness is empty and silent. It is perfect. It is complete.

Calm

"Are you calm now?" Celia asks.

"No thanks to you."

But I say this quietly and slowly. I do feel calm, clear. I'm not sure what was in that powder that Van gave me— more than just sleeping potion, I think. I'm feeling remarkably level-headed and in control. Even so, I've stayed away from camp for most of the day, only returning in the evening. Nesbitt walked back with me, and for once he kept relatively quiet.

"I only used my Gift on you because I thought things might get out of control," Celia says. "The trainees don't know you like I do. They might have thought you were going to hurt me. But I trust you, Nathan."

I remember her face when she was frozen in time and she's being honest, as she always is. She looked calm, like she was making a calculation.

I nod over to the trainees sitting across the fire from us and say, "I get the feeling everyone else expects me to rip their heart out and eat it for supper."

"The question is, what would you do if you saw Annalise?"

"I hate her and want her dead. I want to avenge my father but I want to see her stand trial. I want justice. I want her to be found guilty. I want her punished. Severely punished. I'm thinking that being shot in the stomach and left to die slowly and painfully would do it."

"But you won't try to kill her the minute you see her?"

"Not that first minute. But if she's found not guilty, or let off . . . I don't know." I shake my head. "What will they do to her if they find her guilty?"

"I think she'll be imprisoned. Probably for years."

"She killed Marcus. She should die. She should be shot."

"I doubt the court will want to shoot her. And if you were to do that, or take the law into your own hands in any way, then I'd have no option but to arrest you. It's the way the Alliance must work, Nathan. Fairness to all."

"Fine." I smile at her. "You'd have to catch me, of course."

"Let's hope it won't come to that."

It's dark when I finish talking with Celia and I can't see Gabriel anywhere. I ask Nesbitt and he says, "Try his tent."

I didn't even know Gabriel had a tent. Nesbitt nods to the one at the end of the row and I can see a green light coming from it.

I go over and drum my fingers on the canvas, saying, "Gabriel?"

He doesn't respond but I'm sure he's in there so I stick my head in. The tent is full of a green haze from the bowl of nightsmoke that's on the ground near Gabriel's head. Gabriel is lying on his side on a mat on the ground, a book open beside him. He doesn't look up.

I say, "Hi."

He doesn't reply and still doesn't look up.

"I hope you're just pretending to read," I say. "And really you can't concentrate on the book because all you can think of is beating the living shit out of me."

"I'm not sure what living shit is, but you're not far from the truth."

Gabriel looks at me now and I can see he's serious. He really would like to beat me up. I'm stooped over into the tent and it isn't very big and I feel awkward, so I kneel down.

"Do you want something?" Gabriel's voice is full of poison.

"Um. Yeah . . . I think we need to talk."

"Ha! Coming from you, that's almost funny. But strangely enough I'm not in a humorous mood."

"I wish you'd told me that you thought Annalise had been caught."

"I wish you'd told me about your attacks on the Hunters."

"I did tell you."

"You told me some things, afterward, when you had to; when you couldn't hide them anymore."

"But you were hiding stuff about Annalise. The Hunters didn't affect you."

"Didn't affect me? A group of eight Hunters that close to our camp? That close to Greatorex and the trainees?"

"But—"

"You could have got killed by them, or wounded, and I would have gone looking for you and probably got killed myself."

"But I was—"

"I haven't finished," Gabriel interrupts. "I admit I hid my thoughts from you. I didn't tell you my suspicions about Annalise being a prisoner, because I was trying to protect you. You know I hate her. I'd love to see her dead. Part of me would love to see you rip her to pieces, but another part of me knows that would be wrong, not for me or for her, but for you. You're not yourself at the moment, Nathan. I didn't want you to kill her and regret it after. Everything I did, I did for you. You hid your thoughts and actions from me because of what you wanted for yourself. You were only thinking of yourself. As usual."

I think I've lost at talking with Gabriel.

"You should go now," he says.

I don't move. I don't want to leave. I still want to talk to him. I need to apologize. This afternoon I worked out what I need to say. I've just got to say it.

I take a deep breath and quietly and sincerely say, "Gabriel, I'm sorry I spat at you."

He stares at me and snorts. "Wow. An apology."

OK. So that's not what I hoped for. I say, "I was angry.

But I shouldn't have done that. I wish I hadn't."

"No, you shouldn't have spat at me. You shouldn't have spat. In. My. Face. And, yes, I'm angry too. And apologizing, unique though I'm sure it is from you, isn't good enough."

"What would be good enough?"

"Nothing. Just go." He takes his eyes off me and goes back to his book.

We sit in silence for a bit. I think he may relent; he has to. He can't really mean this. Then he closes the book and looks up. "You still here?" His voice is nasty.

"Gabriel, I—"

"Nathan, I'm really, really pissed at you. I want you to go." And I know he's serious.

I get up and leave the tent, walk out of the camp, and keep going.

I run and keep running. I can run for hours, letting my body take over.

I stay away for the next day, and the next, and then more. I spend most of the time as an animal but some time as the human me, to think.

I'm scared that Gabriel has already come to dread me, like he was afraid he would. And I think about all the stories of Black Witches and how their relationships never last and always end violently. And then I remember how he looked at me and was so angry.

I think of my father and I want to be like him, as strong as him. In many ways he was honorable and totally honest.

And I know he loved me. But he could be cruel and harsh and terrifying. I remember the story Mercury wrote in her diary about Marcus killing the witch called Toro. I never asked my father about that. I didn't want to hear the answer, because I think Mercury was right: he killed Toro simply because Toro annoyed him and because he could, because he really didn't care any more for Toro's life than for a fly's. And I love Marcus but I don't want to be like that. I don't want people to dread me.

Gabriel respected my father, but he also respects my White side, my mother's side. I never knew her, except through Gran, Arran, and Deborah, all kind and thoughtful and caring people. I know I've come so far from them but I don't want to lose that half of myself.

I want to be a Half Code. I want to be Black *and* White, the best of both.

And now I want to see Gabriel, to tell him I'm not lost, that I do know who I am. So I head back to Camp Three. I'm not sure how many days I've been away, four or maybe five. It's a long way and though I run fast the weather turns bad, with snow and freezing wind. It takes me another two days. When I approach the camp it's dark and snowing lightly, though the wind has died to nothing.

I'm exhausted, dirty, and hungry but all I want is to see Gabriel. This time I know the password for the sentry and give it properly and then walk slowly into the camp.

I go straight to Gabriel's tent and with each step I feel

more sick with worry. What if he still won't talk to me? What if he hates me?

I see his tent but even from a distance I can tell there is no green light. And then my stomach is in knots, hurting me. I look inside the tent. There's nothing in there, not even his sleeping bag or book. What if he's left the Alliance without me? I wonder where Nesbitt is. He'll know. But it's late and snowing and there's no one around. And now I want to be sick. I know I've really fucked up this time. I go to the center of camp, to the fire, maybe Nesbitt's there . . . There's a figure, lying near the fire, alone, snow dusting his sleeping bag. Gabriel? I think it's him and I rush to him, scared I'm mistaken.

It's him. He's asleep.

I sit down near his feet. I'm so relieved, my stomach painful with tension. The snow is coming down in tiny, fine flakes. I add a couple of logs to the embers but the fire is nearly out. I still feel like I'm going to be sick.

Gabriel stirs and sits up. Maybe he wasn't asleep after all. He wraps his sleeping bag round his shoulders, though he doesn't move closer to me. We're a meter or so apart.

I stare at the fire and try to work out what to say, maybe apologize again or maybe say something about how I'm glad he's still here.

He says, "You've been away a long time. Were you lost?"

And I feel like crying because his voice is still hard.

I say, "Wounded, not lost . . . maybe lost too. I dunno."

I turn to him. "But I don't want you to be. Wounded, I mean. By anyone, especially not by me."

"Then don't lie to me. Don't hide things from me."

"I won't."

"And don't ever spit at me again."

"I won't." And I know I won't. I couldn't. Not now. I can't take back what I've done to him but I can behave better and I want to desperately.

He says, "You know I love you. Still. Forever."

"So . . . I'm forgiven?"

"I didn't say *that*."

We sit and look at the fire, which is beginning to burn stronger. Gabriel says, "You wound me in other ways, Nathan."

I think of drawing the knife on him, all the times I've sworn at him and just been plain nasty.

He says, "When we first met, you told me all about yourself. Recently, you've hardly told me anything. I mean, I don't want you ever to be a chatterbox, but you say I'm your friend. You need to talk to your friends."

And it's true, of course; when we first met I did tell him about me, my life.

I shuffle over closer to him and say, "OK. So what do you want me to talk about?"

"Tell me things, important things."

"Like what?" And I wonder if he means about my father or my visions.

"Tell me about Wales. I want to go to Wales with you one day."

And I smile and want to cry too. And I tell him about this special place in the mountains that I went to one summer: there was a small lake and I could climb the cliff behind it and dive into the water. And I tell him I'll take him there when the war's over. And I watch the flames some of the time and watch Gabriel the rest of the time and I know I never want to hurt him again.

Golden

I'm awake before dawn. The sky is brightening and Gabriel is asleep by me. The camp is still quiet. I've got the fire going. And I'm actually looking forward to the porridge when I feel a chill creeping into my bones and the grayness gradually slides over everything that I see. My vision, again.

The golden glow fills half the sky and the forest seems to glow with it. I'm walking slowly through the trees. It's as if I'm newborn and seeing the world for the first time. The air around me seems alive. It's all amazing. All beautiful. Every detail is amazing. And the details go on and on. The colors, patterns, shapes, sounds, temperature, air. I turn and see Gabriel. And he is beautiful too. He waves at me to come. He holds his gun loosely at his side. Nesbitt is the dark figure disappearing beyond him. I look back at the beautiful meadow and trees and sun and then turn to go to Gabriel. And I'm flying backward through the air and the world changes to noise and pain and chaos and I land on the ground and look up and see sky and then see Gabriel's face. And the pain in my stomach is intense, burning, and moving to my heart. It's killing me and I know it.

I'm dying.

Camp One

Me, Gabriel, Nesbitt, Celia, Adele, Kirsty, and Donna are on the way to Camp One. Celia seems to have taken Adele on as her personal assistant. Donna is being brought so that Van can make up a special truth potion that will give an answer one way or the other as to Donna's loyalties. Her hands aren't tied but Kirsty is glued to her side and, as Kirsty is almost twice the size of Donna, I'm fairly sure Kirsty can deal with her if she tries anything. Not that I think that's going to happen.

We will have to go through two cuts to get to Camp One, with a bit of a run in between them, but even so it will only be a few hours before I see Annalise. I'm not sure how I feel, other than impatient.

At the first cut Gabriel grasps my left hand in his right and we interlock fingers while Celia guides Gabriel's left hand to the cut. I take a deep breath as Gabriel is sucked through and I'm pulled after him and I breathe out as we slide through the darkness. The cut is so short that a faint light appears ahead immediately and then we're out and on the forest floor at the other side. The others come through and Celia sets off again. We keep close to her. The pace is slower than I'd like but we quickly settle into a rhythm. The woodland thins out to open meadows and there's snow on the ground.

I ask Celia, "How far to the next cut?"

"A mile, beyond the river."

I'm about to ask how far to the river when the ground steepens and we're jumping down a riverbank into freezing-cold water. The current is strong. And then we're scrambling up the other bank and running through knee-deep wet snow to a stand of trees.

At the next cut, Celia guides everyone through, holding me back. She says, "Nathan, you wait and go with me."

Once the others have gone through, Celia says, "I need you to be clear on what you'll do when you see Annalise."

"Don't worry—I'm clear."

"And what is it that you're clear about?"

"I told you: I want her to go to trial."

Celia studies me. "Is that the full truth of it?"

"I won't kill her unless the trial fails to provide me with justice. If they let her go, then I'll . . . reestablish justice."

"What if they say she should be imprisoned?"

"You want the full truth of it, Celia? I don't know what I'll do. But if they let her go then I will do something."

"She won't go free. Not if the system works."

Celia grabs hold of my jacket and slides her free hand through the cut.

At the other side of the cut it's raining a fine drizzle.

Celia says, "Nathan, stay close to me. It's a fifteen-minute run to the camp." It's only when I say "OK" that she lets go of my arm. Then she sets off hard.

Soon I'll see Annalise. I want to see her. I hope she's chained up. I want her to see me looking at her.

We must be almost at Camp One when Celia slows the pace, then stops. She looks around and I know from the way she stands and moves that something's wrong.

"What?" I ask her.

"There should be a lookout here."

The others join us and Nesbitt asks, "What's up?"

"I'm not sure," Celia replies. "The camp's four hundred meters ahead. Nathan, use your invisibility and check out the camp. Nesbitt, Gabriel, you scout the perimeter to the left. I'll go to the right with Adele. Kirsty, you wait here with Donna. Meet back here in five minutes."

I go invisible and set off cautiously. I've only gone about a hundred meters when I hear a faint hiss. It's the noise that mobile phones set off in my head. No one in the Alliance uses phones. *Shit!*

I keep going, slowly. The hissing from the phones is barely there. But I creep onwards and it gets a little stronger. I'm still about two hundred meters from the camp. There have to be Hunters ahead. I move forward, not seeing any sign of them. Everything is still and quiet except for the faint hissing in my head.

Shit! It's too still, too quiet.

I run back to Kirsty and Donna. Gabriel is there as well but none of the others. I tell Gabriel, "I can hear a hissing. It must be Hunters, but I don't know how many. I think they might be on the far side of the camp, getting ready to attack. I need to get in there and warn them. You tell Celia."

"No, Nathan, wait."

But I've already turned invisible again and am running. I go fast, listening and looking all the time. I'm scanning for Hunters but see none. I slow at the edge of the camp. Camp One is not set in a clearing but the tents are dotted among the trees. There's no noise of people. No noise of birds or anything. The only sound is the electric hiss of mobile phones in my head. But it's very faint, fainter than before, as if the Hunters are moving away.

I go closer to the tents, slowly, looking around all the time.

Then I see someone. Her eyes are on me, wide open, but she's not seeing anything and as I get closer to her I see there are no glints in her eyes. But I don't need that to tell me she's dead: the way she lies, so still, so awkward, says it all. She's been shot in the head. I only see the wound when I move round her, neat and clean to the back of her skull. A few flies on it. I stare at her face, trying to remember if I've seen her before, but I'm not sure. She's a member of the Alliance, not a Hunter.

I move to a tent. Slowly, silently. I'm still invisible but I don't want to risk anything.

The tent seems to hold stores: cans, boxes, and blankets are scattered around its broken, collapsed frame. But then I spot someone I do recognize, his body half hidden by the tent canvas. Gus has a bullet hole in his chest. There are ants crawling across him.

And at the next tent I see another body.

And another.

They're all around.

My heart races. This happened recently, but not that recently. Maybe this morning.

But if it happened this morning and I can hear hissing then . . . I think the Hunters are leaving. They're leaving but they're not rushing. They don't know we've arrived. Maybe we can follow them . . .

I move through the camp, trying to locate where the hissing is coming from. Then I see a wooden building, a hut: the prison? I move closer, slow and steady. The door is broken down. Is Annalise in here?

I lean inside the hut.

Empty except for chains. They're unlocked. Annalise must have been kept here. Did she go invisible and escape? More likely they have her.

Then I hear a noise, footsteps behind me, and I turn to see Nesbitt racing through the camp, clearly not caring about the noise he makes. He looks panicked. Behind him in the distance are Gabriel and the others, fanning out through the trees.

I become visible and say to Nesbitt, "I think the Hunters have only just left."

"Have you seen Van?"

"No."

"She—"

An explosion fills the air behind Nesbitt. He cowers and as he goes down I see Kirsty fly through the air, her body cartwheeling high and then falling to the ground.

I've crouched down too.

The sudden noise slowly drifts away. I look around for Hunters. Listen for them. Nothing.

Celia shouts, "Booby traps! Don't touch anything."

Donna is a pace or two from Kirsty's body and she looks toward me. Her face is pale. Gabriel joins them and bends down. He calls to Celia, "Kirsty's dead."

Nesbitt is already moving again. The ground is bare here, and there are numerous footprints: Hunter boot prints.

I follow Nesbitt through the camp and into the trees beyond. I ask him, "How many?"

"Lots. Twenty, maybe more." His voice is different, shaky as he adds, "They're dragging someone, maybe two people. Prisoners. Or wounded."

We're moving away from the camp now, through the trees, and Nesbitt speeds up to a jog and then slows and he groans.

I see past him to the body lying on the ground. Her hair is glistening with fine raindrops. Her eyes are open, the sapphire blue is still strong, but there are no glints in them. Her skin is pale. Her stomach is a mass of blood.

"Van!"

Nesbitt stumbles forward and I grab him in case he goes too close.

She's holding her cigarette case in her hand and I know he wants to take it but I say, "Don't touch her, Nesbitt. They might have booby-trapped her body too."

He sits on the ground by her.

I can't hear hissing anymore. The Hunters are leaving but they still can't be too far ahead.

"Nesbitt, I think they have Annalise. We can still catch them if we keep going."

Nesbitt lets out a faint groan that gets louder and louder as he gets to his feet, roaring. He sets off fast, his rage taking him over. And I can tell he's struggling to keep his breath, but on we go. He's panting and grunting as we reach a small stream, and he leaps over it and goes uphill, through thin trees until we reach an open scrubby area and he stops. He's panting hard and I realize he's crying too.

"That way," he says, pointing.

I go fast, Nesbitt behind me. I don't think the Hunters will be invisible unless they're attacking or think they are in danger so I'm hoping to catch sight of them soon. My breathing is slow and controlled. Uphill now. It's hard, but we've got to be gaining on them, though Nesbitt has dropped well back.

Then I hear it: a hiss.

And over the next rise I see them. Distant black specks. Lots of them lined up at the edge of the bare rocks ahead. They're going through a cut.

I go invisible and run as hard as I can. Not thinking, just running. Eyes fixed on the line of black Hunters getting closer but also reducing in length.

I can see the figures clearly now: there are nine, then seven. All in black except one. Annalise!

I'm running hard. Breathing hard. Legs burning.

I'm staring at Annalise, but then one more Hunter disappears and so does she.

There're four figures . . . three . . . two . . .

One.

And I recognize her. Jessica. But I'm too far away to hit her with my lightning. She looks toward me but doesn't see me. I'm still invisible. Then she disappears.

I keep my eyes locked on the cleft in the rock where she was standing. My legs are giving out now but I push them on and on and then I'm there. I slide my hand through the air, feeling for the cut.

Nothing.

And again. Nothing.

And again.

And again.

Finding cuts is hard enough when you know exactly where they are. And I know it's been too long. They'll have closed it by now. But I keep trying. Sliding my hand through the air.

I was so close to them. So close to Annalise.

"Shit, shit, and fuck!"

I try again and again.

Nesbitt drops beside me, breathing heavily.

It doesn't matter that we were right behind them. The cut is closed.

They're gone.

Every Second Is Precious

It's raining heavily as me and Nesbitt walk back to the camp. Celia and Adele are there, cautiously walking around. Donna is standing by one of the tents. She looks somber. Everyone is quiet, taking it all in: death and destruction, and the ground turning to mud. I go to Kirsty. Gabriel's jacket covers the top half of her body; one of her legs is bloodied and bent horribly.

Gabriel is sheltering under a tree. I tell him, "Van's dead."

"Yes. But we can't move her. Can't bury her. Can't even put a blanket over her in case her body has been booby-trapped." He looks up at me and asks, "How can people do this?"

And I think of the Hunters I killed in their sleep and say, "I don't know."

But I know how to do it, how to be a brute, and Gabriel's done plenty of it himself. And then I realize that's what he's thinking: that we've done this before, he's done it before—killed groups of Hunters and left ten or twenty bodies.

"And Annalise?" Gabriel asks.

"She's alive. I saw her in the distance. They've taken her prisoner."

"Or just taken her," Gabriel says.

And I know he's right. She'll either be chained and tortured, or showered with praise and glory: a prisoner or a hero. But much as I hate her I still don't believe she's Soul's spy.

Gabriel says, "Let's go away. Leave. Now. There's nothing to keep us here."

And maybe the sensible thing is to walk away but I'm not sure where I'd go. And much as I want to live in a quiet place by a river, to do that while Soul carries on killing and torturing doesn't seem possible. This is about more than Annalise; it's about Soul and his system of persecution and terror.

Celia comes to stand by us and asks what I've seen. I tell her about Annalise and how close we were to the Hunters.

"Did they see you?" Celia asks.

"No. I was invisible." But then I add, "Nesbitt wasn't. They might have seen him. I don't think so but . . ."

Celia rubs her face and looks around, saying, "They can't have planned to come back or they wouldn't have closed the cut. But, still, if they did see Nesbitt or hear the explosion . . . We need to leave anyway. There's nothing we can do here."

Me and Gabriel go to find Nesbitt. He's sitting on the ground by Van. I crouch down on the other side of her body and glance at him, expecting to see tears, but there are none. The rain on Van's face makes it look like it's her who's crying.

I remember the first time I saw her, at the house in

Geneva when I thought she was a man. She was always so beautiful: stunning, literally breathtaking at times. So sharp and quick and clever. And I remember the stakes and potions she made to help Gabriel recover from being stuck as a fain. How cool she was in that whole process. And then with Pilot and Mercury and with Annalise too. She was always calm and calculating, but also wise and funny. And now she's nothing. She'll be pecked at by birds, eaten by insects. And the Alliance has lost another important person. Another Black Witch gone. Another witch with huge power and it's all lost, lost to the Alliance and lost to the world. And instead all we have is a corpse lying in the mud. There is only Soul to blame for this. He's to blame for it all: for my father's death, for driving Annalise and me apart, for the deaths of so many Black and White Witches. Soul is the root of the problem.

Adele comes and says, "Celia says we have to move out. Now." And Gabriel and I go with her, leaving Nesbitt alone with Van for the last time. Celia is waiting at the side of the camp near where we entered it. She looks impatient.

Gabriel says, "Nesbitt's just coming." But I know he won't want to leave Van. It's not good having to rush away.

"Have you seen Donna?" Celia asks.

"Not for a while," Gabriel replies.

We stand there and wait. No one comes. Celia mutters something about discipline.

"What do you want to do?" Gabriel asks her.

"I want us to leave five minutes ago." Celia shakes

her head. "Gabriel, go and find Donna. She can't be far. Nathan, tell Nesbitt we're going. We leave in ten minutes, with or without them."

I trudge back toward Van's body and am not surprised to see Nesbitt still by her side.

I tell him, "We have to go."

He leans over Van and says something to her quietly. I step back, not wanting to hear. Then he stands but keeps his back to me. I think he's crying again.

I tell him, "Donna's disappeared. We need to find her."

Nesbitt says, "I saw her a few minutes ago. This way." And he sets off into the trees, scanning the ground. I think he's looking for her tracks.

"What do you think?" I ask him. "Has she run off?"

"Wouldn't blame her. She's hardly been welcomed into the Alliance and now she's seen that this is what's in store for her if she's given the grand honor of joining . . ."

We reach the edge of the trees the way the Hunters went.

"You don't think they're back already, do you?" Nesbitt asks, looking to the distant hillside.

"They closed the cut. They can't get back so quickly."

But I'm wondering if they have another cut, or if the cut they went through only took them a mile or two away and they're already on their way back.

Nesbitt curses the Hunters under his breath.

"We need to find Donna," I remind him.

"She was here." He points at the ground and I see the smudge of a trainer print. "But ..." He glances up and around and says, "She could be anywhere by now."

"What do you think?" I ask him.

"She'll come with us if she wants to. It's up to her," Nesbitt says, and he heads back to the camp. I stare out over the fields, wondering if Donna has run off and given up on the Alliance. She's spent the last few weeks as a prisoner, and today she came a meter away from being blown up. I wouldn't blame her for leaving.

I'm about to turn to follow Nesbitt when the sun comes out to my left, low in the sky and partially hidden by a long bank of clouds. The clouds are clearing already and the meadow in front of me is flooded with warm light. After the rain it's a good thing to feel sunlight on my skin. The land around looks lush, smells fresh. And even with all this death so close to us—because of the death—it's amazing to see the beauty of the world. It's so beautiful and so brutal. It's a reminder that every second of life is precious.

I turn to see Nesbitt disappear into the trees. And further to my right is Gabriel, waving me over to join him. I look back one last time the way the Hunters went and the sun dips below the cloud, turning it red and orange and lighting up the grass and trees and everything, and I'm lit up as well. It's all golden. It's beautiful. And then I realize where I've seen this glow before. I turn to Gabriel.

The blow to my stomach is a surprise, though I know it

shouldn't be, and I'm aware that my body is flying up and backward and through the air. I'm still in the air when the sound of the shot reaches my ears, and another shot follows as I fall and I'm not sure if I've been shot once or twice as the ground rises up and forces the air out of me.

I try to take a breath but my lungs won't do it.

I can't breathe. And I know it's the same as my vision. And I know I'm dying.

The Magic Bullet

Can't breathe properly. Not enough air.

More shooting. Shouting.

Can't breathe.

Gabriel is above me.

Can't breathe. Can't breathe ... can't breathe ... can't breathe.

"Heal, Nathan. Keep healing."

I concentrate on my lungs. Heal them ... fill them with air.

Better.

Gabriel's ripping at my shirt, saying, "You're going to be OK. You're going to be OK."

I can't breathe again. Already!

Heal my lungs again.

Better.

Breathe.

Breathe.

But my stomach's on fire.

I try to look at my stomach but can't lift my head. *Fuck! Fuck!* I move my hands to my stomach. It's hot and wet and Gabriel pushes my hands away, saying, "Lie still, Nathan."

"It's hot."

And my gut burns and burns and I know it's a Hunter bullet and poison but worse than ever.

"It's burning me. Get it out!"

Gabriel holds my wrists down and shouts for Celia.

I heal again. I tell Gabriel, "My healing isn't strong enough."

And already the burning is coming back.

I clench my fists and stare at the sky and think of something that isn't burning.

Then when I can't stand it anymore I heal again.

The burning goes.

"Gabriel, if I—" But the burning is back already.

I stay with it, let it build. I can heal once more maybe.

Let the burning build.

And build.

Shit!

And build.

Gabriel is looking at me.

Now heal. Relief. That's so good.

"Gabriel. I don't think I can do it anymore."

"Yes, you can. Celia's coming. She'll get the bullet out."

"Gabriel . . . I can't."

"Nathan. Don't give up. You can do it, Nathan. Please."

And the burning is back.

And building. Faster and hotter.

Why aren't they coming?

It's too hot. Too hot.

Concentrate on not screaming.

Don't scream. Don't scream.

Concentrate on breathing.

Count.

One.

Two.

Fuck.

Fuck.

Try to heal. Try.

Celia's calm voice: "I'll be quick. Keep him still. Hold his legs."

Celia's face. "Nathan, try to hold still. I've got to cut the bullet out."

And my arms and legs are pulled down and my stomach burns hotter.

And I don't want to scream.

"I said hold him still!"

I feel the knife in my stomach.

I don't want to scream.

"It's not here."

"What? What?"

"I can't find the bullet!"

"It's still in there. It hasn't gone through him."

"I know, but I can't find it."

And the burning is spreading up to my chest.

Celia says, "I think it's moving. I think the bullet is moving inside him."

A magic fucking bullet.

And Gabriel is there telling me, "We'll get it out. You'll

be OK." And our eyes meet and I try to tell him that I want to stay with him but I can't heal anymore and it's so hot.

And I feel like there are flames burning through my stomach and chest.

And every breath is like fire inside me.

I don't want it to hurt anymore.

And I close my eyes and Gabriel is shouting at me to open them and to heal.

I want it to stop hurting.

Celia says she's going to try next to my heart.

And Gabriel's shouts get fainter.

Wallend appears above me. I don't know how he got here. Wallend, who tattooed me and tested me; he must be back to do more. He's bent over me and I'm tied down on the ground. Wallend has a branding iron, its end heated to white. He holds it up to show me and then puts the iron to my stomach and I'm burning up, writhing as much as I can to get away from him, but the iron goes in further and deeper. And all I know is that I want to die. But I don't tell him that. It's my secret. I know I'll die soon.

Hurry up and die!

Wallend has gone. Gone! I need him to kill me and I scream at him, "Kill me!"

Or am I already dead?

It's dark. I must be buried in the earth. Good.

It's cold.

Am I dead?

I'm in a cell in the Council building: no windows, cement floor, brick walls. It's gloomy but there's light enough to see a figure kneeling in front of me. I walk up to her. Annalise. Her hands are tied. I take the Fairborn out of its sheath. And she looks me in the eyes and says, "I love you. You're my prince. You saved me." And the Fairborn is in my hands, wanting blood. And I don't know what to do. *Do I kill Annalise?*

Blackness. Peace.

Am I alive or dead?

I hope I'm dead.

I'm cold. In the cell, not chained to the wall. I look for Annalise but she isn't here. There's a different figure kneeling on the floor. Soul. And now I see that kneeling next to him is Wallend and then I see Jessica and next to her a Hunter I don't recognize and next to the Hunter another Hunter. There's lots of Hunters. The cell is much bigger than I remember. I walk along the line of kneeling prisoners. They're all dressed in black. All kneeling. Heads bowed. I have to kill them all. But the line is long, never-ending. The Fairborn is in my hand but I can't do this with the Fairborn; I need a gun. Where's a gun?

"I need a gun."

"Shhhh, Nathan. Shhhh."

"Give me a gun."

"Shshsh. Rest."

It's black again. Maybe that means I'm dead. *Good.*

Peace.

I'm in the cell again. I don't want to be back here. It's cold. I don't like it. The prisoners are all kneeling, hands tied behind their backs. I walk along the line of Hunters, hundreds of them, thousands, a never-ending line. But now I've got a gun in my hand. I go back to the first Hunter and shoot her in the back of the head. As her body falls, I press the barrel of the gun to the back of the next head. Squeeze. As I squeeze I say the word: "Die."

"Die."

"Die."

"Shhhh, Nathan. It's just a dream. Shhhh. You're safe. You're safe."

And I want to cry. I want it to go black. "I don't want to go back there."

"Shhhh. You're safe, Nathan."

Gabriel. I want to tell him something but I've forgotten what. I try to move my arm but it's so heavy.

"Rest, Nathan. Rest."

I need to get moving. Do something. I need to go.

"Nathan. Rest. Try to be calm."

I'm not dead. I wish I was dead. I don't want to go back to that cell.

It's dark. I look up and see the full moon.

"Gabriel?"

"I'm here."

"Gabriel."

"It's OK. You've been ill. You're getting better now."

"Why can't I heal?"

"You are healing, Nathan. Slowly. There was a lot of poison. A special bullet. Try to stay calm. Please."

"I could . . ." I'm not sure what I could do. I've forgotten. The sky is lighter now.

"Gabriel?"

"Yes, I'm here." I feel his hand move a little; his fingers are intertwined with mine.

"Don't leave me."

He holds me, putting his hand gently on the side of my chest. His breath is on my neck and it's good. He's good.

"I mean, don't leave me ever."

"I know, Nathan. I won't."

"I wanted to die."

He whispers, "Rest now. Rest."

He stays close to me and his breathing by me is good.

And later I remember what I could do. It's easy. I could kill them all.

Tired

⁘

I wake to see sky. Pale blue. Treetops. Arran's face. He's real. Not a dream. I'm not in a cell. I've not killed any Hunters. It was all just the poison, worse poison than when I was shot in Geneva, but just poison.

"Don't try to move," Arran says.

"Gabriel?"

"I'm here." And he touches my hand. And then I realize I don't have the strength to turn my head.

"You're looking better," Arran says. "How are you feeling?"

I think about it and say, "Better. Not great." Even speaking is exhausting. "Tired."

"I need to check this." And Arran gently pulls back the bandage on my stomach. "It's healing. Slowly. The bullet's out of you but the poison is still in. You have to drive it out. You have to heal yourself. Can you do that?"

I concentrate on healing. Nothing happens.

"Not working," I manage to mumble.

"It will work. You haven't lost the ability; you've just used up all your energy. You need more rest, more time."

Arran puts some cold gunk on my wounds, on my stomach and chest, and then a new set of bandages over the top.

He says to Gabriel, "I'll give him more of the potion to-night, to help him sleep. Try to keep him still." And then to me he says, "You will heal, Nathan. But don't be impatient."

I close my eyes for a bit. I've never felt like this before. Even when I was shot in Geneva and had to walk back to Mercury's cottage it wasn't as bad as this. That was a magic bullet too. A Hunter bullet. But this is stronger magic.

"Do you want me to talk to you?" Gabriel asks. "Or do you want silence?"

"Talk."

"OK. What shall I talk about? Do you want me to tell you what happened?"

I nod.

"Was that a nod or a shake of the head?"

"Nod."

"OK. Well, Donna shot you. She was an infiltrator after all. Celia thinks the whole thing was a set-up—like the Trojan Horse. You were always meant to find that Hunter camp. If the Hunters didn't kill or capture you, they knew you'd take Donna back to the Alliance. She was supposed to join up, gain our trust, and wait for the chance to kill you, but she never got the opportunity until we were at Camp One. After Kirsty was killed, she took her knife and gun. Cut out the special bullet that had been sealed in plastic and sewn into the skin of her thigh."

Gabriel holds up a small round reddish-brown ball: the bullet. "New magic. And seriously bad. The bullet seems to know where to go once it's inside you. It was heading for your heart, spreading poison as it moved. Eating away at your insides. It took Celia three attempts to cut it out."

"Urgh."

"Exactly. Everyone's very interested in the bullet. A particularly strong magic. A bit like the magic of the Fairborn, Celia thinks. The bullet wants to kill."

I close my eyes.

"You OK?" Gabriel asks.

"Tired." And it sounds more like "Tyrrr . . ."

"You want me to talk more or do you want to rest?"

Talk more, I mouth.

He smiles. "I like this Nathan who is quiet and enjoys listening to me talk."

I want to tell Gabriel things, how I like listening to him and like him being here. I can't think what to say in one simple word but I manage to mouth, *Good*.

"And who doesn't swear at me or walk away. This is a situation that has advantages."

I try to smile, but have to close my eyes I'm so tired. I feel Gabriel stroke my forehead.

"OK. Where was I up to? The bullet. Concealed in her thigh. So Donna cut the bullet out, loaded the gun, and waited for you. She shot you in the stomach. Got the edge of your left lung. She was aiming for a body shot. She knew the bullet would do the rest."

Gabriel is silent for a few seconds.

"Then it went mad. She'd taken another gun too, with the usual Hunter bullets in it. Nesbitt got hit. Not seriously, just in the arm. But I'm sure he'll let you know that he took a bullet for you. Adele used her Gift, made her skin like metal and protected Nesbitt and shot Donna. Donna's dead. I didn't see it. I didn't see much of the fight I mean. I . . . the way you flew through the air, the way you landed and then . . . you screamed. You screamed a lot."

I thought I'd held it back.

"Hurt," I tell him.

He pauses then asks, "Does it still hurt?"

I think about it. Think about my body. The bad pain has gone. I ache all over but nothing bad. I force myself to sound stronger and say, "Just tired."

"So. Let me finish the story. You were shot. Nesbitt was shot. Adele was the heroine of the day. Celia cut into you three times and eventually got the bullet out. You were a mess. A bloody mess. Adele cut the bullet out of Nesbitt's arm, only it seems that she's less good at first aid and she took a big chunk out of Nesbitt too. Stop smiling! He has a really ugly scar."

I wonder what new scars I've got from all this.

"Anyway, Celia made this stretcher out of wood and our jackets in about ten seconds and we carried you back to the cut. Do you remember that?"

I think about it and then shake my head.

"Well, you were out of it by then. Anyway, we came through the cut and made camp where we came out. And here we still are, exactly where we landed ten days ago."

"Ten?"

"Ten."

"Urgh."

"Celia sent Adele to get Arran and he started work on a cure for the poison. The magic is in making the bullet move to your heart. The poison is straight poison, but powerful."

Gabriel talks some more about the poison but I can't concentrate. He goes quiet and then says, "You should sleep now."

But I don't want to sleep, I don't want to go back to the cell. I tell him, "Bad dreams."

I close my eyes and feel him stroke the hair from my forehead. He says, "I'll stay with you."

I want to thank him and I open my eyes to see him looking at me. His eyes are full of tears.

I Want It to Be True

I have three more scars, though typical of Celia they're straight and neat. The wounds are almost healed but it's another four days before I've got the energy to get up and move slowly around camp. And we are in a camp now. One that has grown around me, it seems. There are some people I recognize and some I don't.

I sit and watch the trainees train. I'm cold and stuff my hands in my jacket pockets. I feel a bullet in each. The original Hunter bullet that Marcus took out of my back in Switzerland is a greeny copper color and the magic bullet that Celia dug out of my chest is a browny red. They are the same size and weight. I expected the magic bullet to have a life about it, a buzz, like the Fairborn does, but it feels like any other bullet: just a dead piece of metal. Maybe it only comes to life when it's inside someone, when it tastes blood. And I know the man who made the Fairborn must have been evil; Wallend made the magic bullet and his magic is evil too.

Nesbitt comes to sit with me. He's healed too now—at least his arm has. He's different: quiet, subdued.

After a few minutes he says, "I'm leaving."

"Leaving?"

"Leaving here, the Alliance. Leaving it all."

It doesn't surprise me as I think he was only ever here because of Van. But I'll miss him and so will the Alliance; he's a great fighter and the best tracker. "Where will you go?"

"Back home. Australia, I mean. Haven't been back there for years." He laughs to himself. "Shit, last time I was there was before you were born."

As usual I don't know what to say. Nesbitt adds, "I won't miss you."

I smile and nudge his shoulder. "Me neither."

We sit quietly for a minute and then I ask, "When are you going?"

"Soon. Can't stand it here now. Need a change of scene." Then quietly he adds, "I want Soul dead and all his evil cronies, but . . . I can't do it, not without Van. I'm . . ."

He shakes his head and rubs his eyes and doesn't finish what he was saying.

The next morning I'm feeling better at last. My healing is finally getting back to its normal strength and by the afternoon I heal myself and get a buzz from it. I actually feel good.

I tell Gabriel, "My healing's working. Back to like it was."

"Good."

"I've been thinking. About the amulet and stuff. I'm going to go for it."

Gabriel frowns.

"I didn't think you'd be pleased, but you must agree it's sensible. If the amulet works I'll be protected. I want to avoid dying. I thought you'd want that too."

"There are other ways of avoiding dying."

"You still want to leave. Like Nesbitt? Go to Australia?"

"I think you should at least consider it. I mean properly consider it. We could go anywhere. It doesn't matter where, but somewhere away from this war."

"I have a feeling that wherever I go the war will follow me."

"You always say that but you never try it. You say they'll follow you. Track you down. Well, maybe they won't."

"My father had to move every few months."

"That was him, not you."

"It would be the same, I know it." And I remember Marcus and his den, the peace of it, and I loved being with him there. But he could never relax, not truly. He was always on the run. Even so, I know he would have continued to evade them. It was me that brought him to the Alliance. It's because of me that Marcus is dead. Annalise shot him but I brought him to the Alliance. I asked for his help. And he asked me for something too.

I tell Gabriel, "My father said I should kill them all."

"It's for you to decide what to do. He shouldn't have said that."

"Part of me is him, Gabriel. Part of me is so like him and that part of me wants to kill them all, wants revenge, in full. No half measures. But another part of me, the White

Witch part, the logical part, says . . . that will only bring on more killing, and it will never end."

"And your father's side is winning the argument but your mother never has a chance to give her side."

I shake my head. "I don't know if she'd disagree. Her life was fucked up by the White Witches as much as mine has been, maybe more."

"And so?"

"And so I intend to fuck theirs up too."

"And would you go if Annalise wasn't there? Is this really about getting her?"

I shake my head. "I hate her and I want justice for my father. But this isn't about Annalise. I'd do it even if she wasn't there. Even if she was already dead. I want an end to the war, an end to Soul, an end to all of those who side with him."

"Well, you might not be able to kill them all, Nathan. You're not all-powerful. And there's only one of you. Soul has a whole army."

"It won't matter how big an army he has if he can't hurt me."

"War hurts, Nathan. It's not just physical wounds. It screws you up. It screws everyone up."

"Even you?"

"Of course even me. I've killed people. I've watched our friends die. I've watched you nearly die and every day it hurts me and . . . I see how it hurts you."

"Would you leave for me, if it was the other way around?"

I don't know why I ask that as I expect him to say yes straightaway but he thinks about his answer and then says, "I'm not sure. I'm not even sure if that question makes sense to me. I think the question should be: what would I do if I was in your shoes? And all I know is that you've been through a lot, you've suffered a lot because of these people, and if I was standing where you are I'd probably do the same thing. I'm not against what you want to do, Nathan. I want you to be sure about it, because you won't be the same person afterward."

"I am sure of it, Gabriel. But I'd like you to stay with me. Help me."

"Of course. You know I'll stay with you. Always."

I go to see Celia to tell her my plan, though as usual it's not much of a plan, more of a vague intention, but I also want to discuss something else with her.

I tell her, "Van thought that Soul wanted me alive. She thought he wanted to use me as a weapon."

"Yes. I discussed that with her and I agree. I don't know Soul well, but the little I saw of him makes me believe that once he sets his mind on something he'll go after it. I think he's set his mind on controlling you. Having you in his power."

"And yet he sent Donna to kill me."

Celia gives a small shake of her head. "No. Donna was

working with the Hunters. She was sent by Jessica. I imagine Jessica spotted her and trained her. I wouldn't be surprised if Soul didn't know anything about her."

"I thought the bullet must have been made by Wallend."

"Possibly it was. I don't know. But I'm sure Soul would rather have you alive and I'm equally sure that Jessica wants you dead. The Hunters and Council work together but the Hunters always believe they are superior to the Council and the Council must always be careful to control the Hunters and not give them too much power."

"I wonder if Jessica would want to take over the Council."

"She's intelligent and ambitious, the youngest-ever leader of the Hunters. There were a few people who were unhappy about her appointment after Clay was removed, but she dealt with them. Clay promoted her and nurtured her career but she did nothing to help him when he was accused of failure when the Fairborn was stolen from him. Jessica's ruthless and a Hunter through and through. She believes in their superiority."

"Ha! She believes in her own superiority and always has."

"Another reason, then, why she might believe she should control both the Hunters and the Council. I wouldn't be surprised if that's her long-term goal. If you were to come under Soul's power it would be much harder for her."

"Another reason for her to want me dead."

"And another reason why Soul would want you alive and under his control: to keep his position safe from the Hunters as well as the Alliance."

"Well, I've no intention of letting either of them get what they want."

And I tell Celia that I'm going to go to Ledger and try to get the amulet. We discuss it briefly and she agrees I should go with Gabriel and get Nesbitt to show us the way before he leaves for Australia.

I tell her, "While we're gone you need to work out stage two of the plan: how we attack Soul once I have the amulet."

"Of course. But you haven't got it yet," she reminds me.

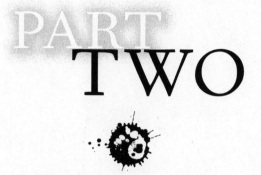

PART
TWO

HALF FOUND

Back to the Bunker

We're back at Mercury's bunker: me, Gabriel, and Nesbitt. We came through the cut in Germany, the one that we used to get to the meetings in Basle. They seem like the distant past, but now that I try to work it out, I think it was only six or seven months ago. Nesbitt has brought us here to show us the way to Ledger but he says he's not coming with us. So this is where we'll finally part.

I've questioned Nesbitt a few times about where Ledger is and all he says is "Patience, kid." Now that we're at the bunker I ask him, "So you went to Ledger from here? Through a cut?"

He says, "Van went. I didn't go with her."

"You didn't tell me that before!"

"I didn't think it was relevant."

"*What?*"

He shrugs.

"But Van told you where she went?"

"Yeah. Kind of."

"Kind of!"

"Look, Van wanted to go on her own. Said there was nothing to fear from Ledger and she could handle it. And I had my own stuff to do. Well, stuff for the Alliance: scouting out camps, checking up on Hunter movements. Van was quite capable of doing it herself. You know, working together is a balance of familiarity and distance. Just like you and me when we're partnered together. I'm friendly and familiar but you're not—"

I swear at him and call him useless.

Nesbitt frowns. "I'm hurt, kid. You know I love you." And the way he says it is real and honest and not joking. "And I was going to say I'm friendly and familiar but you're not the sort of person who would want me treading on his toes." He grins at me and I'm not sure if he's kidding about the whole thing or what.

"What exactly do you know, Nesbitt?"

"Enough to get you there, so stop your flapping."

"Good." I stomp off, saying, "We need to check the bunker first. Make sure it's secure."

It's unlikely that Hunters have been here and laid a trap since Van and Nesbitt were last here, but we can take nothing for granted so we check it out, room by room, from the kitchen on the top level, down through the bedrooms and into the numerous storerooms on the lower levels. Everywhere seems the same as when we left it months ago. The great hallway is still a mess from the fight when Mercury died, when I killed her. In the blood room, where all the bottles of witch blood are stored, everything looks undisturbed.

There'll be a bottle with my mother's name on it here.

A small amount of blood, stolen by Mercury from the larger samples kept by the Council. Soul would have used it to perform my Giving. I'm sure Celia's right: Soul wants to control me; he has always wanted that.

Nesbitt says, "This stuff's valuable." He's right. The Alliance could use it to help Half Bloods, or any young witches, Black or White, if their parents aren't around to give them blood at their Giving.

"Does Celia know about it?" I ask.

"Van told her. I guess she's got other things on her mind right now."

"I'm sure she'll have a plan for it. And it's probably safest left here for the moment."

When we've been through the whole place and are satisfied that there aren't any Hunters hiding in cupboards, we go to the library.

Nesbitt says, "Before Van went to Ledger we came here and went through Mercury's diaries and maps. I'll show you the stuff Van read before she left. It might give you an idea about what to expect from Ledger." He opens the hidden bookshelf at the back of the room and retrieves a sheaf of large parchments.

Me and Gabriel sit on the floor and Nesbitt drops them in front of us. The first parchment is one I've seen before: a plan of Mercury's bunker and the location of eleven cuts that lead to different places in the world.

Nesbitt jabs his finger on one of the lower-level rooms and says, "She went through that cut to New York."

Then he spreads the other parchments in front of us, saying, "These maps show territories: areas belonging to White Witches and those belonging to Blacks. They're all dated and go back two hundred years."

I love looking at maps. I can't read books; most sentences are beyond me and I struggle to even make sense of some words, but maps are something that I can read easily. Looking through them, it's obvious that the extent of White Witch territory has grown in Europe. Britain has become a place only for Whites, and there are smaller changes in other places too, but this change only happened in the last forty years. Before that, for decades—in fact, for over a century—the areas seem to have hardly changed, and on some older maps the White and Black territories even overlap. There's a similar pattern in Australia, Africa, the Far East, and the USA. But in the rest of America, from Mexico and through South America, and in Canada and Russia, the territory of the Black Witches has grown. The major change is that two hundred years ago there were more and bigger areas that overlapped, and some are labeled "mixed," which I guess means Blacks and Whites lived together, and amazingly Britain was one of those places. But on the map made last year there are only five areas where this is still true. I'd like to visit them and see what they're like but it looks as if I'd need to go a long way: China, India, Tasmania, Mexico, or Zambia.

Nesbitt flicks through the top of the pile of maps, saying, "It's these recent ones that show the map room."

"The what?" I'm thinking of the rooms in Mercury's bunker and which one the map room might be.

But before I can ask Nesbitt pulls out a map from 1973, saying, "To get to Ledger you have to go to the map room. It's in Philadelphia. Here." And he points to a brown dot, barely visible, that's marked near the east coast of the USA. "The key says what it is: it's the 'Map Room.'"

I look to Gabriel and ask him, "Do you follow this at all?"

He shrugs and smiles. "If it was easy everyone would go there."

"Exactamundo," Nesbitt agrees. "I don't know where Ledger lives but I know that Van got there through the map room." He goes to the hidden shelf again, coming back with a few of Mercury's handwritten diaries, saying, "These are what Van got really excited about." He clears his throat and starts to read, then stops and looks at Gabriel and me and says, "It doesn't tell you much but I reckon it'll be useful for you guys. But if you'd rather I didn't bother . . ."

"Nesbitt, just read it," I tell him.

And he reads:

"First of January, 2005. Dawn of the new year for some, though the end of an era for others. Another Black territory in Mississippi was abandoned last month after the oldest of them, Destra, died. She was a fine witch. Destra's Gift was a strong ability to heal others, an unusual Gift for a Black Witch. I met her a few times. She was confident, serene, and capable—an

impressive witch. I heard that Marcus and Destra have become
acquainted in the last year. Destra is supposed by some to be the
mother of Ledger, though I don't believe this. I've heard sev-
eral other stories about Ledger's parentage and Destra indicated
to me when I met her that she had no children. I wonder why
Marcus was interested in Destra; because she was an interesting
woman or because he's trying to find out about Ledger? If so,
he's wasting his time. Destra can't help him. I met Ledger once,
years ago—awful woman (man? thing?)—though one rarely
hears of her these days and I rather hope never to hear of her
again."

Nesbitt closes that diary and puts it on the floor. He looks from me to Gabriel, saying, "Good, huh?"

We both look blankly at him.

"Knew you'd appreciate it, boys. So we found that and then we checked back through all the diaries looking for when Mercury had met Ledger. And we found this from 1973." Again he starts to read and then stops, saying, "You keeping up with me? The map"—and he points to the parchment—"is from 1973."

I resist rolling my eyes.

Nesbitt smooths the diary open and reads:

"Finally found the map room in the cellar of the house in
P and it was simple from there. She loves that: mixing the ex-
tremely complex spells of the maps with a simple request to gain
access to them. The map room is very much Ledger's style: her
idea of being clever. And her way of screening visitors—if you
can find the map room, work out how to enter it and how to use

the map, then you are worthy of visiting her. I'm not sure what would happen if you used the wrong map. I suspect you'd go to that place and be unable to get back, at least not without a long walk. The maps are impressive. Their magic is complex and Ledger is, I admit, powerful. Indeed, she has more power than I thought possible. But what is the point of having that power if she never uses it?

"Ledger and I talked for a while, though most of what she spouts is almost unbearable waffle. I asked her about the loss of Black territories and her concerns. She said, 'I have none. All will come back to balance in the end.' I replied, 'How exactly will that happen when the Blacks are being wiped out?' And she said, 'Because it must be so. The nature of our Gifts means it will be so. The world will become more unbalanced but then . . . we have to believe that balance will return.'

"I was getting extremely bored with her at this stage and I said, 'Well, I don't see that happening. I see the Whites wiping everyone out. Everyone except me, you understand.' And she looked at me for a long time and said, 'No. I don't see a White Witch wiping you out, Mercury.'

"At another point she asked me, 'Who is your mother, Mercury? The wind or the rain?'

"I told her that my mother was Saffron, a fine Black Witch.

"Ledger said, 'Isn't your Gift like a parent to you now? Teaching, guiding, helping, and, even for you with all your power, a source of comfort?'

"It took a huge amount of self-control to resist the urge to freeze her jaw shut at that point.

"I asked her what her Gift was and if it was her mother. I wasn't sure I wanted a reply as I was sure it would be more nonsense and I'd already had to put up with hours of it. She replied with a non-answer, as ever. She said, 'I'm still learning about my Gift, Mercury, and still it eludes me.'

"Of course she was being 'humble.' She has learned many Gifts, and I am trying to copy her in that, I admit. She delights in disguise and shape-shifting. (I won't bother to say what appearance she took on for me, except that it was extremely tiresome.) In any case, she is the most powerful witch I know of. The irony is that although she has learned to access many powers she has failed completely to be anything but tedious and absurd. She says things like 'The Essence is our true home' and that she is 'merely climbing through a window to steal a few gems.' To many questions she simply replies, 'The Essence is the source of all Gifts.'

"At one stage she said, 'Whoever can access the Essence, all power is theirs. There will be no limit to it.' She knelt and touched the ground with the flat of both her hands (I had to stifle my laughter), saying, 'It's here somewhere.' Then she looked up at me and said, 'But perhaps, as your Gift is weather, you think it's in the air?' And for the first time I thought that she was genuinely interested in me, or rather in my Gift. That is her weakness: she is desperate for more knowledge.

"I replied, 'Of course the air is the answer for me.'

"But now I'm back in my home and I press my hands to the walls of stone, I think that perhaps she is right and the earth is the answer."

Nesbitt closes the diary and says something but I'm thinking about the earth holding the secret of witch powers. I feel that is true: the earth is the answer. It's through the earth that I helped Gabriel get his Gift back. When we were in the trance and our hands were staked together, we were transported to Wales, at least in our minds we were. I'm not sure what happened then but when the stake went into the earth and into my chest, my heart, we connected with something. I touch my chest, feel the slight indentation scar left from the stake, and I look at Gabriel and he says, "The earth is the answer for me."

Mercury was clearly jealous of Ledger but also impressed by her. She does sound completely unlike any White or Black Witch I've ever come across.

I ask Nesbitt, "Did Van say what Ledger was like?"

"Glad you asked that, 'cause as it happens I asked that very question and Van said, 'She's remarkably calm, pleasant, and reasonable.'"

So this is beginning to look more straightforward. Calm, pleasant, and reasonable: at least it doesn't sound like I'm going to have to fight her.

I say, "So we get to Ledger through the map room, and the map room is here," and I point to the map.

Nesbitt grins. "Yep. In the cellar of the house in Philadelphia. The address is here in the diary."

"Easy then," I say. "Are you sure you're not going to come?"

Gabriel sees that Nesbitt's considering it and adds,

"I don't think there'll be any Hunters there. Might be interesting."

Nesbitt smiles and says, "I'm sure it will be interesting." But he shakes his head. "If you don't mind, fellas, I'll leave it to you." He gets up and makes to leave, then turns back, saying, "Nearly forgot. You need to be thinking about what to take with you. A token, I mean. Something to show you're making a peaceful visit."

"What did Van take?" I ask.

"She took a fancy diamond necklace from Mercury's collection," he says. "It was a weapon—kills anyone who puts it on."

"Nice."

"Van brought the necklace back."

"She did give Ledger half of the Vardian amulet. That's probably more rare and precious than diamonds," Gabriel reminds us.

"True. Well, I'll leave that with you. I'm going to cook dinner. The last supper together, eh, boys?" And he wanders out, saying, "Mercury has some decent wine here as I recall."

The Last Night

After Nesbitt goes to the kitchen, I leave Gabriel in the library and wander around the bunker. But really I'm not wandering; I know where I'm heading.

The bedroom that Annalise and I shared is just as we left it. The bedclothes are rumpled and creased; there's even a dip in the pillow. I remember lying there, Annalise's head on my chest. There's the small vial of potion on the chest of drawers: the one I used to wake her. The bowl of nightsmoke is still there too. We stood here in front of the bowl and kissed and caressed and I loved her. I loved her so much. She was gentle and kind and sweet. It was a beautiful time we had together here—only a few days but special. And I can't work out if she changed or I changed or we both did or what. I don't think I changed that much but maybe I did. From the age of eleven we knew each other but maybe not that well. Maybe we just saw in each other what we wanted to see.

I look at the bed. It seems strange to think that I lay there with Annalise, talked with her, kissed her, and now I feel nothing for her at all except loathing. My anger, my fury, has changed to simple hate.

There's something on the floor under the bed and I pull

it out. It's the silk nightdress Annalise took from Mercury's wardrobe. She looked amazing in it. I remember holding her, the silk against her skin, against my skin. And kissing her and everything we did was so good.

And now I detest her and I wonder how she feels about me. I know she thought I was getting more like my father. Marcus was always the problem. We never spoke about him but she knew I loved him and she didn't understand that. I think she hated her own father and expected me to feel the same way about mine.

I remember a conversation we had about Marcus when we were working for the Alliance. She asked me where he slept. I told her, "Away from everyone. Where he won't be disturbed. Where he feels safe."

"In a tent?" And I think she asked that because she knew it was unlikely.

"No. In . . ." And I was going to tell her about his den that he grew around himself. A thicket of brambles like the one I stayed in with him. I said, "I'll take you sometime."

"I've never even spoken to him."

"He doesn't like it in camp."

And the next day I went to see my father, sat with him in his den. Felt how good it was to be there. I told him Annalise would like to meet him and he said, "If you really mean that, then bring her here."

But I never did. That was a few days before things started to go wrong between me and Annalise, and bringing Marcus into the problem didn't seem like a good idea. And, if I'm honest, I knew she wouldn't have understood him and so wouldn't understand that part of me. And I knew in my heart that she wouldn't feel at home in the den.

I hold the nightdress to my face, feel its softness, and then I let it drop back to the floor.

The meal Nesbitt has cooked is typically huge, enough for eight of us, and it's good. Soup and fresh bread, followed by stew and lots of veg, and for Nesbitt a lot of wine too. I don't drink and Gabriel's small glass lasts all evening. We talk about the food and the bunker and then Mercury and Van. Nesbitt tells us stories of things he and Van did together, of places they went all over the world. Of how Van helped him when he was young and trained him and how she loved his soufflé but would never even try banoffee pie. He is nearly crying at the end of it. I'm glad for his sake that he's leaving the Alliance and hope he finds something better, something he believes in. He says he wants to settle down, find "the right woman" and have kids, which I'm surprised to realize he'd be great at. We talk a little about people we have known but who have gone, most killed at BB. Sameen and Claudia and some of the others we trained with, Ellen, my Half Blood friend from London, who was a scout for the Alliance and who was killed in the aftermath of BB, and others we never had the chance to bury or even remember properly. And I wonder how many more of us will die in this war.

Eventually, however, Nesbitt's talk makes no sense at all and he begins to fall asleep at the table. Gabriel says we should put him to bed, though I really don't see what's wrong with letting him sleep on the kitchen floor. But Gabriel has this idea that it's our last night together and we should look after him, so we take an arm each round our shoulders, Gabriel grabs the bowl of nightsmoke and we walk Nesbitt down to one of the bedrooms and drop him on the bed. Gabriel throws me some blankets and I make a bed up for myself on the floor. Gabriel does the same.

And I sleep.

A wonderful sleep that must last all of half an hour because I wake to the sound of snoring. Snoring that is loud, irregular, and unmistakably Australian.

Bastard!

I get up. It's impossible to ignore snoring, especially when you know it can be stopped by smothering the idiot who's doing it.

The light from the nightsmoke gives the room a faint green glow and Nesbitt looks ghostly in the light. He's lying on his back, his mouth wide open. I roll him onto his side. He mutters, but doesn't wake. I stand by him and wait, and he sighs. The snoring has stopped. He breathes quietly.

I go back to my blanket on the floor and am about to lie down when the snoring starts again.

A new kind of nightmare!

I haven't had a vision of me killing Nesbitt but there's a chance it might happen unless I get out of the room. I look over to Gabriel but he seems to be asleep so I take a small bowl of the nightsmoke and go looking for somewhere quiet. The next room down the corridor is a bedroom with a comfy-looking bed, but I have the urge to go somewhere else: to the room I've avoided since we came back.

It's just a bathroom. Very cold now. The bath is dirty, still lined with bloodstains. Mercury's blood. This is where I came after I killed her. I washed here and I kissed Gabriel here.

I walk over to the basin and look in the mirror. I look older and strangely unreal in the greenish light of the night-smoke. I touch my face and feel the small scar on my cheek where Jessica caught me with the photo frame when I was a child. I guess I was about three or four, so Jessica would have been ten or eleven. She's oldest of us four children, though she'd just say three children and a half Black. I can't remember any occasion when she was nice to me. She hated me from birth. And in a way it's understandable; my father killed her father. And yet Deborah and Arran didn't blame me for what Marcus did. And they must have wondered about me, wondered about my Black Witch side.

I pull my hair back to see my eyes. They're the same as ever: black, and the empty triangles in the blackness tumble around slowly and steadily. And the tattoo on my neck is the same: **B 0.5**.

I feel my cheek and the stubble there, but I don't need to shave much. I'm still only seventeen. My chin and my patchy beard say seventeen but my eyes, and maybe my soul, say one hundred and seventeen. I guess I've done a lot more than the average seventeen-year-old.

I see my father in my face too: a younger version of him. I'm not sure if that's part of my problem. That what everyone sees when they look at me is his name, his myth, the people he's killed and eaten. And maybe that's what happened with Annalise. She began to see not me but only Marcus and the stories about him.

And part of me is proud Marcus was—is—my father. I'm proud that I'm like him. We're alike in so many ways. Fighting, yes; being good at drawing; our Gift to turn animal; and our appreciation of solitude. But I'm unlike him too. I had a White Witch for a mother and a grandmother. I've got—

"Hi."

I look in the mirror and see Gabriel is standing in the doorway. "Nesbitt wake you as well?"

It's not really a question and Gabriel doesn't answer; he stays in the doorway and I stay leaned over the sink.

"You OK?" he asks. A genuine question.

I speak to my reflection as I reply. "Yeah, great."

He doesn't say anything.

So I look up again at his reflection and ask him, "How old are you, Gabriel?"

"Umm . . . nineteen."

I turn to face him. "You look older. Twenty or twenty-one maybe."

He shakes his head. "Turned nineteen a couple of months ago. You missed the big party."

And for a brief second I'm jealous to think there was a party, with Greatorex and the trainees and I didn't get an invite, but of course he's joking. But then again a couple of months ago I was with Annalise and I've no idea what Gabriel was doing when I was with her.

"Wish I'd known. I'd have done something. For your birthday, I mean."

"I doubt it." And he leans against the door frame, clearly not going to come into the room, and says, "Anyway, it doesn't matter. I really don't care about my birthday."

And I'm irritated. I think he does care, maybe not about his birthday but about me not even knowing or asking before now.

And I suppose I can still give him a present. He bought me a knife for no other reason than he wanted to give me something. And, typical of Gabriel, it was a perfect present, beautiful and useful. But less typical was how nervous he was when he gave it to me. I'd like to do that: give him something and make it so clear it was special, that it was important.

I say, "I can still give you something."

"Yeah?" He sounds skeptical.

"A knife or . . . I don't know . . . a book or . . . or something."

"That would be nice," he says, and then adds, "Nice isn't normally one of your strong points."

"No . . . Sorry."

"And did you say sorry then?" He shakes his head as if clearing his ears. "That's the second time you've said that to me."

I know that I owe him lots of "sorry"s. He once said he liked how I was honest with him and recently, since I last said sorry to him, I've tried harder, but I never tell him half of what I think, not a fraction. And I wish he'd come into the room but he's still standing there in the doorway. And I know he won't come in because of what happened last time we were here and I kissed him.

I think about it a lot, that kiss, and how it was good. And I think a lot too about how I fucked it up.

I'm not sorry I kissed him. I wanted to, and it felt good, and mostly when I think about it I wish I'd done it better and not stopped so soon and not, definitely not, walked out and left him. But then there was Annalise and I'd just killed Mercury and I was freaking out and . . . and mainly there was Annalise.

But I wanted to kiss him then and I did and it was good and I'd like to do it again.

But he doesn't take a step into the room and I think he's staying away from me because I fucked up last time. But the kiss wasn't fucked up. And I'm not sure he'd let me do it again, but I'd like to try. I'd like to do it better.

But, oh shit, it seems a long way from the basin to the doorway. And I really don't want to mess this up.

But I want to touch him, kiss him.

I turn to the mirror and stare at myself. I look a mess so I close my eyes and I'm not sure what I'm thinking except that I want to kiss him. So I turn round and take a step toward him and then another and another, and with each step I'm feeling less clumsy, less unsure, until I reach him and stand in front of him.

I raise my left hand and with my fingertip touch the scar that runs through his eyebrow. "I always meant to say sorry about that. About your eye, I mean. About beating you up."

He doesn't move. I don't think he's even breathing.

"I could have blinded you," I say, and stroke the scar. It's pale and wide despite being only a couple of centimeters long.

And, oh shit this is difficult, and I think I might be shaking but I move my left hand down, touching his cheek with my fingertips, then his jaw, his neck, and feel his hair on his shoulder. I move my lips to his and then, with my lips brushing his, I say, "Sorry." And I caress his lips with mine. And now I feel him breathing onto my mouth, and his breath mixes with mine, our mouths slightly open. And I say, "Sorry about the scar." And his lips feel good on mine and I have to kiss him, but very gently. He doesn't kiss me back and I open my eyes to see his but his eyes are closed. I say, "Sorry I beat you up." And as I speak my lips brush his again and I kiss him again. And I check his eyes, and they're still closed and he still hasn't kissed me back. He hasn't moved away, but not into me either.

My hand is on his neck and his hair and I want to kiss him again but I daren't now.

All I can do is say, "Sorry. Sorry I hurt you." My lips still brush his as I say it, and I do that on purpose, because I like doing it and I'm desperate for him to do something.

But he still does nothing.

"Gabriel, I'm sorry. This is me being as nice as I can."

And still nothing.

"I'll wait here forever, if that's what you want. I'll say sorry again and again."

And then I feel his hand on my waist, first one side gently, barely touching, and then the other. And he pulls me to him, our hips together, and he says, "You should be nice more often," and he says it so slowly and his lips brush mine as he speaks, and he says some stuff in French and all the time his lips are brushing against my lips and then finally he kisses me.

We kiss a lot. And Gabriel takes me to one of the bedrooms and we kiss more, undress each other and do stuff, nice stuff, making-love stuff. And it's good. Very good. Very sweaty. And then we sleep together. Naked, sweaty-type sleeping. We wake in the night and start kissing again and more making love. Then he kisses my scars, kisses me everywhere, and I fall asleep.

Later I wake and he's asleep and I move over him gently to kiss across his chest and listen to his slow heartbeat, and

I want to stay there, listening to his heart. I feel strange. I can't remember ever feeling like this. I think I'm sort of happy. I close my eyes but even so I know it's not sleep that's coming but a cool darkness. A vision.

There's a river and trees and gentle hills and the sound of birds and sun on my skin. It's a beautiful place. A place I've always dreamed of being. And I'm with Gabriel and he's with me.

Maps

•..•

Nesbitt is standing in the kitchen, his back to us. He's swaying slightly. I think he's still drunk. He's knocked back two large glasses of water and groaned quite a bit but not done much else since we woke him and dragged him out of bed.

Now he straightens himself and says, "Let this be a lesson to you, boys. The evils of alcohol."

I say, "I don't think it's us that need the lesson."

"I admit I'm feeling a bit rough."

"You look like shit too." And then I add, "And you don't smell that great either."

"Thanks, mate." Nesbitt turns to face us. He really is looking bad: sort of pale gray, with pinprick red eyes and stubble. He looks ten years older. He says, "Can't even remember that much."

"You cooked, we talked and you drank, and then you talked more and drank more, all the way through three bottles of wine and some of this." Gabriel smiles and lifts an empty bottle of whisky.

Nesbitt shudders again and says, "I'm going back to bed."

"You can do that after we've gone," I tell him.

"Hurry up and piss off then." He fishes in his trouser pockets and pulls out a wad of US dollars. "Found these in Mercury's room yesterday. Have you decided on the token you're going to give Ledger?"

Gabriel pats my backpack, saying, "I've put in a few of Mercury's diaries, the ones with comments about Ledger and the maps that show where the map room is. I think she'd like to know we're keeping her location as private as possible."

Me and Gabriel discussed this and agreed that the token should not have a monetary value and we couldn't think of anything magical that was appropriate so this was the best we could come up with.

Nesbitt takes us to the cut that links to New York. And then we have to say good-bye and I'm not sure if we'll ever see Nesbitt again. I have a feeling we won't but maybe that's just the somber mood we're all in. Nesbitt says, "If I do get married you'll have to come to the wedding. It'll be a big do. I know how you love a good party, kid."

"I've never been to a party."

Nesbitt shakes his head. "Why does that not surprise me?" And he hugs me and says, "I'll miss you."

Then he releases me and hugs Gabriel as well. "I'll miss you too, Gab. Look after yourself and look after him."

Then he stands back and says, "Now, if you don't mind, I think I'm going to go and throw up."

Gabriel takes my right hand in his left and interlocks

his fingers in mine, then reaches for the cut. I look back to Nesbitt standing alone and pale in the room and my body slides into the cut and then darkness.

It's completely black and yet I know I'm moving because I'm feeling dizzy. I know I should breathe out to stop that, so I do and I concentrate on what I feel, which is cold—cold to my bones on all parts of my body except my hand where Gabriel holds me. I look ahead, or at least where I think ahead is, but there is no light. I'm running out of air. It must be over a minute now.

Then we're slammed onto a hard floor. I can breathe again. We're in a dark corner of an alley, squeezed behind a massive dumpster. It's dirty but not like the dirt in the woods. That is good dirt; this is grime.

We head off to a main street to get our bearings and Gabriel says we need to go to the railway station. I've not been to many cities and this is different from London and very different from Basle and Barcelona. But the hiss of the electricity is the same, a constant noise in my head. It doesn't bother me, or stop me concentrating on what we're doing, but it does make me think that I'll never notice a Hunter here.

We walk, as we can't go by underground or even by taxi while it's dark, and we keep a lookout for witches—Gabriel reminds me this is White Witch territory—but we don't see many people. At one point a police car blares past and Gabriel pulls me into a side street, pushes me up against the wall and holds me there. I let him. I know we're in no danger; they're just fains, but Gabriel's being Gabriel. And it's nice to feel his body warm against me in the cold air, the wall cold on my back. He kisses me, pressing his body against me. And then he moves to set off but I pull him back and kiss him, pushing him against the wall now. I kiss his lips, his cheek, his neck, his ear.

"Do you kiss all your friends like that?" he asks. It's the question he asked after I kissed him the first time, all those months ago, and I kiss down his chest and then work my way back to his mouth and with my lips close to his I say, "Only you." I'm trying not to be too serious but he looks at me serious now. I tell him, "And I'll always be your friend."

"I know."

I kiss him gently and then we set off again, walking fast. There are more people and more cars on the streets now. It's beginning to get light by the time we get to the railway station. Inside we find out when there's a train and then go to a café to wait.

We have our coffee, hot chocolate, croissants, and fruit. I end up messing with the packets of sugar, ripping them open and tipping the contents into my mug, ripping the paper up into bits and adding that to the mug too. Gabriel reaches over and touches the back of my hand with his fingertips, so I stop messing and we stay like that, me holding a packet of sugar and him caressing the back of my hand. He talks to me, tells me about his family and how they came to live in America, in Florida, and how he shot the girl who betrayed his sister, Michèle, and I look at my hands and think of all the people they've killed and wonder how many more there are to come.

We catch the train and sit next to each other, close, and stare out of the window as the world goes by and changes from pale gray skies to blue skies. The buildings gradually fall away to fields and snow and then turn back to houses and then Gabriel says, "We need to get off."

A cab driver says he knows the address and ten minutes later we're going through the suburbs, snow piled up along the roadside. And then we're in the country and the roads are icy. The driver complains that it hasn't snowed for days and the roads are still not cleared properly. And then he stops the car and says, "This is it."

There's a house set back from the road that looks unoccupied—the snow around it is pristine. Gabriel pays the driver and we stand in the road while he takes forever to turn round and drive back the way he came.

We walk up to the front of the house, the snow squeaking beneath our feet. It really is cold and we have to shield our eyes and squint in the low, bright sun.

The front door is locked, as is the back. Gabriel has one of Mercury's magic hairpins, though, and it opens the back door without a problem. Before he goes in, I hold his arm and ask, "What about protection spells?"

He shrugs. "Nesbitt didn't say there were any."

"He never came here."

"But Van did. She would have been caught by them."

And before I can stop him he steps in. I wait and look around me. But it's all quiet and I follow Gabriel in.

The house is old and run-down and smells of damp. There are carpets in some rooms and the curtains are still hanging and drawn shut but the only furniture is a broken chair in one bedroom. We check upstairs and on the ground floor to make sure that no one and nothing else is here before going down the wooden steps to the cellar. The light doesn't work so we have to use our torches.

The cellar is exactly that: one room with a lowish ceiling and a cement floor. There's nothing in it.

I tell Gabriel, "I admit I wasn't sure what a map room was but I sort of expected a room with maps."

"Yeah."

Gabriel shines his torch over all the walls.

I ask, "Do you think someone's taken them?"

"I don't know. If Ledger's so powerful I think there'll be some magic involved."

"Maybe there's another cut in here that leads to the map room."

"This is where it's meant to be. It was on Mercury's map. It's this address. The cellar."

I walk around the room but there really isn't anything to see. I check the ceiling and the floor and the walls, but there is nothing here. The room is empty.

Gabriel says, "They must be here. We're just not seeing them."

"Maybe we have to say a magic word and the maps appear," I suggest.

"Mercury doesn't mention that in her diary." Gabriel starts feeling the walls, saying, "Maybe there's a hidden room."

"She doesn't mention that either."

I lean against the wall and watch Gabriel wander around the room, pressing at the walls, tapping them and coming up with nothing. "This can't be right," he says. "We're missing something."

"Obviously."

"Maybe they were here and Van saw them and Ledger decided to move them after that."

I have a bad feeling he's right and we've wasted a trip. I growl in frustration and scrape my forehead against the wall. Then something catches my eye. My face is against the wall and the wall of cement or plaster, or whatever it is, is lit from below by my torch. From this angle I can see that the walls aren't perfectly flat; they are covered in tiny humps and dips, like hills and valleys.

"Gabriel, bring your torch here and shine the light sideways."

I stand against the wall, my cheek on the cement. "What do you think? Does it look like . . . a landscape?"

And as I stare more detail appears: I can see mountains and then I spot darker veins in the plaster that could be rivers, patches of dark that could be forests, or towns perhaps.

I take my face off the wall and the picture fades but when I touch it with my skin it comes back.

I move along the wall a little to see more. "This looks like a mountain with a river running down it."

I peer closer and it's as if I'm looking down from high up, the view I have when I'm in the body of an eagle. The detail is amazing. The closer I look, the more I see: plains, trees, and lakes. I even think I can see birds flying, circling below me.

This is a map and it's powerful magic.

I look over to Gabriel and he's touching a different wall and I go to check it out. This too is a map but seems to be a different place: a desert, with sand, boulders, and scrubby vegetation. He says, "This is beautiful."

I remember it from old cowboy movies that I watched with Arran. I say, "Yeah. It's the badlands."

Badlands

I reach out to touch the map but Gabriel snatches my hand back.

"It's just a wall," I say. I've been touching it for the last ten minutes and nothing bad has happened.

"It's a map. And magical. And we don't know how it works or what's in there. Except that Mercury said that if you went to the wrong map you'd get stuck."

I back off a little from the wall. "So? How do you think it works?" I ask. "Is there an on switch or a spell you have to do?"

Gabriel gets Mercury's diaries out of my backpack and reads: *"Finally found the map room in the cellar of the house in P and it was simple from there. She loves that: mixing the extremely complex spells of the maps with a simple request to gain access to them."*

"So 'a simple request to gain access' is what we need."

"Sounds like it."

"Any ideas? I mean, it couldn't be as easy as asking, 'Can we come in?' Could it?"

"I have a feeling it really is as simple as that." Gabriel looks at the wall and says, "I would guess that you touch where you want to go on the map and ask to gain access and . . . maybe it sucks you in, like a cut or something."

"OK, but which map?" And I move round the room, studying all four walls, all four maps, but I've no idea which is the right one. There's the badlands, a snowy mountainous place, a desert, and a city by a lake.

Gabriel looks at them all too and then goes back to Mercury's diary. He says, "There's nothing more. What we need to do is give 'a simple request to gain access.'"

"Right. So we ask the map something like, 'If you can take me to Ledger, then please let me in.'" I look at Gabriel to see what he thinks.

He nods.

"So which one do we try first?"

"Badlands," he says.

"Why?"

He smiles. "I like the sound of it."

"All right." And I move to the wall and flex my fingers. "But where do we touch?"

We inspect the map but there's no obvious sign to help us. "I think we pick a spot in the middle and ask to go in."

Gabriel doesn't look too impressed but says, "OK. But we go together."

"No."

"Yes. If you go alone, I'll come straight after you anyway so we might as well go together." I know he'd do it too, so I take his hand and then put my finger to the midpoint of the map and touch it gently.

Gabriel jerks my hand off the map, saying, "You have to

mention Ledger's name. You have to say to give us access to Ledger. I think if you just ask for access then we *will* go in but it might be the wrong map."

"OK." I smile at him. "Is English the right language? Or do you want to try French?"

"If she's that powerful, I imagine it works whatever language you use."

"You ready?"

Gabriel nods and I say, "Map, please take us to Ledger."

And, of course, nothing happens and so I say, "Map, if Ledger is . . ." but then something does start to happen. I feel warmth. Heat reaching up my arm, which seems to be disintegrating and dissolving into the map.

There's heat and a yellow glow all around me and I'm floating in it like a warm bath. It's not like traveling through a cut but like sinking into warm mud.

But then the yellow glow clears like mist and the world comes back into focus. The rock beneath my feet is beige and the blue sky above is clear. The sun is high in the sky and the dry heat around me is intense. I'm standing in a narrow, steep valley, a badlands valley. Behind me, the slope climbs even more steeply; ahead of me it widens out as it drops to the valley floor. But I'm alone. Gabriel isn't here.

Shit!

I don't know if I said it wrong. I don't remember letting go of his hand. And now I've no idea what to do. I don't know how to get back to the cellar or anywhere else come to that. I can only hope that Gabriel is back in the cellar, frustrated but safe. There's nothing I can do about it and I have to get on with sorting my own mess out.

My options seem to be to climb up or walk down. I try both but neither work. If I try walking down to the valley floor, I seem to tread on the same spot. I focus on a distant place, the brown and red stone walls of the valley below, and run at them. But I don't move more than a meter. The same happens if I try to move uphill focusing on the ridge above me. So then I try focusing on a spot ten paces away and try to get to that but I don't make it. I consider throwing my backpack to see what would happen but instead decide to throw something I don't care if I lose.

I feel my pockets and all I've got are the Hunter bullets and the white stone for Annalise. I get the bullets out; they may as well be useful for once. I throw the first uphill, aiming to get it as near to the ridge as possible. It seems to fly off away from me, but then I see that it is on the ground a meter from my feet. I pick it up and try again with the same result. Then I try rolling it downhill and it rolls for a meter and then stops. I give it a nudge with my toe and it rolls downhill a few centimeters and then rolls back uphill to where it was.

So it seems we're stuck here, me and my bullets.

And now I'm sitting on the dry, uneven ground and waiting. The ground is hard, the sun is hot, and there's no breeze. I've got a small water canister with me, enough for a few days, if I'm careful.

I'm still by my backpack a long time later, but although

hours seem to have passed the sun hasn't moved. Perhaps I'm stuck in the map, but when we looked at it in the map room the birds and animals and rivers were alive and moving. Here it feels like time has stopped. It has that same quality of silence and stillness. Ledger must be powerful to do this: make the maps, keep me stuck here, and stop time. And I think back to what Mercury said about Ledger, that she is the most powerful, but what's the point of it? And I think that's like saying what's the point of anything? Of life, of being able to run, to turn into an animal, to go invisible, to change appearance. The ability is the thing. And here Ledger is showing off her ability but so far not harming me by doing so. I just have to hope that doesn't change when time starts up again.

If time starts up again.

And so I wait. I try to work out what to say to Ledger if she turns up but I've no idea what to say and I end up thinking about Gabriel, wishing he was here with me.

And then something changes.

In the distance I see movement.

A figure: slowly walking up the valley toward me. Whoever it is—and I assume it's Ledger—isn't in a hurry. Then the figure waves an arm, indicating I should come down. I get up and walk and find that I can make progress now, so I go downhill. There's a slight breeze. Time has started up again.

As I get nearer to the figure I see it's a young man and, as I get closer, he turns and walks ahead of me. He's slim and agile. I speed up to get close to him and he disappears.

Fuck!

I keep my eyes on where he was. I could see that he was dragged away through a cut. I walk on, my arm out feeling for it. I think I'm at the same spot but nothing happens and I can feel my heart beginning to race. But I keep trying and then I feel my arm and then my whole body being sucked through and then I'm spat out on to my knees on warm grass.

Birds are singing. I'm on a grassy meadow, distant hills and trees off to my left. There's a warm breeze and the sun is low in the sky. There's a wide river to my left and up ahead is a large stone-built cabin, and I can see that the door is open and the boy is disappearing inside. I walk to it slowly, looking around all the time, but there isn't anyone else to see. I consider going invisible to have a proper scout but I don't think that would be polite and might cause more trouble than it solves. At the end of the day, if Ledger is so powerful and she wants to kill me, she probably will.

The Cabin

I push the cabin door wide open. There's a sitting room and beyond that a kitchen. The boy's in the kitchen. His dark blond hair is cut short at the back but falls in front of his face. I can't quite see his eyes. He's maybe eighteen or nineteen. He's nice-looking but nothing special.

I take a deep breath and go in. "I'm looking for Ledger," I say, not sure if this is her in disguise.

"You're Nathan," he replies. He gives me a shy smile and I see one of his front teeth is a little crooked. He blinks through his hair, then extends his hand to shake mine, saying, "I'm Ledger. I've been looking forward to you coming. Welcome."

I'm not sure what I was expecting from Ledger, but a boy not much older than me wasn't it. I shake his hand, though, and he looks into my eyes. His are similar to mine, though steel gray, not black, but he has triangles turning in them; the more I look, the more I'm drawn to them—to how empty they seem. Then he takes his hand away and turns his back on me, saying, "I'm making coffee. Do you want some?"

"Ummm. No."

"Tea your thing? Or something stronger?"

"No." Though I'm thirsty. I've been sitting in the dry heat of the badlands for hours. "A glass of water?"

Ledger lets the tap run and then fills a glass and passes it to me.

I say, "I have a friend, Gabriel. I was with him but we got separated."

"Yes."

"Is he still in the map room?"

"He's safe."

"Safe where?"

"The map only allows one person in at a time. After you came through he tried to follow you but put his finger on the map a centimeter or two further west."

"And where is he now?"

"As I said, he's safe." Ledger looks me in the eye again and says, "I've no reason to lie. He'll join us soon enough." And I know all I can do is trust that Ledger is telling me the truth.

Ledger makes the coffee and puts it on the table and gets milk and sugar. And then sits down opposite me.

I remember the tokens and fish them out of my backpack. "Umm . . . I've brought some things for you. Tokens of friendship. The map was Mercury's; it shows where your map room is, and there's a couple of her diaries that record her meeting you and talking about you. They helped Van find the way here, and helped me too. We, I mean, me and Gabriel thought you might . . . anyway, they're for you." I lay them on the table as I say this.

Ledger says, "Thank you," but makes no move to take the map or diaries or even to look at them. He pours his coffee, adds milk and then sugar.

I say, "Van told me about you. Well, she didn't say much but she did say that I should come to see you." I hesitate and then add, "She was killed a couple of weeks ago. Killed by Hunters. They were sent by Soul, the leader of the White Witches in Britain. They wiped out the Alliance camp she was in."

I watch Ledger to see what effect this news has, but he shows no reaction. He watches me too and I feel like everything I do and say is being assessed.

I continue. "Van said you had half of the Vardian amulet and that she'd given you her half. She thought that the amulet would protect me when I fight Soul and the Hunters. She said that you'd give it to the right person."

Ledger doesn't react to that either but just sips his coffee, his eyes not leaving mine. He says, "You don't believe in small talk, it seems."

I hesitate. "Do you?"

"Well, at some stage I'm sure it will be useful to get to know each other." He takes another sip of his coffee. "But let's stay on the subject you've raised for now. You want to kill Soul . . . Put an end to his terrible reign." And he looks at me now, right in the eyes, and it's as if he's reading my mind. "Do you believe it's right to kill people?"

"Killing Soul is the right thing to do."

"I can understand your reason for thinking that, for believing that. But as someone wise once said, 'There's no truth, only perspective.'"

I try to work that out and say, "I don't . . ."

"It means that I'm entitled to have a different view and it's equally valid."

"And what is your view?"

"My view about Soul is that he's a man . . . out of balance. My view on killing him, on killing anyone, is that I don't approve of it. I'm not a great believer in killing people at all, and if I was to help you I'd be helping you kill. Not just Soul, I think, but many more besides."

"You'd be helping me survive. And by helping me you'd be saving the many people Soul is killing."

"So, to save some people I don't know, I have to kill some other people I don't know?"

"You don't have to kill anyone. And I intend to kill them all one way or the other."

"All?"

I hesitate, thinking of my dream and the never-ending line of Hunters kneeling on the floor.

Ledger looks at me and I get the feeling he's seen inside my head, seen my thoughts. He says, "And you're OK with that, Nathan? Killing all those people?"

"They're evil."

"So you say. But isn't life sacred?"

"Life is life, death is death. Don't make it what it isn't.

We all die. Some people live lives that cause harm."

"Including you perhaps." And I feel his eyes on me still.

I shrug and look away and then look back at him and meet his gaze and say, "I'm not a hero but I can end the war. And the Alliance, if they win, can maybe bring some stability, maybe allow White Witches and Black Witches to live together peacefully."

"And do you think it's possible for Black Witches and White Witches to live together in peace and harmony?"

"I'm not sure. But it has to be worth trying. It has to be better than what we've got at the moment."

"I agree, but it's how to get there that's the point of this discussion, I think."

Ledger leans back in his seat, saying, "You know, the thing I've learned over many, many years"—he waits for me to look up at him and then he smiles as if to acknowledge how young he looks—"is that things turn round anyway. Nothing, however bad or, sadly, however good, lasts forever. All is ephemeral. Including us."

"So do nothing is your answer? Wait for it to happen naturally!"

"It's an option. You could leave them to it, Soul and the Alliance, and find a quiet place to live. I see you by a river, trees, mountains . . . a place very much like my home here in Montana." He leans forward to look into my eyes. "Yes, trees, and a river for sure, though I'm not so certain about a cabin."

Ledger reaches out to touch me. "May I?" he asks, and then he lays his hand on top of mine. "You're an interesting boy, Nathan. So young and yet bursting with magical powers. But your own Gift is powerful and yet it feels small: buried under all these other desires and emotions."

"I've had other things to think about. I'm learning to use all my Gifts. I need them all to fight Soul. But I need the amulet too."

"We seem to be back where we started."

For lack of anything better to say, I add, "Life—death. I mean everything, the whole system, is fucked up anyway."

"Out of balance is the phrase we older people would use," he replies, but he's smiling again.

I ask him, "Why are you in that disguise? I mean, why appear as a young man? I know you're not young and I don't think you're a man."

"Does it matter what I appear to be? I thought you might enjoy talking to someone more like yourself. And I have to say that being young and healthy and full of vigor is so much more pleasurable than not."

"When Van came did you appear to her as a sophisticated woman?"

"Yes, as a matter of fact, I did."

"And when Mercury was here?"

"Oh that was fun. I remember it like yesterday. I took on the look of Thetis, which Mercury didn't like at all. Too much competition."

"I've no idea who Thetis is."

"You should Google her sometime."

I don't reply and he says, "You don't like phones, computers . . . electricity?"

I hesitate, then explain. "It sets off noises in my head, hissing."

"Ah, a few of us Black Witches have that sensitivity. At first I battled against it myself. Then I learned to ignore it: for years I ignored it, was very pleased with myself that I could ignore it and get on with my life. I thought about it, meditated on it, meditated with it. And then finally, *finally* . . . the lightbulb moment, as they say."

"I've no idea what you're talking about."

I look away from Ledger and out of the window. I say, "Where are we? I mean, we're not really in Montana, are we?"

He looks out of the window too, as if to check and consider the question carefully, before saying, "Well, it certainly looks like Montana."

I'm not sure what or where we are. It could all be some kind of dream or illusion. But Ledger is real enough. I sip my water. It's cold and seems real too.

"I'm glad you've come, Nathan. I don't get many visitors."

"That's not surprising. You're not easy to find."

"No. That's true, I suppose. I complain but I don't do anything about it." He gives a thoughtful smile as if considering this. "We missed out on the get-to-know-you small talk, but I should say that I am against killing, against violence. And you, Nathan, have a lot of violence in your past and in yourself."

Ledger leans across the table and takes my hand. His is cool and dry but with a firm grip. "And yet I am also a believer in balance, in the power of our Gifts through harmony. Nathan, you have so many strengths, from your mother, your father, and I think from your own self. Though at the moment I don't sense much harmony." He rubs my palm and looks at it. "You have a long lifeline, curiously long . . ." Then he looks up at me, as if confused. "And I feel that your future is ultimately a peaceful one."

"Ultimately?"

"As I said, I see you by a river . . ."

It feels strange to sit here with my hand being held by Ledger but I try to forget about that and concentrate on what I've got to say. I continue. "And that's what I want. I believe in good things, in peace. But we don't have peace. We have war and torture and persecution. Everything is fucked up at the moment—out of balance. And it's all very well saying you don't believe in killing people but Soul is killing people. He has to be stopped and you're helping him if you don't try to stop him. He's evil."

Ledger looks into my eyes and says, "The only thing necessary for the triumph of evil is that good men do nothing."

"I'm not sure what all that means but I know I have to do something. That I can do something. Van told me that you'd be able to get the amulet to work and that you would give it to the right person. Am I that person?"

Ledger lets go of my hand, saying, "We'll see."

"Can you get the amulet to work?"

"I've been giving it a lot of thought. But, as ever with magic, thought is one thing, though feeling and intuition are more vital. My intuition is that it will work as all magic does when things are balanced in a certain way, when the right things have fallen into place."

"And have they? Fallen into place?"

"Perhaps. I'm not sure yet. You coming here *may* be significant. I have wanted the other half of the amulet for a long, long time. I wanted to see it out of curiosity, you understand, to see it whole. It's a historic object as well as a powerful one. To see it, to hold both halves, is wonderful. I never saw the point in chasing all over for it. I knew it would eventually come to me."

"Ha, that's not mystical or significant. Of course whoever had the other half would want your half."

"Really? Many people have owned that other half of the amulet before it came into Van's hands and none of them searched me out. Only Van did that, but she didn't want the amulet for herself; it was for you. She told me about you." Ledger sips his coffee and then says, "The amulet is a wonderful object containing great magic. At first I thought it didn't work because it was damaged, but I could still feel the magic in it. If we are to believe the story, the White Witch Vardia ripped it in two but intended that it would still protect Linus, a Black Witch, if she and he were reunited. Those are its origins and I sense the magic will still work but only for the right person, a person in whom Black and White are united."

"Me?"

Ledger gives me a brief smile. "I'm not sure you should be so pleased. The amulet, if it works, will give you protection from many things but it will demand huge responsibility to use your power well. I can assure you that living quietly by a river, studying your powers, learning about your Gifts and developing them over years, will ultimately result in greater strength and far greater happiness."

"In the meantime people are dying."

"People are always dying. It's a terrible habit they have and nothing you can do will change that."

"I can change it for some of them."

"Perhaps. But you are very young; you're only seventeen; you've only just received your Gift. You still have a huge amount to learn."

"I've learned enough to fight Soul."

"You think so? I don't think you even have a clue how much more there is."

And the house in Montana disappears and we're sitting at the same table and chair but on a huge ship, an ocean liner, and we're on the top deck and the wind is blowing fiercely and in the distance the water ruffles as dolphins break the surface; then we're surrounded by snow and ice and the chill makes the condensation in my nose freeze; and then we're sitting in a restaurant, surrounded by other people and other tables, and to my side is a huge window looking down on a harbor and across to skyscrapers.

"Very impressive. I take it we've not really moved. You've just made it look and feel like that."

And with that we're back in the house in Montana.

"I'm not trying to impress you, but to show you how much there is to learn. With that Gift I offer your mind suggestions of images and you see them. It's a rare one and difficult to control, but I have learned to do it. There is so much that you too can learn, Nathan. You have great potential."

"You've learned how to use other Gifts? But did you take them from someone else?"

"No, Nathan. I haven't taken anything from anyone. I access . . . the source of it all. And I think you could learn to do that too. And there is true joy in discovering more, in learning."

"That's really not me. I was never that good at school."

"I'm sure school didn't suit you at all, but you learn quickly about Gifts. You're intuitive. And remarkably trusting and honest, given your background. Oh yes, Van told me all about you. Everything she knew, which was quite a lot. About your parents, your brother and sisters, your time in a cage, your escape; and since then too—your father and what happened to him. You've overcome so many challenges, Nathan, but there is still more potential in you— that I know. Perhaps it's this wildness that you have."

He takes my hands again and looks into my eyes, and I wonder if the amulet can be made to help me, a Half Code, fight Soul and the Hunters.

Ledger sits back in his chair, saying, "Your thoughts are always going back to this war and the amulet. But, Nathan, the amulet is a trinket. I admit a very special one, but it's still a magical thing and the thing is of little interest; it's the magic itself that you should be interested in. The creator of the amulet locked that magic within it, but it's the same magic as is in you and in me. There is the same core of power that moves through it all. The Essence, as I call it. The Essence of it all. The Essence of us all."

Impressing Ledger

"So you've found it, the Essence?" I ask Ledger as we walk along the riverbank.

"I've found many things and have many abilities and I like to think I'm plucking away at the edge of the blanket of the Essence."

"What was your one Gift? The original one."

"Mind control. I was an intelligent child and confident in many ways and I knew, absolutely knew, that I would have a strong Gift. And yet in other ways, socially, one might say, I was neither confident nor happy. I had many strengths but they were out of balance. I was a small girl, not that attractive and very boyish. I wasn't interested in dressing nicely or fashionably. I found boys' clothes more comfortable. One boy in particular, Jack, he called me a boy. Said I wasn't a girl at all. I ignored his comments, my intellectual self telling me that he was stupid, a fain, and what did it matter what he thought or said? And yet inside I was hurt. I didn't realize how much until I found my Gift, a few weeks after my seventeenth birthday. It was a tiny incident. I was sitting on the school bus, near the front, reading a book, and Jack got on, walked past me, and called me a freak the way he always did. 'How's it going, freak?' And I remember not even looking up from my book but thinking, 'Go away, asshole!' And he turned round, got off the bus, and walked away.

"That's how I knew what my Gift was. Within a few weeks I discovered that not only could I make Jack walk away but I could make him do other things as well. It was a long time ago. Attitudes were different . . . maybe. I made him tell his friends that he preferred boys; I think I knew that he did, that he was trying to cover this up. He was seventeen too. I thought I was very clever. It seemed the perfect revenge." Ledger glances at me. "I'm not sure exactly what happened after that. He ended up sitting at the front of the bus but not with me, not with anyone. Then he started missing school, and when I did see him his face was bruised. I felt guilt but couldn't think how to make it right. A few weeks later he committed suicide.

"Was it my fault that he died? I think so. Did he deserve to die? No. Was he evil? From my perspective, not far off it—he made my life miserable. But I felt guilt then and still do. Because of me a boy died. I swore then that I would never use my Gift to harm anyone, not witch, not fain or Half Blood, no one."

"It wasn't your fault. You didn't beat him up or make his life hell. Society did that."

Ledger smiles at me. "Trust you to see that. But still I was using my power in a negative way."

"Society needed to change. Not you, not him." We walk on a little and I ask, "Is that story even true?"

Ledger laughs but doesn't answer the question. Instead he says, "What is true is that after I found my Gift I left home and traveled, meeting people, thinking, reading, and learning as I went. We are told that witches each have only one Gift, unless they steal them from others, but I began to question that. Healing is a kind of Gift, after all, and all witches have that power too. If we have two Gifts, why not three? Why not more?

"I realized that the Gifts themselves aren't important, but the underlying power is. And then I began to believe that if the power is there in all of us then we all have every Gift within our grasp anyway, but we need patience and work to find them."

"I'm not sure," I say. "The Gifts I have from my father I definitely didn't have to find. They came to me after I . . . ate his heart."

"But I'm saying that you could have found them this other way too. It would take longer but it's possible."

"So you can access any Gift now?"

"There are many things I can do, and many I can't. But I'd like to work with you, Nathan. I'd like you to stay here where I can share my knowledge and perhaps even learn from you." Ledger pauses and then asks, "Have you never felt something more than your Gift? Something more than any of the Gifts you've acquired?"

He looks at me intensely now. "I think you have. What was it?"

"My friend, Gabriel, he can transform, but he got stuck as a fain and couldn't transform back. Van helped us, gave us a potion to drink and we went into a sort of trance and Gabriel found his way back."

"How?"

"In the trance we went to Wales. Gabriel says it wasn't part of the trance, that it was real, but I'm not sure. Anyway, we had a stake joining us, me and Gabriel, and I fell on it, the stake, I mean, and it went into my chest, my heart, and into the earth." I shrug. I hate talking about this; words don't describe it properly at all. "Anyway, Gabriel found his way back."

"And you felt something more?"

"Yes . . . but I don't know what. All I know is that there was something outside my Gift, a strength, a power, and the stake linking me to the earth was part of that."

Ledger smiles. "I think the earth is the key to so much of our power. And that links to you too, Nathan. Your connection with nature is strong."

"Maybe."

"And isn't the thought of learning about that so much more exciting than fighting Hunters, some stupid witches who have lost their way to the extent that they have no idea of what they are missing?"

I don't know. I don't feel that excited. "Look, I appreciate that you're offering me something special and I'm sure you're right but . . . it's just not me. I can't ignore the people who are destroying so many other witches."

"Has it ever occurred to you that you may fail?"

"Of course! Do you think I'm *stupid*? I know I could be killed. No one goes into a battle without that possibility going through their head a million times. That's why I need the amulet. And why I'm working on the Gifts I have, trying to get better with them."

"Really? Then show me some of your magic, Nathan." He folds his arms. "Your turn to impress me."

For a second I feel like I'm back with Celia, Clay, and Wallend, having to show them what I can do. I tell myself this is different, Ledger is different and I should just get it over with: I go invisible for a few seconds, throw out a bolt of lightning, become visible again and breathe flames from my mouth.

I fold my arms and wait. Ledger doesn't react.

"You don't look impressed," I say.

"Probably because I'm not. Can you transform into an animal for me?"

"No." It takes all my effort not to swear at him.

He stares into my eyes, reading my mind again no doubt, and in my head I *do* tell him to fuck off.

"It seems you're in the mood to show me your fighting skills, though." He moves away from me, saying, "You'd better protect yourself." But before I can do anything he runs at me and kicks at my chest. I sidestep and send a flash of lightning, which Ledger dodges, but he releases a rolling ball of flames from his arms toward me and, feeling the heat on my face, I roll away sending more lightning from both my hands. Ledger jogs to safety. I send a long streak of lightning out to where I think he's going next, but he dodges back and is running at me again, but this time he somersaults over me, and I see he's smiling as he sails overhead. I send flames at him from my mouth. Ledger lands and opens his arms, stepping toward me, the flames engulfing him. Except I don't think he's burning; he seems serene and calm. He's certainly not panicking or screaming. And I'm pissed off enough to keep the flames going . . . as long as I can.

When the flames stop, Ledger smiles at me but then notices a wisp of smoke from his jacket pocket and frowns as he pats it to ensure any fire is put out.

"It's lucky that I put the amulet in the other pocket," he says, and winks at me.

"You don't need the amulet for protection. You're powerful enough without it."

"I can defend myself against you, even two like you, possibly three . . . but four might be stretching it. And although that seems unlikely, well, bombs are only going to get more powerful, guns more efficient, poisons more insidious. And the amulet is the only thing that can defend against them."

I kick Ledger in the chest. My fast kick really is fast. No one, no Hunter, has ever outmaneuvered it. But now I hit air. Ledger has sidestepped it with ease. I try a different kick. Air again. My next kick is like my first but aimed at where I expect him to go. Still I don't connect. I try twice more. The final time, he retaliates, and I move back; I've been expecting his counter-attack and only his boot heel catches my arm.

"You're very quick." He smiles.

I throw the lightning again and he dodges to the side, but his sleeve has a burn on it. I throw another and another. He dodges each one but I think he's tiring and I throw another, the biggest. And he disappears completely. Then from behind me he says, "Nathan." And I feel like a brick wall has hit me.

The sky is blue and clear of clouds, the sun low in the sky. I'm lying on the ground looking at the sky and feeling the grass underneath me, and part of me wants to get up and punch Ledger and another part says it's wise to stay down. Maybe that's balance.

I'm aching and before I heal myself I want to remind myself how bad it is to hurt. This is bad. Every muscle feels like it's been ripped from my bones and then put back.

"Ah, you've woken up." Ledger is standing to the side of me.

"So, you impressed yet?" I say.

He looks serious. "You fight well and you're fast, but you're vulnerable too."

"What did you hit me with?"

He looks to the large tree trunk at his feet.

"*Really?*" It looks too big to lift.

And, as if reading my thoughts, which I suspect he is, he says, "I move it magically, by thought."

"Do you think my enemies will have similar Gifts to that?"

"Undoubtedly."

"I need the amulet," I say, and get up.

"Why don't you stay here a while and think about it?"

"You talk about respecting intuition and that is what I'm doing. My future isn't here with you. I've . . ." I hesitate whether to tell him but I carry on: "I've had a vision, and you're right; it is by a river, a beautiful place, but it's not here and it's not with you."

"Visions can be misleading."

"I know that," I say, "but I also believe they have an underlying truth. There's an inevitability about it. I'll go this way or that, fight now or stay with you, but somehow or other I'll end up at the place by the river."

Ledger nods. "Well, I hope after you've fought Soul you will come back here. If you're right, then a few years with me won't change your final destiny."

"After I've fought Soul?"

"You seem determined to do that."

"And will you help me? Will you give me the amulet?"

He gives the smallest of nods and says, "I've no intention of doing nothing, but evil can triumph if good men do the wrong thing as much as if they do nothing. I intend to do the right thing and I think you are the right person to give the amulet to."

"Thank you. And I'm not promising that I will come back but it's a possibility."

"Life is full of possibilities. Let's return to the cabin and take a look at the amulet. Gabriel will be waiting for you, I think."

"He's there?"

"I took Gabriel to the cabin before I met you. We had a coffee, though I admit I slipped a few drops of sleeping potion in his. I left him safely asleep before going to collect you."

I speed up—it's all I can do not to break into a run—and then I see Gabriel standing outside the cabin staring at us. I slow as I near him and give him a grin. "You OK?"

He nods. "And you?"

"Yeah . . . good. I lost at fighting and I've talked more in the last few hours than in the previous six months."

Both Barrels?

The two pieces of the amulet are lying on the table next to each other. The parchment is yellowed and it looks like each piece has been crumpled up at some time in the past. The pieces clearly fit together; there's nothing missing. Ledger says that the writing on the paper is the magical element. That's all the amulet is: writing on a piece of parchment. The writing is strange, not letters I recognize so much as shapes, and they form three circles, one inside the other, when the two pieces are joined together.

We're back in the cabin. Ledger is sitting across the table from me, and Gabriel is at my side. Along with the amulet, on the table is a pot of herbal tea, an empty bottle with a round base, a cork, a stick of sealing wax, string, a candle, and some matches.

I say to Ledger, "I take it we can't use Sellotape?"

Ledger smiles. "If only it was that easy. The amulet can't be repaired at all, or at least if it was repaired the magic would be changed by that. But that doesn't mean the two halves can't work together. And it is meant to be that way. Everything about the amulet is about balance; you will represent that balance yourself."

"The two halves of me, you mean?"

"That and much more. Show me the tattoos on your finger."

I hold out my right hand. The three small tattoos of **B 0.5** are on my little finger. Ledger says, "Van told me that a man called Wallend made those tattoos and each one on your finger mirrors one on your body. Wallend was going to cut off your finger and put it in a witch's bottle as a way of controlling you, a way of forcing you to do his will. I believe that fate is now turning full circle. There's a certain balance of life and death, of good and bad. Do you see?"

"Yin and yang. Tit for tat. Give and take. That sort of thing?"

"That's not exactly how I'd put it, but a balance between each side, yes. Wallend was going to use this to gain power over you, but equally you have the ability to use it to have power over him." Ledger sips his tea. "The amulet cannot be joined up, cannot be glued together again, but it can be made to protect your finger and thus your whole body, if we put the amulet in the bottle with your finger."

"So . . . I have to cut my finger off?"

"Well, I don't see how it will get into the bottle otherwise."

"And what if it doesn't work?"

"Then you'll have an interesting ornament for your mantelpiece."

"And is there a spell or something to go with it?"

"I don't see that being necessary. There's the magic of the amulet, the White and Black Witch blood that is mixed together in you, your tattooed finger, and your history. Feels like enough magic to me."

"OK. So, once they're all in there, that's it? I'll be protected wherever I go?"

"Yes. Until the bottle is broken open."

"So the bottle can be destroyed?"

"Of course. It's just a bottle. If the bottle was broken open and the amulet removed, you'd be vulnerable again. But if the bottle is safe you are protected. The bottle could be used against you. If it was heated up, you'd burn; if it was frozen, you'd freeze. But I will keep it safe. You will have to trust me, Nathan. That is the price for my help. I'll keep the bottle safe until it's no longer needed. When you've killed Soul, I'll break it open and you'll be vulnerable again. Then I'll keep the amulet and you can have your finger back." He pauses before asking, "Is that a deal?"

I want the amulet but I don't like the idea of a witch's bottle. The thought that I'm giving myself over to using something that Wallend wanted to use makes me uncomfortable. But I guess I don't have a lot of choice. I nod.

"Good," Ledger says, looking from me to Gabriel. "So, who's got a knife?"

I don't want to use the Fairborn—somehow I feel its magic will be bad luck or may interfere—so I pull out the knife Gabriel gave me. I always carry it on my belt, even though I rarely use it.

My right hand is flat on the table. I'll have to cut the little finger at the base, at the knuckle, and I position the knife but it's awkward and I want to do it quick and clean.

"Shall I do the honors?" Ledger asks, reaching for the knife.

But Gabriel says, "No." And he puts his hand on mine, our fingers overlapping round the hilt of the blade. He says, "You sure?"

I nod and he pushes the knife down.

Blood seeps out on the table and my finger looks tiny and strange. I wait for the pain to hit. And now it does. I heal my hand and the bleeding stops and the wound scabs over and then heals completely to a white scar, not even a stub of my finger left as the cut has been made so close to the palm of my hand.

Ledger picks my finger up and carefully places it on top of one of the amulet halves and then rolls the finger up and wraps the other amulet half round that. Blood stains the paper but Ledger doesn't seem bothered and I think possibly it's a good thing.

"Now tie it up." He holds the finger and I take the string and carefully wrap it round and round the bundle, making sure it's tight and securing it with a knot. I tie another piece of string the other way to make sure that the finger can't slide out. Ledger drops the little bundle into the bottle and puts the cork in. Then he lights a candle. He holds the block of red wax over the flame and lets the wax dribble onto the top of the bottle, sealing the cork in place.

Ledger glances up at me, then back at the bottle to admire it.

"So that's it?" I ask.

"Well, I think it would be sensible to test it." And he turns to Gabriel, saying, "Would you like to go first?"

Gabriel smiles at me and reaches for the knife.

"Hold on. This isn't a game!" I say to them both. "I don't want to find out it doesn't work seconds before I die!"

"I won't stab you in the heart, maybe just try to cut your skin," Gabriel says. He looks to Ledger, asking, "The amulet will protect against any injury, won't it?"

"That's the idea."

And before I can object Gabriel pulls the knife across the back of my hand. Normally I'd have a deep cut from that, but there is no wound and I felt nothing at all, as if the blade didn't touch me.

"Try stabbing my hand. Gently."

"Stabbing gently? I'll do my best."

Gabriel stabs at my right hand. The knife slides off it and again I feel nothing and there's no mark on my skin.

"Try again, harder," I say. "With this." And I give him the Fairborn.

Gabriel rises out of his chair and quickly brings the Fairborn directly down onto my hand but it doesn't connect at all. The Fairborn slides past me and embeds itself in the table.

"OK. So knives, even the Fairborn, don't seem to hold

much of a problem for you. But Hunters generally use guns." And Gabriel pulls his gun from his jacket and twirls it round his finger, smiling.

"I don't see why you find this so amusing."

Gabriel says, "Well, I could try strangling you instead. Always wanted to do that."

"Very funny. Get on with it and shoot me."

He points the gun at my shoulder, stomach and then leg. "Leg, I think. Right or left?"

"Just get it over with." And I do feel nervous and want it done.

He fires. The bang is loud.

I look down.

"Did you aim properly?" I ask. I'm not hit and didn't feel a thing.

Gabriel looks irritated. "My aim is fine."

"Well, where's the bullet gone?"

We spend a few minutes looking and find that it's buried in the door.

Ledger says, "It must have ricocheted off you. This is getting dangerous. I'll leave you to it. There's a shotgun up there, Gabriel, cartridges in the drawer, but do stand well back."

Gabriel reaches up to the wall and pulls down a very old-looking gun. He loads it and smiles at me again.

"Both barrels?" he asks.

"Maybe we should go outside."

Outside, Gabriel aims at my waist and keeps a distance.

He fires. The noise is the most painful thing. Shotgun pellets shower around me and I cower and close my eyes. When I open them I see that Gabriel is on his back but he's laughing. "This gun is a monster. Almost dislocated my shoulder. You didn't get hit?"

"No. I did feel something, but I think it was the air moving past my skin. You want to try to hit me?" I ask. "I mean, punch me?"

Gabriel sits up. "No. I have a feeling it'll hurt me more than it'll hurt you." But he stands and turns the shotgun round to swing it from the barrel. "How about this?" he grins.

"Do your worst."

And he comes at me, swinging the shotgun at my shoulder and it sort of slides past and he spins in a circle and I really try not to laugh, which seems to irritate him, and he drops the gun and tries to punch my face and then my stomach in a quick one-two. And to my surprise the punches land and I feel the touch of his fist on my jaw, but it's as gentle as a caress and the same for my stomach. He, on the other hand, is rubbing his fist in an exaggerated way.

"I think strangling would be interesting after all," I say.

"A pleasure," he replies, and he grabs me round my throat. I feel his hands, warm on my skin, gentle at first and then I see he's applying as much pressure as he can but all I feel is his warm skin.

I tell him, "It feels a little ticklish."

Gabriel laughs and drops his hands. "Hmm, what

about . . . I know, come back inside." He goes to the sink, puts the plug in and runs the tap.

"You want to drown me?" I ask.

"Stick your head in and I'll hold you under," he says.

"What if I can't breathe?"

"Then we'll know the amulet's weakness."

I go to the sink, bend over it, and put my head under the water. Gabriel places his hands on the back of my neck and holds me there. I breathe out, letting all my air go. But I have no desire to breathe in. I feel strange, a little light-headed, but basically I hold my breath. I wait. Surely it can't go on forever? I wait. And wait. I know I've been under for minutes now, lots of minutes.

Then I get the urge to breathe and it gets harder now. I move and squirm but Gabriel is still holding me down. I'm running out of oxygen. I'm getting dizzy, blackness is closing in. I kick back at Gabriel and he pulls my head out of the water.

"You OK?" he asks. But he's laughing as I cough and splutter.

"I ran out of air at the end," I say. "I could drown."

"But not quickly. You were under for nearly ten minutes."

"Any other ideas?" I ask.

"I wish Mercury was here to freeze you to death."

"Somehow I think I'd be OK with that too."

Gabriel goes to my backpack and opens it, but then stops and says, "Close your eyes. I do have another idea."

I do as he asks.

A few seconds later he says, "Put your hands behind your back. I'm going to hit you with something but not let you see it or know where it's coming from."

"I don't think it'll make a difference," I say, but I do as I'm told and put my hands behind my back.

And then I feel the zip tie round my wrists, tight.

"Get out of that," Gabriel says.

I pull my hands but I'm stuck and I turn round to face him. "Very funny. I thought you were going to try to hurt me?"

"No. But I see the weakness. You can be tricked and you can be captured." He looks serious. "Both the sorts of things Soul enjoys doing."

Too Precious

•..◆

We stay with Ledger a few more days. The real world of war and fighting seems unreal here but that doesn't mean I've changed my mind about wanting to go back. Ledger doesn't try to persuade me to stay but he does say I need to work on my Gifts. I can stop time for short periods, almost a minute if I concentrate. I'm not sure I could do it in a fight, though. Even Marcus only used it once in a battle—when he was dying. It takes energy and concentration and I think it took the last of his.

Ledger leaves me to practice my Gifts on my own, which surprises me; I thought he'd give me advice. All he says is, "Listen to everything, observe the earth in particular, and you will learn all you need." But he shows me a range of other Gifts to give me an idea of what I might be up against. He throws everything at me: lightning, flames, water, sound, light, colors, and objects. And he throws me too: at water, trees, and the ground. None of it hurts me, but it's distracting and it shows I can be put off.

Ledger's mind control works on me too. I stop attacking when he tells me to stop. And, most frighteningly, I even attack Gabriel if he tells me to. Ledger makes sure he doesn't get hurt, but the point is made. My mind can be controlled.

Gabriel practices his Gift too, though it seems pretty perfect to me already, except for when he transforms into me, which I hate. I'm sure he makes me look better than I am, nicer, happier. Although I am happier here. Not because of Ledger or learning or any of that but because me and Gabriel are back like we used to be, better than we used to be.

In spare moments I think about the present I said I'd give Gabriel. I know he thinks I'll forget or not bother, and that's making me more determined to find the right thing. But the options don't seem that inspiring: knife, book, watch, necklace, bracelet. They're all fine and he'd like them but none of them seem good enough. I want to give him something special.

And each morning I transform into my animal self and spend time as an eagle, and usually afterward I think of my father and the time we had together, remembering all the details of him. One day after I've transformed back I realize what I should give Gabriel. I feel stupid for not thinking of it before: it's so obvious, so perfect.

We sleep outside at night, although Ledger has made it so we could stay in the cabin. The first night we sleep by a fire but the second night I make a bramble den like my father had. I've found the Gift now that means I can make plants grow fast or die. The den is just a simple dome of brambles with a short tunnel as an entrance. It isn't big enough to stand up in but feels cozy. We have a fire there and there are gaps in the roof we can see the stars through and the smoke finds its way up through the branches. Me and Gabriel lie together and look at the stars.

On the fifth night I say, "We should go back tomorrow."

"If that's what you want."

"You like it here?"

"I like you here."

We kiss and make love and Gabriel falls asleep. I listen to his heartbeat some more.

I've decided on the present I'm going to give him, but the problem now is how to do it. I don't want to do the wrapping-in-paper-and-waiting-to-see-what-he-thinks-of-it thing and yet I do want it to be special.

I hold my right hand up and in the glow from the fire the skin on my wrist is warped and smooth. The shape of my hand looks odd with the missing finger. On my index finger is the ring my father gave me. I remember being amazed that he'd given me something so special and how proud I was of it, of having him for my father, of him giving it to me. I slide the ring off and hold it to my lips and kiss it. I remember the first time I saw Gabriel at Geneva Airport, the time Rose told me he loved me and the first time *he* told me he loved me. And I know I love Gabriel more than I've ever loved anyone, more than I thought was possible for me. He makes me a better person. I slide the ring onto Gabriel's finger. It looks good on his hand. And I lie down close to Gabriel, and imagine our future together living peacefully in a beautiful place by a river.

The next morning I wake to Gabriel saying my name

quietly. I'm lying on my back and I can feel Gabriel's body next to mine.

"Nathan?"

I open my eyes. He's propped up on his arm, looking at me, all serious but also nervous. He says, "I need to talk to you." Then he looks away—he really is nervous. And he holds his hand up, the gold ring on his finger and says, "About this."

"I said I'd give you a present. That's my present to you."

He looks at me and he really is serious and he doesn't say anything and then he looks down and turns the ring round his finger as if he's thinking about it and he opens his mouth to say something but before he does I say what I planned to say.

"You're pissed off, aren't you? I knew you would be."

He looks confused. "I'm not pissed off." And he says it sincerely with a small shake of his head. "I'm definitely not pissed off."

"And I can understand that you are, because you think you're good at presents and niceness and all that shit, and I've actually outdone you and given you an even better present than what you gave me."

He smiles now, realizing I'm teasing him, and shakes his head again. "I admit you've outdone me. I never thought you'd give me anything like this. In fact, if I'm honest about it, I never thought you'd give me anything at all. But this was your father's and . . ."

"It was my father's and my grandfather's before that and

probably his father's too. It's an ancient and valuable Edge family heirloom." I'm teasing him but it's also the truth.

"Nathan, it's too precious."

"It's precious, yes, and it's important to me: it's the only thing I have that my father gave me. Well, apart from the Fairborn and a Hunter bullet. Anyway, it's the one good thing that my father gave me; that's why I want you to have it."

"Nathan . . ."

"I've thought about it carefully and I'm sure. I want you to have it and I know that my father would approve too."

Gabriel's eyes fill with tears.

"It's yours. Forever."

And now his tears spill out and we kiss and kiss more.

PART THREE

HALF LOST

The Fifty-First Problem

We're back at Celia's camp, the new Camp One. We stayed at Ledger's cabin for a week in total, resting, learning, working on my Gifts, and testing the amulet's protection as much as we could. Then Ledger guided us back to the map room and from there we made our way to New York and then another day later we arrived here.

I don't tell Celia much about Ledger—he likes his privacy— but I tell her about the amulet and my invulnerability.

I'm curious to see what will happen if Celia tries her Gift on me. I hate her noise. If there's one thing I dread, it's that. It's not just the pain but the memories, the shame, the number of times I've been left sniveling and groaning on the floor because of it. But now I want her to use it on me. She is also keen to try it, it seems.

I grin at her and say, "But first punch me in the face."

She cracks her knuckles, makes a fist, and swings at me, a solid right hook.

And I do feel something: not pain but a thrill at seeing Celia double over holding her hand to her body. She stands up, healing as fast as she can, no doubt. "It's like hitting steel," she says.

Of course that doesn't stop her trying more things:

stabbing and shooting, though I draw the line at her hanging me. I tell her to use her noise.

She says, "You're ready? You don't need to prepare or
anything?"

"No, the protection is like armor I'm always wearing."

And then the noise hits me. Only it isn't painful, and
hit isn't the right word. It's a faint sound, high-pitched, un-
pleasant, and screeching, but no more likely to stop me in
my tracks than someone singing out of tune.

I fold my arms and say to her, "Are you actually trying?"

She ignores my comment and looks to Gabriel and says,
"Have you found any weakness to the protection?"

"He can drown, but it would take a long time. He can be
tied up or imprisoned. He can't fight mind control. If someone with the Gift for mind control suggested he surrender,
Nathan would do it. But in a battle, in a straight fight, he
can't be hurt."

"Bombs?" Celia asks.

I roll my eyes. "We haven't tried them."

"You could get buried by rubble?"

"Yes. But I'd be buried alive, if that's any comfort to you."

"Are you expecting bombs?" Gabriel asks.

"Explosives, possibly," Celia says. "Booby traps, like
the one that killed Kirsty."

"I'll be fine against that."

"You want to try?" Celia asks, taking a grenade from
her pocket and holding it out to me.

I admit I'm nervous now. But then again bullets didn't

penetrate the amulet's protection so the grenade shouldn't be able to either.

I take the grenade and pull the pin. Celia and Gabriel rapidly back away. My heart is racing and I look at my hand, my arm, wondering if I'll lose both.

The explosion is blinding and loud and I stagger back, my eyes closed.

My heart is still racing and my hand and my arm are tingling, but I'm relieved to see they are both still attached to me. I flex my fingers and they still work. It's not an experience I'm desperate to repeat, though.

Later that night I'm sitting with Gabriel, Celia, and Greatorex by the fire and I'm laughing. Celia has been outlining her plan for the attack on Soul: the plan she has been formulating while we have been away.

When I stop laughing, I say, "It's taken you a week to come up with that? Walk into the Council building and kill everyone. That's the plan?!"

Celia says, "I'd thought you'd appreciate its simplicity."

I resist swearing at her and just glare.

"The annual Council meeting is coming up. It hasn't been hard to find out the date. It's an important event to reelect Council members and the Council Leader. Soul, Wallend, and Jessica will be there. It's a perfect opportunity to remove them. You go in first. Take out those key personnel and then we come in and deal with the Council members and Hunters who are there."

Gabriel frowns. "And what if they're not there? If you've got the date wrong?"

"If they're not there, then Nathan will have to make the best decisions in the circumstances. Which I have every confidence he will do."

I'm thinking already that I know what I'll do if that is the case: I'll burn the Council building. Destroy everything that I can.

Celia continues. "The major problem with any attack is that the Hunters can become invisible. With that Gift they will always have the upper hand. Whatever happens to Soul, the Hunters will carry on fighting and we can't win against an invisible army: we can't catch or kill what we can't see.

"We have used truth potions on two Hunters we caught but haven't found out much. It seems that even the Hunters don't know a lot about how the magic is made to work, but we do know that Wallend controls the ability through the use of witch's bottles. The Hunters who have the power to go invisible control it themselves but Wallend gives them the Gift."

Much as I want to kill Soul, I agree with Celia. I say, "So getting rid of the Hunters' power of invisibility is the first objective, then Soul."

"Yes."

"What's Soul's Gift?"

"Potions. The same as Wallend. But Soul doesn't have

a strong Gift; that's why he uses Wallend. Wallend has an exceptional Gift."

"And Wallend works from the Council buildings, does he?"

"Yes, all the information we have received about him shows that he spends most of his time there. I can see no reason why he would change his habits."

Nor can I. He always struck me as someone who was obsessed with his job and had no life outside it. With the success of the Council he's had no reason or need to move.

Celia goes on. "Knowing Soul's desire for control and also his lack of trust in the Hunters, I'm sure he will be keeping whatever magic it is that gives the Hunters their powers of invisibility close to himself. It's all got to be in that building somewhere. If all you do is get in, find the witch's bottles or whatever they are, and neutralize the Hunters' ability to go invisible, I'd count the mission as a success."

"You might; I won't."

"Well, I agree; we should aim for more. We need to remove Soul, Wallend, and Jessica, and we need to ensure no one escapes the building: capture all those in it."

"I thought the plan was to walk in and kill them?" And I'm reminded again of my father's advice to kill them all. I've killed so many minor players, unimportant Hunters, that it would almost be an insult to them if I let Soul, Wallend, and Jessica off.

"Kill or capture," Celia says.

"Fine."

Celia continues. "There are several problem areas, of course."

"Of course."

"The first problem is getting into the Council building. There are three entrances. The main entrance, the one on the high street, is the simplest way in but is too public. The last thing we want is some fains noticing something."

I know that entrance. It's open and clearly going to be guarded and protected. Even invisible, I don't fancy that route.

"OK, I agree with that," I say.

"The rear entrance isn't used now and is sealed off as far as we can tell. I think they saw it as a weak spot: it was always difficult to guard, with poor sight lines and fain properties very close all around. Anyway, it's no longer an option."

The back entrance is the one Gran and I used to use when we went for my Assessments and is a way I know well but that doesn't matter now, it seems.

"The entrance in Cobalt Alley is still in use but too dangerous."

"They're all dangerous," I say, "but I know how the magic in the alley works. It draws you into the building, right? Can't we use that to our advantage?"

Celia shakes her head. "The alley leads into an internal courtyard, which is an exposed area where we could be contained and picked off. If I was in charge of security I'd make this option look tempting but the next access door would be impenetrable. I'm certain that is what Soul will have done."

"So what's it to be then? The roof? The windows?" I'm only joking a little. I'm sure the whole place will be protected against intruders.

"We go in through a cut from another Council property. From the Tower."

"The Tower?"

"Roman Tower, to give it its full name. It's the Council-run prison for White Witches. I know it well. So does Greatorex, so do all the Hunters. Part of Hunter duty every year is spent there working as a guard. There's a cut from the Tower into the Council building."

"And you can get us into the Tower?"

"I've had it watched for weeks. We know the routines of the guards, the numbers and times they change. There is a system of passwords and checks but you, Nathan, will be able to enter with the guards while you're invisible. Once you're inside, you overpower the guards and let us in."

"How many guards are there?"

"Six Council guards and four Hunters at any time. Each on eight-hour shifts. The prison is easy to guard and patrol. None of the prisoners are ever let out of their cells."

"Nice."

"It's not meant to be nice."

"OK. So I slip in, deal with the guards, and let you guys in. Then what? I go through the cut to the Council building and find Wallend, Soul, and Jessica?"

"Precisely. But that brings us to the second problem: Jessica."

Celia rubs her face with her hand, then says, "Even if Soul, Wallend, and the Council are defeated, the Hunters will still be against us. The Hunters do the bidding of the Council but they don't follow Soul; their true loyalty is only to their leader, to Jessica. While Jessica is alive, the Hunters will fight. Whatever has happened to Soul or Wallend, she'll never surrender."

"And?"

"You let her live in Geneva," Celia says.

I laugh. "Oh. So the problem is that you think I *won't* kill her?"

"Is it a valid problem?"

"No." At least I don't think it is. Jessica is my half-sister, the daughter of my mother, but I hate her. I do believe she's evil. And I know she'd kill me without a second thought. It's true I let her go in Geneva. But we weren't at war then. Things have changed, and I've changed too.

I tell Celia, "Don't worry. I'll kill or capture her."

Celia nods and moves swiftly on. "Problem three is also to do with Hunters. There is a myth about them that they won't surrender or run—ever. But, as you know, that isn't totally true. Many will die rather than surrender but the truth is that they are all human. Some will choose to live. And I think when they see that they can't win they will make a tactical withdrawal, and they may even surrender. If they do, then we don't harm them. The organization will need to be disbanded. We need to break the history of the Hunters."

I remember my dream of a long line of Hunter prisoners.

"Executing them all would be a good way to do that."

"No it wouldn't. Hunters come from virtually every family of White Witches. We need to show tolerance and fairness. They are soldiers. They aren't evil."

I shake my head at Celia.

"We don't kill prisoners, Nathan. And we don't kill those who surrender."

"So what exactly is the third problem?"

"Nathan, I need to be sure that you won't kill them if they've surrendered, and if they want to surrender you let them. I need to believe that you know it would be wrong to execute prisoners."

"You mean you need to believe I'm not like my father. That I don't want revenge for my ancestors who were all killed by them. And what about all the other Black Witches who've been killed by Hunters? Can't I get a little revenge for them too?"

"I want us to win this battle, not get revenge."

"'Kill them *all*' is my motto."

"Even if they've surrendered? That makes you no better than Soul."

"Yes . . . No." I'm not sure how I feel except that I'm pissed off. I sneer at her and say, "You can try them all first for war crimes if that makes you feel any better. Then execute them."

Celia says, "My plan is to run the Alliance with Whites and Blacks and Half Bloods working together. We will have to investigate carefully and publicly the crimes that the Council and its members have committed. But we must all be careful not to commit similar ones. Or we too will be in the dock.

"We will work together and we will have to be, and be seen to be, fair to all. Just and fair. To *all*, including you, Nathan. I'm warning you that this will happen. That is the society that we need to establish and we all must be subject to the same rules. The battle is the easy bit; what comes after will be the real challenge."

"Thanks," I say. "Glad everyone appreciates what a doddle of a job I've got on my hands."

Celia says, "So, back to our attack. Is the third problem a valid one?"

I tell her, "My objective is to win the battle and remove, one way or the other, Soul and Wallend and Jessica. I'll kill anyone who gets in the way of that or who tries to kill me or any Alliance fighters. If we win and there are any Hunters or Council members alive, I'm going to leave them to you to sort out. You can sit in the Council building in meetings all day playing with your conscience; I'll be living quietly by a river."

"And Annalise?"

"I won't forget my mission and go hunting her down. Wallend, Soul, and Jessica are my priority."

"If Annalise is alive she should go on trial as the Alliance originally planned."

"Well, let's just hope she's been tortured to death by now."

Celia doesn't respond to that so I say, "The next problem?"

She starts to get up, saying, "It's late; we'll go through them tomorrow. We all meet here first thing. There's one more thing you should know. I'm going to tell everyone about your invulnerability. It will give them confidence going into the fight."

I think about it, but I don't suppose it'll make any difference to me what they know.

"Fine," I say.

She takes a step away and then turns back to me. "I suspect the major problem will be problem fifty-one, so don't be complacent with your new Gift." And then she walks off to her tent.

I shake my head. I'm not feeling the least bit complacent.

"What's she talking about?" Gabriel asks. "Problem fifty-one?"

I tell him, "It's one of her things. She always used to say there were many problems in any battle and she could always come up with fifty things that could go wrong. Problem fifty-one was slightly different; it was always there, but even she couldn't think what it could be."

Never-Ending Problems

The annual meeting of the Council is a big affair and will include the key Council members from Britain and possibly a few from Europe. But it's such an obvious target that it's bound to be well guarded. We can only hope that they think the Alliance is so weak and depleted it will be unable to attack.

Problem four is the date. The meeting is usually held on the last day of April but it would be typical of Soul to change this.

Problem five is the layout of the Council building, which is a labyrinth of corridors. I've been there every birthday from age eight to age fourteen but I've only seen a fraction of the building; even from my limited experience I realize it's vast and the corridors complex. Celia, Greatorex, and some of the other members of the Alliance do know the building, or at least parts of it, and they've drawn up a plan from the cells in the basement to the attic rooms. There are some areas on the top floors that they don't know and of course they think that is where Wallend has his laboratory.

All the Alliance trainee fighters from Camps One to Seven are here now. There are more than I hoped but fewer than we need: twenty-seven. Most faces I don't recognize. We all spend time learning the layout of the building. The plan is for me to go in first and for the other members of the Alliance to come in only if I can remove the Hunters' invisibility and after I've killed or captured Soul. Greatorex keeps saying to the trainees, "You must be able to find your way if it's dark and smoke-filled. You must know it better than any place you've ever been." And that's true for me as well.

To help us learn the layout of the building, each floor has been marked out on the ground, and key areas have been replicated with walls made of wood and canvas. These are the basement, ground floor, and top floor. The basement is where we will enter. The cut from the Tower goes in there, to make it easier to move prisoners between the cells and the Tower. The ground floor has all the main offices and meeting rooms, including Soul's private office.

They've been working on the replica while I've been away but when I go round it some things don't seem right to me. The stairs down to the basement should be narrower. I remember the guards had to push me ahead of them and it was really cramped.

I go into the replica of the cell that I was kept in. The walls are canvas and there's no roof. It's morning and the sky is blue above. I pace out the cell as I remember it. Where I was chained up, how far I could move along the wall. I walk out of the cell and go to Room 2C. This seems more like the real place; the canvas walls remind me of the white of the room. I lie down in it and remember Wallend bending over me, tattooing me. I wonder how many others he's done that to by now.

I wander around the whole cell area. Learning the layout but wondering, too, how many people they will be holding in each cell. Just one in solitary or twenty squeezed in with no space to lie down? I remember all the stories Celia used to read me about the gulags and the punishments and interrogations, and I'm sure they'll be making each place as bad as they can.

I sit in my old cell again, up against the wall in the corner where I sat the first night I was forced to stay indoors as my witch powers grew. I remember how sick I was, how frightened. I was sixteen, which sounds so young, but I'm only seventeen now and I realize that I was in the cell a year ago, less than a year ago. Shit, it feels like twenty years. And I've changed, experienced so much. Back then all I wanted was to escape and be given three gifts on my birthday; all I wanted was to live free. And here I am, and I've got my Gift and many more besides. I've got more power than I'd have thought possible and I'm risking it all. And yet I feel confident about the attack. I am invulnerable after all. I know we have a good chance. Soul and Wallend and Jessica will be there for sure. And Annalise, if she's still alive, may be down here somewhere, in this cell or a prisoner in the Tower. I tell myself that but I also know there's a chance she isn't a prisoner, isn't being tortured, but being kept in comfort because she shot Marcus, because she's a spy.

"I wondered where you were. It's getting late." Gabriel comes and sits by me.

It's dark. The day's gone and the last few hours I've been lying here in the cell, thinking.

"What's bothering you?" Gabriel asks.

"You want the full list or just the top ten?"

I'm surprised that my voice is shaking. Saying it makes me realize how close to the edge I am. And I know soon I'm going to step off it completely.

Gabriel leans close to me, his voice quiet as he says, "Give me the full list."

"Am I bad for killing people? For wanting to kill them?"

"You have the power to fight. You do what other people can't do. You're not bad, Nathan. But do what you believe in; only do that. You have to live with your conscience. Only you can know what's in there and only you have to live with it."

I rub my face in my hands. And I suddenly want my father back with me to help me.

"I never thought I'd kill people. A year ago I was being kept in this cell and I didn't want to kill anyone, not even the people who held me prisoner. I just wanted to escape, just wanted freedom. And now I have that; I have my freedom."

"Do you? Sometimes I think you're still a prisoner. You're not free of this place in your head, Nathan. And you're definitely not free of those people. They haunt you."

"Maybe. I dream about them a lot. Bad dreams. In my

dream there's a long line of prisoners kneeling on the floor, hands tied behind their backs. And when I say a long line I mean *long*, never-endingly long. And I walk behind them and I have a gun and I shoot each one in the back of the head. And as each one slumps to the ground I step forward and execute the next one."

"And this is a dream? Not a vision?"

I shake my head. "Visions feel different. This is a dream. But I hate it more than anything. I hear my father's voice telling me, *Kill them all. Kill them all.* And he's not angry or mad or anything like that: he's calm and logical, and he fills me with confidence that I can do it. And I know when I get to the end of the line I'll be able to stop, and my father will be quiet." I look at Gabriel and say, "But I never get to the end of the line. I'm never able to stop."

"You have to stop at some point, Nathan, but because you choose to. You'll never kill them all. It's impossible. And . . . I think it's wrong. I mean it's wrong for you. It's a path your father would have gone down, did go down. But you have to choose what is right for you. You aren't disrespecting your father by following your own path. He knew you loved him. He knows it still. You don't have to do this for him."

I nod. I know Gabriel is right. Everything he says is right. But just now I feel more lost than ever.

He takes my hand and weaves his fingers with mine and says, "You will stop, Nathan. I'll help you stop. And you will live a quiet life by your river and I'll be there with you."

It's three days to the attack. We're all ready. Even the train-ees look pretty good. Every day, Gabriel and I train to-gether. For fitness we run and climb in the forest and then we practice in the Council building mock-up. We test each other in there. Trying to confuse each other, put each other off with noises, shots, but we know we've got it sussed. Today we're going to the Tower. I want to see it before the attack anyway but Celia is taking us there so we can find out the passwords.

Me, Celia, and Gabriel go through a cut to London and make our way to a grim residential estate that is a waste-land of mud, sparse grass, litter, and broken tarmac. There are five towers, each seemingly separate and unconnected to the others and anything else around them. Celia has al-ready had someone check out the guards' movements but she wants me to check again, closer, using my invisibility.

Roman Tower looks nothing like a fain prison, at least not in the ordinary sense of the word: it's orange for a start. All five towers are seventies-style blocks, each one with its panels painted a different color: red, yellow, orange, lime green, and pale blue. The colors and the concrete are all dirtied and worn. Roman Tower is five stories taller than the others and the prison occupies the top five floors. Below live ordinary fain residents. How or why they don't notice who lives above them I haven't asked. I guess it's a mixture of magic and general apathy.

The guards mostly live in the other towers, and they use

the ordinary fain entrance to get to the prison. The Hunters get to work through the Council building, through the cut. In Celia's day there were six guards and four Hunters on each shift. The guards are not trained to fight, but the Hunters are Hunters. Each floor can house up to twenty prisoners, so there might be as many as a hundred in there.

Anyway, we're here to watch the guards and confirm their pattern of movement. I'm standing with Gabriel in the shelter of a building that's occupied by a series of shops and a launderette. All have their graffitied shutters down but even here the graffiti isn't up to much: like no one could really be bothered with that either. Gabriel is standing close to me. We're eating a takeaway curry, which isn't as disgusting as its green color would suggest, but then any food is good food to us.

Celia is at the other end of the wasteland. The guards change over three times a day. We're waiting for the four p.m. changeover, or rather *I'm* waiting for it as it's only me that's going to go in. We've agreed I'll go into the Tower at three thirty and suss it out and most importantly suss out the entrance to the top five floors. Celia says that the entrance to the prison has an outer and an inner door. The first door is opened from the outside by the person saying the password and using a key and this leads to a holding area. The next door is opened from the inside, again with a key and a password. There's a peephole to check the incomers are who they are supposed to be. All I've got to do is shadow the guards as they go in, check that the system is still in place, and find out what the password to the outer door is.

At three thirty, I set off, walking slowly across the expanse of open ground to the Tower. There's a number-code system to gain entry, but the door is broken anyway so I go straight in. There's a lift but I go up the stairs. In the stairwell the smell of stale urine is strong but the steps are clear of rubbish, just dirty with years of grime. I become invisible now and move silently and quickly. I check out each floor, looking for anything that might be out of place; any sign that Hunters are watching or setting a trap. I don't see anything and I don't get any feeling that Hunters are here or things are out of place.

On the eleventh floor there is only one door: the entrance to the prison. I realize I'm tense, holding my breath. I stand in the furthest corner, back against the wall, and concentrate on breathing slow and staying invisible while I wait for the guards.

It's not long before I hear the lift crank into gear. There's no lift door on this floor. It might be them or it might not. I find I'm holding my breath again. Then the lift doors open on the floor below and I hear footsteps coming up the stairs. No one talks. There're five of them but they're typical of the guards used in the Council building—huge. Not dressed like guards or Hunters, though, but like fains, in jeans, jumpers, and jackets.

When they're at the door to the prison, all I can see is the backs of five massive men. One of them says something—"Ring ray," it sounds like. Then the door opens and they move through into another room but I can't see much and the door shuts.

Shit, that was useless.

Now what?

Then I hear more footsteps on the stairs. They get louder and slower and finally another guard appears. The sixth one.

He goes to the door, puts a small key in the lock, and leans to the hinged side, not the side that opens, and says, "Spring day." He has his left hand on the key and as he says the words he turns the key and the door opens. I get a brief look inside to a small room, painted in shiny orange paint with an orange door beyond it. Then the outer door closes.

I make my way back to Gabriel and Celia slowly, still checking each of the floors of the Tower again for anything that might feel out of place, but I don't spot anything.

Celia seems pleased, if she ever seems pleased about anything. She says, "The system is working the same as in the past. You'll be able to get in. Of course, once you're in you have to deal with the guards, et cetera, et cetera."

I turn to Gabriel, saying, "Et cetera, et cetera: that's my specialty."

Celia replies, "It'd better be."

Scum

When we get back from our trip to the Tower, I go to the mock-up of the Council building. I know I have to keep practicing and double-checking my knowledge of the layout, and it's reassuring to go over it again and again. It's night, so a good time to practice in the dark.

I'll get into the Council building through the cut in the basement, invisible, and I do that now: go invisible and go through the basement and its narrow corridors, then up to the ground floor and then up the main staircase to the fifth floor, the top floor. It's the place we know least about but I go through where I'll look for Wallend. Then I have to deal with Soul. And so now I make my way back through the corridors to Soul's private office on the ground floor, as I plan to do it: walking quiet and fast. This part of the mock-up re-creates the corridors, meeting rooms, and offices with walls of tarpaulin across wooden frames.

There's a strong wind and the tarp is flapping and snapping. I slow as I get closer to Soul's office, looking and listening, imagining where guards would be positioned, staying invisible as I move past them. I'm almost at the doorway to Soul's office when I hear the voices of some trainees. Greatorex encourages them to practice constantly so I shouldn't be surprised they're here, but I don't want to go in there with them around. Anyway, I've done most of my route; I can start again from the beginning. I'm about to retrace my steps along the tarpaulin-lined corridor when I hear my name and I stop. I realize they're not practicing but talking. I go back to listen.

"If he does manage to kill Soul, then this could all be over. Soon."

"It's a big if."

"Well, he's got more chance than anyone. And look on the bright side: if he fails at least he'll be killed."

"He's invulnerable. He can't be killed."

"Exactly what I've been saying. No one can kill him. So what's to stop him turning round and killing us after he's killed all of Soul's people?"

"He's on our side, guys!"

"Yeah? The way he looks at us, I think he wants us all dead. Remember he almost killed Celia with those flames from his mouth? Look at us. We're all Whites. What's to stop him executing us after all this is over?"

"Celia believes in him. So does Greatorex. They know what they're doing, Felicity. Our fight's against Soul, not against Nathan. Soul's the evil one."

"And what's Nathan?"

"Scum."

"Black, blood-sucking, heart-eating scum."

"Come on, guys. He's on our side."

"He's not Black anyway; he's half Black."

"Oh, sorry. Correction! Half-Black, blood-sucking, heart-eating scum."

Someone laughs.

"Not jealous, are you?"

"*What?* Of him? Pleeeaase!"

"Everyone knows you adore Gabriel. And didn't he turn you down?"

"He didn't turn me down. Do you really think I'd throw myself after some Black Witch?"

"Well, whether you did or not, he's not interested in anyone but Nathan."

"Yeah, have you seen the way they look at each other?"

"Nathan looks like he wants to kill everyone all the time."

"Maybe that's his plan. He'll kill everyone, until there's only the two of them left, just him and Gabriel."

"Correction on the correction. He's *gay*, half-Black, blood-sucking, heart-eating scum."

"I heard he had a girlfriend before. A White. Annalise O'Brien. She's Soul's niece."

"I don't get it—is he gay or what?"

"Annalise? Isn't she the one who was being held prisoner at Camp One?"

"Yeah, everyone at Camp One was killed."

"I heard *he* killed her."

"Maybe she caught him with Gabriel."

Laughter.

"And he killed all Annalise's family. Her brothers were Hunters. He ripped them apart."

"Yeah, I heard that too. He ate their hearts."

I don't know why I'm still here listening to this rubbish and I'm about to leave when I change my mind and walk round the corner slowly so they see me, so that they know I've heard everything.

They all go quiet and I say to them, "As far as I know Annalise is still alive. And for the record I've only killed one of her brothers. My father killed another one. The third one's still alive, but don't worry—if I get the chance I'll gladly rip him to pieces. Annalise shot my father. Because of her he's dead. And, yes, he was a murdering Black Witch but he was also a great man and you are so stupid that you will never have a chance of understanding one molecule of his being. And as for me . . . mind your own fucking business." I turn to go then turn back and say, "I'm not scum but, yes, I'm a fucking blood-sucking, heart-eating half-Black so I suggest you keep out of my way."

I'm back in the cell. I've been sitting here for a few hours. I keep going over what I said to those trainees, wishing I hadn't said anything or wishing I'd said it better. I go over it all again and again and again.

A silhouette appears in the cell doorway.

"Ah, found you," Arran says, and sits down next to me. He's been in the camp since I was shot and I see him most days but we hardly ever have time alone together.

"Hi."

"You've been frightening some of the trainees, I hear."

Oh, so that's it. They've been talking about me. I say, "I had an argument with them, but you'd have been proud of me, Arran; I didn't hit them. I was incredibly calm."

"No wonder they're so scared."

I smile despite myself.

"They said you threatened to kill them."

"*What?*"

"Celia didn't think it was true. She said you'd either do it or you wouldn't. I said I'd find out your side of the story. Want to tell me what happened?"

"Not really." Then I add, "They were saying stupid things about me. So I said stupid things to them. I didn't threaten to kill them, but I did tell them to keep out of my way."

"Ah. A sort of veiled threat."

Maybe they saw it as that. "I won't kill them, Arran. However stupid they are."

"Good. Not that I thought you would."

"Can we talk about something else?"

"Of course."

We sit for a while and talk about what he's been doing, which is learning about healing. He ends by saying, "Van taught me a lot. I've still got loads to learn but she really helped me. Anyway, at the moment there's no one left to heal. They're either alive and well, or dead." He looks at me. "I'm not sure if I should count that as a success or failure."

"When they're all dead, that's failure," I say. But then I think about it and add, "No, even then it's not a failure. You do what you can, Arran."

We sit for a while and then he waves his arms at the canvas walls, "All this is for some big attack, I guess."

So Celia hasn't told him. And I'm going to kill more people and one of them will be Jessica, his sister, my half-sister.

"Arran . . ."

"Yeah."

"Don't hate me."

"I don't hate you."

"I mean whatever I do. Please. I know you can't understand me but please . . ." And I look at him and he looks back at me the same way he always has done. Meeting my gaze so honestly and openly. He says, "You're my brother. My kid brother. I can't hate you. Ever."

I shuffle closer to him and he hugs me and keeps hold of me.

"There is something I was going to tell you"—his voice is really quiet and a bit shaky—"I mean I want to tell you and it's good but . . ."

I move back to look at his face and he's smiling a little but also not meeting my gaze.

I can't think of anything other than he's found a girl. Arran has never really had a girlfriend. Or at least not when I was at home with him. And I realize I've no idea whether he's had girlfriends or boyfriends or anyone since I left home.

"So?" I ask, leaning forward and peering at his face. I can't help grinning.

"Well, yeah . . . I've got a girlfriend." He cringes. "I hate that word. I mean I'm with someone . . . there's someone I like and she likes me and . . . we're friends, more than friends. It's nice. A bit of a surprise. I wasn't really . . ."

I try not to smile too much. "Anyone I know?" I ask. It has to be someone I know. And then I feel sick. Oh no, it must have been one of the trainees who were talking about me. "Oh shit! Have I messed it up? I mean if I have I'll . . . but she . . . I mean you . . ." But, really, what is he doing with one of those girls?

Arran looks confused. "You've not messed anything up. Adele's far too sensible to let anyone mess her up, even you."

"Adele. The-one-whose-skin-turns-to-metal Adele?"

"She doesn't do that very often with me."

"She's a good fighter."

"And that's not really what attracted me to her either."

I snigger. "What did attract you?"

"She's kind and thoughtful and funny. And pretty and I like her hair . . ."

We sit in silence for another minute while I process that. But I can see why Arran would like her. Adele is smart and attractive. She's also a Black Witch.

I say, "She's Black, you know. If you have kids they'll be—"

"We only met each other a few weeks ago, when you were injured. We're not planning a family just yet!"

"No, but you know what I mean." I smile at him.

"I know what you mean. Maybe in the future, under the Alliance, there'll be lots of little Half Codes. But, as I said, we've only just met."

"I hope she makes you happy."

"Thanks. She does."

He smiles and looks embarrassed and then he goes quiet and for a few seconds I look at him happily and he looks so cute and innocent and then I realize that he's probably been discussing me with her. I'm the subject of long conversations.

"You want to go back and find her?" I ask.

"No. I want to stay with you."

And he's got that Arran thing about him. That slow, easy, comfortable quietness. A gentleness like no one else has.

After a while he says, "I still have that drawing you did of you and me in the woods, the one you left with me before my Giving."

I remember it. Remember drawing it, remember rolling it up and laying it on Arran's bed and leaning over to kiss his head before I left. Only it seems like a different me who did that.

"Do you still draw?" he asks.

"Haven't done for a long time."

"You should do."

"You still watch old movies?"

"I wish. When this is over I'm definitely having a day in

front of the telly. A comedy marathon: Buster Keaton and Charlie Chaplin, the really old stuff. I love those."

"You love them all." And I love being with him.

"I miss those days," he says.

And I realize something for the first time.

"I don't. I mean, they were great times. And I love you and you're the best brother, and I loved living with you and Gran and Deborah. But now I know that behind it all the Council was watching me, my father wanted to see me but couldn't. Our mother . . . There was a lot of bad stuff."

He nods.

I say, "And I know you've had it tough. But you're still the same. It's great for you that you are. But I'm not and I was pretty messed up to start with."

He shakes his head now.

"You've no idea, Arran. So much has happened to me. I'm not the person who used to watch films with you. I wish I was but . . . that'll never happen again. Never. I'm different. And I can't go back. I don't want to go back."

"I know."

"The fourteen-year-old me was taken, Arran. And he's gone. He can't come back." Then I feel like I should be more positive so I say, "When the Alliance wins. When it's over. Then I'm going to live quietly by a river."

"I can imagine that. You should draw too."

"Yeah, that'd be good. I will."

Into the Woods

•..⚫

It's two days until the attack on the Council building. After my confrontation with the trainees I sleep in the woods outside the camp. Gabriel says I shouldn't let them bother me, shouldn't let them drive me out. He thinks that him saying that will annoy me enough to make me stay; it annoys me a lot but not enough. I make a den by growing brambles, have a small fire, and Gabriel stays with me. In the morning we go for a run. I go ahead and then drop back and stay with him for a while and then peel off to the left or right and go faster before dropping back again. Gabriel keeps up a good steady pace. Finally he slows and I race off and come round to his left to sneak up on him: it's what we do.

I go fast but not far before looping back round. He'll know what I'm up to, and will probably expect me to come from the high ground, but I'm hoping he might discount it for that reason—my double bluff. I move across and up the slope, expecting to get sight of him down to my right, but can't see him yet. I stop. The forest is still and silent.

I'm still too now. Which way will he have gone? I have an idea he might have worked out what I'm doing and be trying to get higher than me. The top of the gentle slope isn't visible through the trees. I move further along and up to the top of the rise. I look back but can't see Gabriel. Everything is very quiet. The slope down into the next valley is much the same as the one I've come up. I move down into that valley thirty meters, intending to come back on myself, but then I hear it. Hissing. A phone.

I freeze.

Listen again.

It's definitely the sound of a mobile phone. Faint. Maybe two hundred meters away.

It could be fains but somehow I know it's not. It's Hunters.

Shit!

And where is Gabriel? Oh shit.

And then I feel an arm round my neck, fingers in my hair pulling my head back. It doesn't hurt; I'm protected but I don't fight. I know it's Gabriel even though I can't see him. It's his signature move.

I relax back into him and say, "Hunters, two hundred meters away."

He holds me still; I think he's unsure if I'm tricking him.

"You win. I give in. I surrender," I say.

"Really?"

"Gabriel. Keep your voice down."

He releases his hold on me and I sink to the ground knowing he'll copy me. I look at him and he sees then that I'm serious.

"Go back to the camp. Warn Celia. I'll try to work out how many there are."

He nods, but hesitates. "You think they're going to attack the camp?"

"I don't know. Go. Be careful. Watch out for more of them."

"They'll be invisible."

"Go back the way we came, fast. I didn't hear anything along that route."

He presses his hand on mine and then leaves, running back up the slope and over the top out of sight.

I become invisible and move further down the slope. Taking it slow, trying to work out where they are, I move in the direction of the sound, scanning left and right as I go. Then I see a footprint. A boot print. Definitely Hunters.

But I still only sense one phone. She must be hunkered down in the trees to my left. I take a couple of steps in that direction. And a few more. And a few more. The hissing is loud now and I should be able to see the Hunter, so I'm pretty sure that whoever is here is invisible. I can't see any signs of a camp. Nothing except that one boot print.

Is this the front of an attack or is it a scouting party? If they were planning on attacking the camp I'd expect there to be loads of Hunters. Tens if not hundreds. I'd have heard something.

I listen again. There is only one phone. Just one Hunter, who is still and invisible.

But they always work in pairs so her partner must be around. And if they're scouting then her partner is probably looking for our camp or already watching it. I have to hope that Gabriel doesn't come across her on his way back. But he should be safe. One won't attack. They're here to watch.

I move slowly away from the Hunter, then go further into the valley, listening for more of them. I make my way back in a curving sweep, trying to cover as much ground as possible, but I find nothing.

Thirty minutes later I'm back at the camp. Gabriel is with Greatorex and Celia. Celia has had the mock-up of the Council building pulled down, but apart from that the camp is behaving much as it always does. I'm surprised. I thought she'd be packed up and ready to go or dug into six-foot-deep trenches by now.

I tell Celia, "I've found one. There's no camp that I can see. I think there is only one pair, very good and very quiet, traveling light. They're not here to attack."

"We'd be fighting by now if they were going to attack," Celia says. "But more will be here soon. And there's no way of knowing how long they've been here, how much they've seen."

Celia turns to Greatorex and says, "Ideas?"

Greatorex replies, "We patrol every morning and evening. The trainees know to look for any sign. They've seen nothing. And if the scouts had found us more than a few hours ago, we'd already be dead. Odds are they arrived this morning but they'll have phoned in a report and more Hunters will be on their way here right now."

"We need to leave. Will they be able to work out what we're planning from that?" Celia nods at the broken-down pile of tarps and wood.

"They'll know we're up to something. They'll go through the possibilities and work out that we're practicing an attack. The Council meeting is the obvious target."

"Will they think we're strong enough to attack it?"

"They'll believe we're desperate enough."

Celia rubs her face. "There's nothing we can do about it. We need to move now. Evacuate the non-combatants to Camp Two immediately. I want them gone in fifteen minutes. Close the cut behind them. All attack personnel prepare to move out on my orders. But first"—and Celia looks at me—"I want those two Hunters. Greatorex, send out your top trackers. Scour the area. I want that second Hunter traced and hounded down. Nathan, you go to the first one and wait there. They'll reunite if they feel threatened. I want you to take them both out. We can't have prisoners; they'll slow us down. If you detect any more Hunters, the start of an attack, you come straight back and we all leave."

I think that this is the first time Celia has given me a direct order to kill someone. And it occurs to me that it's a strange thing to be ordered to do.

"Are you OK with that?" Celia asks.

I meet her gaze and say, "Sure."

I leave without a word to Gabriel, without even looking at him. What can I say? "Back soon—I've got to go and kill two people."

I go quickly back to the Hunter, turning invisible before I leave the camp. I can't think about right or wrong, just about doing the task. For all I know, a hundred Hunters might already be waiting for me.

I slow when I reach the rise and then stop and listen. The hiss of the phone is still there. I get my breath. I've run flat out most of the way. I calm my breath to make it slow, smooth, silent, and regular. Then I move closer to the source of the hissing. The Hunter is still and silent, possibly asleep. I consider killing her now, but then she'll be visible and I think the other Hunter will come back to warn her once she knows the Alliance fighters are onto them.

I decide to wait. If she moves I'll kill her.

It's not long before I hear footsteps coming from behind me and I'm not sure if this Hunter will be visible or not.

Visible! A woman in black. She runs close to me and straight to her invisible partner. Then stops and says, "Floss? Floss, are you here? We need to move out."

Floss appears close to the other girl's feet. She's dressed in the same way and is sitting on the ground, back against a tree.

The Fairborn is in my hands without me thinking about it and I stride up to them and slit the throat of the one standing. I'm still invisible and Floss probably can't work it out; all she sees is blood and her dying partner, who now falls to the ground. But Floss is a Hunter and her automatic reaction is to pull her gun and shoot. I stab her in the neck. She shoots again and the bullet taps my shoulder and she lashes out at my face with her other hand, a final strong swipe with all her energy, but it feels like a gentle pat to me and she bleeds out over my hands.

I let her body fall. I know they couldn't have hurt me but my orders were to kill them. That's what I've done. And they would have killed me without a second thought. They're Hunters, the enemy. But . . . *Shit, I can't think about this now. I've got to get moving.*

I check their pockets. Floss has energy bars, a phone, and lip salve. The second girl has no orders, no maps, but she does have a notebook and a phone. It looks like she's been writing up times and then notes against those, but I haven't got time to spell out any of the words. The phone is locked, but I bet she's taken photos on it. I put the blood-covered phones and notebook in my pocket and head back to camp.

They were sixty-five and sixty-six. I repeat it as I run. *Sixty-five and sixty-six.* If I say numbers, I think numbers, not bodies, not blood, not dead people caressing my face.

Sixty-five, sixty-six. Sixty-five, sixty-six.

The Break-In

We're in a new camp, only established a few hours ago but already looking organized. Celia has been through the things I've brought from the Hunters. From the notebook she works out that the Hunters had only found us that morning, like Greatorex thought. They'd been traveling alone and were many miles from any cut. But they had phoned in that they'd found a camp, had our numbers and location, with comments about the replica of the Council building, though they hadn't guessed what it was.

"We're still going on with the attack?" I ask.

"You want to call it off?" Celia replies.

"No."

"Neither do I. We stick to the plan. The Council meeting will go ahead. They may expect you to get in. Soul might even want that, but they don't know you're indestructible. That's the advantage we have. Just make sure you use it to maximum effect."

We all patrol the area that day, everyone nervous that we've been followed, but Celia's system of moving and closing cuts seems to have worked. At night, me and Gabriel stay in the camp with the others. We don't talk. He lies down by the fire and I sit and watch it. I go for a run in the dark to tire myself out and then come back to him. I know I'm doing the right thing. If this can be over soon, then me and Gabriel can leave here for good and find somewhere to live together.

We're on our way to the Tower. "We" being all the members of the Alliance who are trained to fight, plus two healers, Arran and another witch, who will tend to any wounded.

Once we're through the cut and in London, Greatorex, Arran, and the trainees go off to some place I don't know, but they aren't with me and I don't need to think about them. The advance party is here: me, Gabriel, and Celia.

It's dark by the time we get to the Tower. There's going to have to be two stages to me getting into it. At the midnight changeover of guards, I need to check if the password has changed; given that Soul probably knows our plans, a change seems guaranteed. To find out the password I'll have to stay inside for about ten minutes, maybe more. I've no idea how I'll cope with that, but I've told Celia I can do it. I did wonder if the amulet might protect me against feeling sick and went inside a shop for a few moments when we got here. Within a minute I felt dizzy and within two I felt like puking. It's a full moon—just my luck.

So, anyway, I have to find out the password at the midnight changeover and then we have to wait until the eight a.m. change of guards for me to go in.

The towers are hard to distinguish from one another in the dark; lights are on in lots of the flats but the top of

Roman Tower is all in darkness. There hasn't been much movement into or out of any of the buildings.

Celia is watching the far side of the residential estate. I'm standing with Gabriel where we had our curry. Now Gabriel has a bottle of cider. Some local yobs hang around near us and Gabriel swigs from the cider and offers me some. I shake my head and say, "It's disgusting."

He smiles. "I'm trying to fit in."

And of course he does fit in, anywhere he likes, but I tell him, "You're very good but not perfect . . . try not to sound so happy."

He laughs. "I could learn so much from you." And now he copies my voice, saying, "Is this better?"

I swear at him and he creases over in laughter. The youths look our way but when I look at them they wander off and Gabriel sniggers again.

There's a cold wind but at least it's not raining. We just have to wait. I pick up the bottle of cider and wander up past all the shopfronts, trying to look natural—bored and mean, I guess. It can't be far off midnight by now. I go back to Gabriel and stand with him.

At 11:47 I go invisible and walk to the Tower. The door is still broken and the stairwell still stinks of piss, but I get to the third floor before I notice my headache. I'm at the seventh floor when I feel the first wave of nausea. I have to hold on to the wall for a second. Then I hear footsteps on the stairs behind me. I take a deep breath and carry on upward, feeling sick but not too dizzy. I get to the top floor and move to the far end of the corridor.

The guards wander up, not in a hurry. I'm wedged in the corner concentrating on breathing, on staying invisible.

"Jez late again?" one says. I look up now and see there's five of them.

"Just get in, will ya?"

But then there's a shout from below in the stairwell. "I'm coming. Hold on."

There's general swearing and complaining. My stomach is churning. The walls are closing in on me and it's taking all my strength to tell myself that walls don't fall in; that it's some kind of mind trick or illusion *but whatever it is the walls are not falling in!*

And I've got to stay invisible. My stomach cramps and I'm bent over, and someone says, "Hurry up, will ya?" And I hear, "Thrott—" and Jez is shouting, "Wait up." And my stomach heaves and I have a taste of sick in my mouth and all I can concentrate on is breathing in and staying invisible. Then they're going inside and the door shuts behind them and I run for the stairs and half run, half fall down them and get to the next level and keep on going down and I throw up. The walls *are* closing in and the noises are starting and my stomach's cramping again and I throw up again and I know I've got to get out but I'm not sure which way is out and I can't stand so I crawl and then I'm rolling downstairs and crawling some more and falling some more and the noises in my head are banging away and I want to shout back at them but I can't here and I can't even crawl now. And the screeching gets louder and my stomach is cramping more and I curl up in a ball and scream back and then I feel hands on my back and Gabriel's voice saying, "I'm here. It's OK." And I'm being pulled up, hands going under my arms, and Gabriel's voice is telling me, "We've just got to get down two flights and then we're out." But I can't stand so he drags me backward down the stairs and through the door and the second I'm outside the cramps ease and I heal myself of the headache and nausea and I feel fine. I feel more than fine. I feel fantastic.

Gabriel doesn't complain, though I know he's desperate to. When we're back at our post by the shops he asks, "Did you get the password?"

"'Throttle back,' I think."

"You think?"

"'Throttle' for sure."

"'Back' not for sure?"

"It might have been 'attack.'"

"Or 'sack'? Or 'hack'? Or 'tack'? Or something else entirely!"

"Throttle back."

I think.

Then it's back to waiting. The shops are shut now. No one and nothing is around except for the cold. Gabriel and I go down an alley and sit on the ground close to the wall. Neither of us can sleep.

Gabriel says, "Someone once said that war is long periods

of boredom punctuated by moments of sheer terror."

"Minutes of terror, I'd say."

"Yes, minutes, maybe hours if it's bad."

"I think today might be bad."

Gabriel takes my hands and interlocks his fingers with mine. "But then it will be over. No more boredom, no more terror, just lots of peace and climbing and coffee and croissants."

"Yeah." But I'm not thinking of peace or climbing or coffee, I'm thinking of hours of terror and all the blood and screams and fear.

It's getting light now. A delivery van comes and drops off newspapers on the street and then the newsagent opens up. Gabriel goes to buy some snack bars. I can hardly swallow them but I force them down. Then there's more waiting.

Celia appears round one of the towers. It's 7:29 and I have to go.

Gabriel says, "I'll join you soon."

I jog across the expanse of open ground to the Tower, through the broken door, up the smelly staircase, past the sick on the seventh-floor landing and already I feel good. The tension in my stomach has gone. I'm dying to get on with it.

I go invisible and carry on up the stairs to the top floor and the door to the prison. I've got one of Mercury's hairpins that magically picks locks and, leaning close to the door, I say quietly, "Throttle back," as I put the tip of the hairpin on the lock and push.

Nothing happens.

My throat is dry and maybe my voice was unclear. Or maybe the password is wrong, but I can't go through lots of options.

I can hear footsteps on the stairs. The guards aren't due to change over for twenty-five minutes so it's probably another resident. But still I need to get through the door. I say "Throttle back" again, a little louder and clearer, but it seems like a shout in the quietness of the building. I put the pin on the lock, push the door, and it opens.

Now I'm standing in the dark. I got a quick glimpse of the next door two or three paces in front of me. But there's no handle on it and I don't know which way it opens, so I can't tell which side of the room I should be on to slide in with the guard. I'm not sure if there's a light in here but I daren't look for one and put it on. I've just got to hope that when the guard arrives I have time to get into a good position. It'll be another twenty minutes or so.

But a minute later the outer door opens. It must have been a guard on the stairs. I have a second to go invisible and the guard pulls a cord that hangs from the ceiling, illuminating a bare bulb, and the outer door swings shut. He knocks on the inner door five times. Two loud and slow and three fast, which I guess is another signal.

After nearly a minute, the peephole in the inner door slides across for the briefest of seconds and then back into place. The lock rattles and then the door opens and the guard on the inside says, "Early for once." He lets the door swing open for my guard to enter. There isn't much room for me, but I slide to the side and hold myself tight against the wall.

I'm in.

The returning guard swears and looks down. A sweet wrapper is stuck to his boot. As he bends forward to pull it off, I shrink further back against the wall. His jacket touches mine. That's all, nothing more. But somehow I know he knows there's something wrong. And he turns round as if to check behind him, staring straight through me, with the sweet wrapper between his fingers. He turns away again and says, "Is Jake here?"

"You're the first. You're half an hour early. Dale's still finishing his rounds."

"I thought I heard Jake . . ." Then he wanders up the corridor, the sweet wrapper held out in front of him. And I have a bad feeling he's working it out.

I follow the sweet-wrapper guy through to a small room with a set of kitchen units along one side and a table with a bench seat along the other. He puts the wrapper in the bin then wipes his hand on his trousers. He takes his jacket off and hangs it on a hook on the wall. The other hooks are full. Another guard comes in and says, "You're early."

"Yeah."

"She throw you out or something?"

The sweet-wrapper guy shakes his head, as if he has other things on his mind. He fills the kettle and makes a tea. Then more of the leaving guards arrive and comment on the sweet-wrapper guard's early arrival. Even I'm getting fed up with their comments now but it seems he's forgotten about hearing me say the password. The room fills up with more of the new shift arriving and I move into the corridor and wait out of the way and concentrate again on staying invisible. I count the old guards out as they leave and I make sure all six go. I then follow the Hunters as they leave too, and see where the cut is that they go through to the Council building.

So now there are four Hunters and six Council guards here. And I've got to remove them without letting any escape or raise the alarm. They all go to a meeting room and the lead guard is giving instructions, comments about prisoners. The guards don't carry guns: they don't need weapons as they don't let the prisoners out. They're just a food-dispensing and waste-disposal system. The Hunters do have weapons, of course.

Luck is now on my side, though. The Hunters are standing together at the side of the room. I'm standing in the doorway. The lead guard is talking about the cleaning rota; the other guards are facing him.

Now I have to begin in earnest.

I send out lightning to all four Hunters.

It takes a few seconds for them to begin to fall.

The guards are surprised. They can't see me. They maybe even think it's a weird electrical malfunction. But one shouts, "Raise the alarm." I blast him too, but with a weaker jolt. I don't want to kill the guards. I let myself become visible and two of the guards come at me but I send lightning to them too. They're stunned and fall but they're not dead. The others are all back against the wall and I hit two of them with more lightning to stun them so that the only people left standing are me and the guard with the clipboard, and he's gripping his clipboard so tight it looks like he's going to twist it in half. He's totally still as if he too is stunned. But then he comes to life and throws the clipboard at me hard. And then other stuff flies at me: pens and handcuffs, mugs and all the stuff that's lying around the room. Of course it doesn't hurt me; it doesn't even land on me, and the guard's Gift isn't that strong. The chairs wobble as if he's trying to move them but they don't lift.

I hold my arms out, saying, "I won't kill you." I wait for him to stop. "Your friends aren't dead. Just stunned."

A set of keys flies at my face but slides on past.

I tell him again, "I won't kill you. But I might hurt you if you keep throwing things at me." And I send a small lightning bolt to his feet to remind him what I can do.

He puts his hands up in defeat. The room goes quiet again. He's shaking.

"What's your name?"

"Sean."

"OK, Sean. Well, I'm serious about not killing you. If you do as I say, you won't get hurt at all."

He doesn't reply, but then bends over and is sick. I take his handcuffs and put them on him and push him out and down the corridor to the front door. Through the peephole I see Celia and Gabriel are already in the small holding room.

I tell Sean, "We've got to let my friends in. I need the password."

He shakes his head.

"If you don't tell me, I'll kill your friends one by one. You understand that?"

The Tower

Sean is surprisingly cooperative. He only needed to be threatened once before telling me the password and that the keys were on his belt. Celia and Gabriel quickly enter and I tell Celia, "This is Sean. He's been very helpful."

Sean says, "You'll all be killed. Or caught. And then you'll end up in here permanently."

And then he surprises me by trying to headbutt me, which feels like a soft kiss on the end of my nose and his head is thrown back. That freaks him out and he kicks me, which obviously hurts him a lot and me not at all, though he still can't work it out. I think he might calm down but he just gets madder and it's a waste of time so I hit him and he falls unconscious.

I tell Celia, "The Hunters are dead but the guards are stunned. I think they'll be waking up soon." And I show her where they are.

"Find a cell to put them in," Celia says.

I go along the corridor to the first cell and look in the peephole. Of course it's occupied and when I see inside I begin to think we should kill the guards after all.

The only things in the cell are a thin mattress, blanket, toilet, and a prisoner. The prisoner is a woman, very thin and very pale. Her eyes are those of a White Witch. She's wearing bright yellow overalls.

I go along the corridor looking for an empty cell, but each one is occupied and they're all the same: small and bare with a mattress, toilet, blanket, one prisoner in yellow overalls. It's grim. At the last cell the prisoner is sitting but looking at me. He smiles in a strange way when I open the peephole. He's old and thin but I recognize him straightaway. I don't even need to say hello, at least not out loud.

I use Mercury's pin to open the cell door and go in and kneel in front of him. He's sitting on the mattress, his back leaned against the wall, a blanket wrapped round him. His bare feet are pale, almost blue-white. He's painfully thin, but then he was never fat. He blinks slowly and stares at me. "Have I gone to heaven, gorgeous boy?"

I shake my head.

"Well, then, this is certainly an unexpectedly pleasant surprise." Bob's voice is still as strong as ever, which is promising. I only met him once, for a short time, when he helped me on my search for Mercury. I hoped he'd escaped from Soul and the Hunters, but obviously not. Now I'm closer to him I see he's got purple bruises on one side of his neck that seem to stretch down to his shoulder.

"Are you OK?" I ask, and feel stupid because he really isn't.

"Old and tired, and a bit battered. But feeling a lot better for seeing you." He tries to get up but has little strength and can't manage it.

"Don't try to move. Stay where you are. You're better here for now. I've dealt with the guards."

"I take it you haven't done all that just to help me."

"We're attacking the Council building."

"Jolly good."

"We need to empty a cell to put the guards in so I'm going to bring another prisoner in here. There'll be some medical help soon. But you have to stay here for now."

I race back down the corridor and, with Gabriel's help, move the female prisoner from the first cell, along with her mattress and blanket, to Bob's cell. Then we drag all the guards into the first cell. They're heavy, fat. They disgust me. Some of them, including Sean, are waking up. And I just want to get them in and shut the door on them before I get too angry.

I go to the guardroom and look for food, finding some biscuits, a banana, and a bottle of water. I take them back to Bob and tell him, "You'll have to share it with your new cellmate."

Celia says, "Time to go, Nathan. We can help the prisoners best by succeeding in our mission."

Bob looks at Celia and says, "The Council meeting is happening. The Hunters on the last shift were whinging about the organization of it: there are a lot of Hunters in the building and not enough bathroom facilities apparently."

I tell Celia, "Bob's Gift is that he can read minds."

"Is there anything else you know that might help us?" Celia asks. "Anything about Soul, Wallend, or Jessica?"

"Not much, and nothing good, I'm afraid. The guards are too lowly to have even seen them. They fear them, though. The Hunters respect Jessica," Bob says, and adds, "Wallend is a bit of a mystery. They all wonder what he's up to but no one seems to know. He's given the Hunters the power to go invisible, which they like. Now he's developing something called blue. A potion, but I don't know much about it."

He pauses and then says, "If you don't mind me asking, are you serious about this attack? There don't seem to be many of you."

I laugh. "Reinforcements are coming. But I better get going."

"There's someone else here who may know more. Though I'm not sure how eager he will be to help."

"Who?" Celia asks.

"Most prisoners I know from their fear. They spend a lot of time thinking about the past and what they shouldn't say. The guards think about the future. But someone else plans escape, plans revenge, plans a future, plans, plans, plans. Clay's mind is hardly ever at rest. He's on the top floor, I think. It's rather nice to know that the man who caused me to be here is now sharing the same fate."

And I'm up and out of the door and down the corridor to the internal metal staircase and taking the steps two at a time until I'm at the top. Celia is close behind me, shouting at me to stop, that Clay won't tell me anyway. I keep moving quickly along, checking the cells, trying not to think about the state of the prisoners I see.

Looking through the peephole to the last cell, I find it's as small and grim as all the others, but the prisoner here is sitting in a lotus position and is chained to the wall by both wrists. I can't help but smile.

I tell Celia, "It's him."

She replies, "We don't have time for this."

I open the door with Mercury's pin. I want him to see me standing over him.

His eyes are different. They still have lots of silver in them, so much that the blue is almost lost, but his right eye is deformed by a mass of scars that run down his face, and as he blinks I see that his eyelid doesn't properly cover his eye. Clay looks at us and says nothing and I keep the silence as long as possible. For fun I take out the Fairborn.

I say to Celia, "I'm not going to use it, just reminding him that I have it, that I took it from him and that because he lost it he's here in this cell."

Clay says, "Celia, what an unexpected surprise." And he stands now. He does it smoothly and slowly, but I detect a stiffness and although he's still big and muscular he's not looking at all like his old self. He's not tall but wide, and his neck is still big, but it's obvious that he's lost a lot of weight. "What brings you here"—and for the first time he looks at me as he says—"with *that*?"

He steps forward, stopping before the chains linking his arms to the wall go tight. And there's an energy to him still.

I say, "You suit the chains, Clay."

His eyes are icy, but I can see emotion in there, lots of it. Lots of hate. And I'm not sure if it's all for me. "Has Jessica been to visit you here? I imagine she likes to see her men in chains."

He ignores me and turns to Celia, asking, "Is there any particular reason for your visit?"

I want to ask Clay about Geneva, about how he knew where the apartment was that had the cut through to Mercury's cottage. Did Annalise tell him? Was she working for him? Was she a spy? Did she betray us?

Celia says, "No. Just checking on you. Time to go, Nathan." And she starts to swing the door shut.

"I need to know something first." And I grab the door and hold it open. "I want some information."

Clay sneers at me.

"The night we stole the Fairborn from you. I was shot and injured but I made my way back to an apartment. There was a cut on the roof that led through to Mercury's cottage in the Swiss mountains. Do you remember it?"

He stares at me unblinking.

"*Do you remember it?*" I repeat. "I got back to the apartment and the place was swarming with Hunters. You drove up. I saw you. I left and then came across Jessica."

"And cut her pretty face."

"Nathan," Celia says, "we haven't got time for this."

"You remember the apartment?" I ask.

"I've lost twenty kilos, not my memory," Clay snaps.

"How did you find it, the apartment?"

He doesn't reply.

"Did Annalise tell you? Was she your spy?"

Clay smiles now. "Ah, Annalise." He moves back to the far wall of the cell and slides down it to sit and look at me. "Where is she now, I wonder? Back with her Uncle Soul, some of the guards say."

"Was she working for you all along?"

"Questions, questions, questions . . ."

"But not answers," I say.

"And no time for them anyway," Celia interjects.

"Let me out of here and I'll tell you," Clay says, staring at me.

"Tell me and I won't kill you."

"Well, you'll never know if you kill me."

"Nathan, there's no time for this. You have to go," Celia says.

Clay smiles at me and says, "Better do as you're told and run along. I'm sure I'll still be here later."

"You'll be here forever," I reply and swing the door shut.

When this is over I want Clay swimming in truth potions. I want Bob to dig through his brain and find out everything he knows, though in honesty I'm not sure what difference it makes anymore what Annalise did or didn't do. She shot my father and that's all that matters.

Thumbs

I go to the cut that leads to the Council building, Celia following close behind barking at me, "I need you to follow my orders. When I say go, you have to go."

"I'm going now. OK?"

Further down the corridor I see Greatorex, Adele, and a couple of the other trainees arriving. Gabriel is waiting for me at the cut in a Hunter uniform.

I turn to Celia and tell her, "I could have killed Clay. I didn't. You told me to go. I went."

"Eventually."

We glare at each other.

Gabriel says, "Did I miss something?"

Celia looks at me and says, "Nothing important."

It was important to me. I say to Celia, "Annalise may be a prisoner here in the Tower. Do you want me to go and look for her?"

"No. I want you to do the mission as we planned."

"OK. I'm going to do the mission as planned. Are you ready, Gabriel?"

He says yes and I say to Celia, "See how good I am at following orders."

I know I haven't got time to look for Annalise and I'm

fairly sure she isn't here in the Tower anyway from what Clay said, and if she is Celia will ensure she stays put.

Celia says, "You both know what to do." And, looking hard at me, she says firmly, "Do it. Stay focused and we can win this."

Gabriel's job is to wait in the Council building, disguised as a Hunter until the fighting starts, then send a text message to Celia, and the Alliance fighters will come through the cut. I know Gabriel will be the first to join the battle. I wish he'd hang back, be last and not take any risks, but there's no point in even suggesting that. The main way to keep him safe is the way to keep everyone safe: get Soul.

Gabriel changes his appearance to a crop-haired Hunter, and I recoil. He looks almost like Kieran. He says, "I've taken the ID of one of the Hunters that were working here. Is it no good?"

"Too good, I think." And I grasp his hand, take a breath, become invisible, and slide into the cut.

The darkness of the cut lasts only a second. Then I'm thrown out into more cold darkness, stumbling to my knees on a stone floor, Gabriel pulling me up. We hardly made a sound, but we hold still, listening.

We're in a dark room but light seeps through the cracks around the door. There are voices on the other side, two of them, but then it goes silent. I think they've left but I wait ten seconds to make sure before using Mercury's pin to pick the lock. We make our way through the corridors and I quickly get my bearings.

We're in the southwest corner of the basement. The cells are to the west, but I have to go east to the stairs that come up into the main foyer. We don't see anyone until we get to the top. Then there are Hunters. Lots of them.

Gabriel pulls me back and whispers, "You think they're here because of the meeting or because they know we're coming?"

"Does it matter?"

"At least I don't stand out so much when there's so many of them." And I know Gabriel will try to mingle with the Hunters, find out what's happening. "You'd better go."

I can only hope his natural ability to fit in anywhere works even here.

I walk slowly and carefully past the Hunters, making sure I don't touch any of them, and I'm in the huge foyer of the Council building. It's not *full* of Hunters but there must be over twenty of them standing to either side of the main door and there's a small, slim man behind an enquiries desk.

I take the stairs three at a time, and on the first-floor landing there are more Hunters again: ten of them. I carry on up, slowly now, to the top floor. There are four Hunters on the second landing and I see two more patrolling the third- and fourth-floor corridors, but the top floor is quiet and empty.

It's different from how I'd imagined it from practicing in the mock-up. The wooden floor has a strip of red carpet leading down the middle but overall it's light, airy, and warm. I'd imagined it to be dark and gray. I go right and to the first door, as I rehearsed in the forest. The room is furnished and doesn't appear to be in use. I work my way along the corridor, checking each room, and every one is similar and similarly unused.

I hope for better luck the other way and turn back to try the corridor that heads left from the top of the stairs into the area that Celia hadn't managed to re-create in the mock-up.

I listen at the first door but there are no sounds except the hiss of phones. That hiss fills the building: there're lots of people with phones, and lots of computers and electrical equipment. I try the handle and it opens. The room beyond is a large book-lined study. There's an old leather briefcase by the side of a wooden desk and a coat thrown over the back of a leather armchair. No one is in here but there's a door to another room. I go to that and listen again. I can hear music. Classical music.

I'm fairly sure that whoever owns the coat is in the room with the music and there has to be a good chance that the owner is Wallend. But I want to get close to him without raising the alarm and I want to find out how many other people there are on this floor.

I go out and try the next door along the corridor. This opens to a smaller office, with a desk and chair, shelves and a small sofa, and some personal things: papers, a laptop, and a handbag. This office also has a door leading to another room, and from it I can hear the classical music again. I think this door leads to the same place as the door in Wallend's office.

I carry on with my check of the corridor, speeding up now. The next door is locked but Mercury's pin opens it easily and I find another unused office. There's one door left to check. There are no sounds coming from behind it. I use Mercury's pin and enter.

This is not an unused office.

There are three gurneys, each with a gray cloth over them, and their shape indicates that a body lies beneath each one.

I go to the first and pull the sheet back. It's a woman. Brown hair, eyes open, staring, no glints in them. Her skin is pale. She has a tattoo on her neck: **W 1.0**. As I pull the sheet further back, I see that her chest is open. There is no blood—that has all been taken out and, as far as I can see, so has her heart. I look at her hands to see if she has similar tattoos to me. Her little finger has a single tattoo on the side of it: **W 1.0**.

I go to the next body. This is also a woman, black-skinned but mutilated the same way as the first.

The last body is different. It's a girl. She can't be more than eleven or twelve. She has a tattoo on her neck and finger as well, and her chest is also open.

The room itself is cold. Very cold. The walls are lined with shelves and bottles that seem to contain parts taken out of these victims. There's drawers of surgical equipment.

There is also a door to another room. I go and listen. Nothing. No music.

I try the knob and am surprised that it's not locked. I go in.

The room is vast and contains rows of metal shelves,

each protected by a glass door. And on each shelf, bottles. And in each bottle . . . parts of bodies. I slide a glass door back and pick one up to check. In the bottle is something fleshy and dark. I think it might be a liver. It has **W 1.0** tattooed on it.

I go to the door at the far end of the room and, yes, at this door I can hear the classical music. I'm sure Wallend and his assistant are inside but there may be guards too. And I know the chances of me getting into this room without Wallend noticing something are slim, so my options are limited. I need to move quickly. But I don't want to raise the alarm if I can avoid it.

I retrace my steps to Wallend's office, making sure the doors are locked behind me. I don't want anyone to run and escape this way. Back in Wallend's office I go to the door in the far wall and listen for the music but a man's talking now, though he's not in the room; he's on the radio introducing some Beethoven.

I take hold of the doorknob, concentrate again to ensure I stay invisible, and slowly and gently open the door far enough to slip inside the room.

Beethoven starts, nice and slow. I close the door quietly.

The room is bright. Skylights line the ceiling. At the far end of the room are two figures sitting at a bench. They are bent over, working. A man and a young woman. The man has his back to me. He's narrow, thin, wearing a white lab coat, and although I can't see his head because he's bent over I know it's him: Wallend.

The woman looks toward me and the door. She must have noticed a movement. She says something to Wallend and he turns as I approach him and he looks right through me.

The room is a laboratory, full of equipment and jars and tubes and stuff that I've no idea about. I daren't use electricity in here. I take the Fairborn and see that Wallend and the girl are not bent over a desk but a body laid out on a bench. The body of a man and on his neck is a tattoo in large letters: **B 1.0**. His chest is cut open, his heart exposed.

I go to Wallend's assistant and neither me nor the Fairborn hesitate. Her blood flows over my hand and the assistant's body slips silently to the floor. I allow myself to become visible.

Wallend stares at me. He has a scalpel in his hand. I hold up the Fairborn and say, "Care to try your luck?"

Wallend steps back between the tables and turns, and I go round fast to follow him and I'm on him in three strides. I grab his arm and pull hard but he squirms round behind a desk. My hand slides down to his wrist and I slam his hand onto the wooden desktop and pin it to the surface with the Fairborn. Wallend's shaking, not resisting, and I use the scalpel to fix his other hand in place. He still hasn't said a word: no scream of pain, no cry for help.

Beethoven is playing, a nice tune—very soothing, gentle, not that funereal stuff.

I say to Wallend, "I have to tell you that I'll probably kill you whether you help me or not. But the longer you live the bigger the chances are that you'll carry on living.

When the rest of the Alliance gets here they'll want you alive. Want to put you on trial and stuff like that."

He doesn't say anything, just shakes.

"I really can't be bothered with all that, though. I mean, as far as I'm concerned, you're guilty of murder. Lots of it."

Now he speaks. "And you're not?"

"We're talking about you today. You're guilty. The question is: can you stop me from executing you?"

"Wh-what?"

"I need you to show me how the Hunters go invisible."

He shakes his head.

I take another scalpel from the end of the bench and go to Wallend. I chop his right thumb off. Now Wallend screams.

"Painful, isn't it?" I say. "How's your healing?"

He's shaking again, worse now. Blood running across the desktop.

"You're not good at healing. What *are* you good at, Wallend? Just chopping people up?"

He looks at me, terrified, then turns away and is sick on the floor.

"You ever get sick when you're cutting up other people, Wallend?"

He doesn't reply, just shakes, which I think is a no.

"So, where are the witch's bottles that you use to make the Hunters invisible? That's how you do it, isn't it? With bottles?"

He nods.

"So?" I ask. "Or are you going to let me take the other thumb?" I smile at him.

He stares. "They'll kill you. Slowly, if I have anything—"

I take his other thumb off and he makes a strange choking cry.

"You want to move to ears and nose next?" I ask. "Or eyes?"

"In the next room! In the next room!"

And I glance over to where he's looking, to another small metal door between the benches.

I pull the Fairborn out of Wallend's hand and then the scalpel, and push him to the door. He's weak and quivering but he goes.

"Open it." I could use Mercury's pin but I need to see if he'll do what I say.

"I can't. My hands . . ." he says, holding them out and staring as if what's happened to them is only now registering.

I open the door. Wallend begins to collapse—it's definitely only hitting him now that he isn't ever going to be able to turn a doorknob again. I push him through into the next room and he crumples into a heap on the floor. And I just stand and stare.

The Dome

It's a pyramid of glass inside a glass dome.

The pyramid is made up of glass bottles, neatly piled up on the floor. There are hundreds of them. I step closer and see that in each bottle is a small piece of flesh about five centimeters across and on it is a tattoo, a circle like the Hunters have over their hearts.

I can't get too close to the pyramid because it's inside the glass dome. There's a narrow, shallow circular channel in the floor in which the dome rests.

I reach toward the dome but hesitate and turn to look at Wallend. He's staring at me, alert now, and I have second thoughts about touching the glass. I walk round the dome. It's about three meters in diameter and seems perfectly shaped and clear, like an upturned glass bowl. But the more I look at it the more I'm sure it's not simply glass. The pyramid of bottles inside is neatly—perfectly—arranged, except for a few gaps, as if some bottles are missing. As I continue to walk round, I spot a few more gaps. Or am I mistaken? One that I thought was missing is there now.

And then I get it. The bottles become invisible as the Hunters they are connected to become invisible. I watch for a moment and see two vanish and one reappear.

I walk back to Wallend. "Open the dome. I want to look at the bottles."

He shakes his head.

I lean forward and hiss at him, "Open it or I cut off your ear."

"I can't."

"I think you can."

I grab hold of his ear and pull it hard, saying, "Last chance or this is going."

He hits out at me now with his arms and then kicks me. I hit him back, let him fall to the floor, and take the scalpel and slice his ear off, even though I know it will not help me one bit. But he has to know that I'll follow through with what I say.

He screams once and clutches at his bleeding head.

I throw the ear at the dome.

Electricity sparks fly around the piece of flesh and it bounces back to land on the floor near Wallend. The dome crackled a blue-white color but only briefly and only in the area where the ear hit it.

I look at the scalpel in my hand and wonder if I should try that.

Why not?

The scalpel hits the dome and for a second seems to fuse with it as the dome changes color around the point of impact. Then the scalpel flies back toward me, landing with a tinkle on the ground.

I make another circuit of the dome, but this time looking

at the other equipment in the room. There's a bench along the wall opposite the door we came through, and there are many things on it: paperwork, surgical equipment, pens, computer, but nothing to indicate how to open the dome.

I say to Wallend, "You must add to the pile of bottles in there. When there are new recruits you want to give the Gift of invisibility. So how do you do it?"

He shrinks lower and I notice the scalpel has disappeared from view.

"And is there a spell that manages the invisibility or does this just give the Hunter whose bottle is in there that Gift?"

He doesn't answer. His ear isn't bleeding as much as I thought it would. Maybe he can heal reasonably well after all. His hands don't look too bad now either.

"If you're not going to talk to me, Wallend, then there isn't much point in you having a tongue."

But I don't want to do any more surgery on him; it's disgusting. "Do you use this to open it up?" I ask, picking up a laptop and weighing it in my hand. "I've never been great at computers but I'll try it."

Wallend cowers but doesn't try to stop me, so I suspect it holds nothing important and I toss the computer at the dome. Again at the impact zone the dome turns blue-white and the laptop is held there for a second, as if caught, before it is rejected and thrown out. There are sparks and a lot of crackling but after a few seconds the dome is back to its quiet, clear norm. And Wallend has taken those few seconds to move round to me, scalpel in his bloodied paw. He must know he doesn't stand a chance.

I step toward him and realize as I do that that's what he wants. His only hope of beating me is to push me into the dome. And I have to admit I'm rather curious myself what would happen.

Wallend charges at me but he's slow and weak and I sidestep him, and although he grabs me I push him off and use his momentum to force him toward the dome.

He clings to me then.

"Really?" I ask him. "You want to fry or should I just hold your face against the dome and see what happens?"

"No!" he whimpers. And at least now he seems to know that I'll do it. "Please. I'll open it. There's a spell. I need the wand."

"The *wand*?" I've never heard of anyone actually using a wand.

"That. On the bench over there."

I drag him with me to where he indicates.

It's a stick. Admittedly it's a nice stick with the bark peeled off and it looks worn and smooth. I pick it up and wonder if I'll feel something, something alive the way the Fairborn feels. But I get nothing.

"How does it work?"

"With the correct words. And the wand."

And now I'm stuck. Do I let him tell me the words or do I let him do it himself? The amulet should protect me either way. I hold the wand out to him and say, "Take it and open the dome. You've got one chance to get it right."

He nods and the tip of his tongue appears and licks his top lip. He takes the wand in his right hand, grasping it between his fingers. He doesn't show any pain or difficulty in doing that. I think he's healed fine.

Instead of touching the dome itself, he touches the point of the wand to the channel it sits in and says, "Dome, liquefy."

The dome becomes opaque white instantly, and the top changes to be like liquid, like milk, and it flows to the floor and into the channel so that it's brimming and looks like a glistening, shining pool. The bottles are two strides away, waiting for me to destroy them.

"Bring me a bottle," I say.

Wallend hesitates and then steps over the channel of milky liquid, reaches slowly up and picks up the topmost bottle from the pile between his two paws. He looks strong and unwavering now, but then goes back to being bent over as he brings the bottle to me. The bottle is plugged with a cork, and tied to the cork is a small label that has a name on it. The Hunter's name, I guess. Inside is a piece of tattooed flesh. I take the bottle and smash it onto the bench. Nothing happens.

It seems that the dome is a way to secure and protect the bottles. Some of the bottles are still invisible but I think that if I break the bottles then the Hunters will lose the ability to go invisible. Only one way to find out. I snatch the wand from Wallend so he can't do anything to the dome and I go to the pyramid and feel for one of the missing bottles near the top of the pile. It's there but invisible. I pull it out and drop it to the floor. The broken glass appears with the flesh and the cork and the label. So, breaking the bottles does break the spell. It's as simple as that. All I've got to do is break all the bottles and Soul's army will lose the ability to go invisible. I swipe at the top of the pyramid, knocking a few bottles, and as they crash down Wallend shouts, "Dome, solidify." I turn and see he's standing, looking strong, and the milky-white wall rises in front of me and I turn and try to move through the liquid except I can't. The dome is already completely white and solid. And then it clears and Wallend stands on the other side, grinning at me victoriously.

I've still got the wand and I hold it up to him.

"It's a stick," he says. "I was trying to enchant it, but couldn't get it to work. It's just a stick."

I touch the stick to the base of the dome and say with as much emotion as I can muster, which is a lot, "Dome, liquefy."

Nothing happens except perhaps that Wallend's grin widens.

He says, "The dome recognizes two masters only. Me and Soul. It won't do what you say."

I pick up two bottles and throw them at the dome. It reacts the same way as when something hit its outer surface, becoming opaque for a second or two and then becoming clear again.

"I'll destroy all the bottles," I say.

"Then the Hunters will lose their ability to turn invisible but they'll still be Hunters. And you will still be my prisoner."

Well, I'd rather the Alliance fought a visible army so I lash out at the bottles, kicking them at the dome. There's glass flying all around me but the dome doesn't show any hint of a weakness.

Eventually I'm done; there are no more bottles to smash. I'm panting with rage and frustration, standing on crushed glass and bits of flesh as the dome returns to its clear smoothness. And Wallend is still there grinning at me. I thought he might take the opportunity to run and get help but he's not in a rush. He's confident I'm not going anywhere.

He sits on a chair and looks at me. "You've made a mess of your new home." He smiles. "Soul would like to see you here. He was expecting you but I'm tempted to not tell him you've arrived until after you run out of air. It'll be a few hours, I think. You lived a long time in a cage and now you're going to spend the rest of your days, or should I say hours, in this one."

I swear at him.

"Soul thinks we can use you, have you work for us, but"—he holds up his hands—"I know you for what you are: an evil Black Witch, just like your father."

"You want to see evil? I've not even started." And I take the Fairborn and leap at the dome with all my strength. Where the knife hits the dome it becomes opaque for a second and then it throws me back so I land among the glass shards, which shatter beneath me but feel like a feather bed. I get up and raise the Fairborn again.

Wallend comes closer now, studying me. I think he's noticed that I'm not cut by the glass.

I move to stand opposite him and stab the Fairborn at the dome. It bounces my arm back again.

He says, "You're wasting your time. You can't break out. It's impossible. The magic is too strong."

Now I grin at him and I say, "Want to bet?"

I try being gentler this time. Slowly putting the tip of the knife to the dome and pushing it down, still using all my strength. I'm thrust back again but not as forcefully.

There's no mark on the dome. It turns opaque briefly and then returns to its clear self. But I can feel the Fairborn in my hand and its desire to cut, to rip the dome. To the Fairborn, the dome is alive, and the Fairborn doesn't like alive.

I repeat the same slow cut and the same thing happens, but I still sense the Fairborn's desire, its fury. It's madder than I am. I make the same cut again, and the dome doesn't throw me back this time, and I see there's a small opaque line that stays longer than last time, and when it disappears there's a fine scratch in the surface of the dome. A weakness. The Fairborn seems to sense it too, and it wants more, wants to go deeper.

I repeat the cut, slowly and forcefully, pushing the Fairborn into the dome and pulling it down. I'm thrown back, almost to the other side of the dome, but this time the opaque color takes longer to clear and the scratch left behind is deeper and longer than before. I stab once more and, with the weight of my body behind it, the Fairborn's tip is embedded in the dome. I lever the knife up and down, my arms shaking, my whole body shaking. The dome has become opaque and white and I lever faster and push harder, and sweat blooms out of me but I keep levering. And then the dome cracks from floor to floor, right over its peak, and is opaque all along that crooked line. I lever the Fairborn from side to side now and the dome cracks again, crossing the first. Then I take the Fairborn out and thrust it hard at the point where the two cracks meet and I kick high at the place where the blade first went in, and a hole appears in the dome and through it I see Wallend already at the door. Leaving.

I send out lightning. Wallend falls, stunned, not dead. I kick at the dome to make a hole big enough to get through. By the time I'm out, Wallend is groaning and trying to crawl.

Kill or capture are the options now, so I go to Wallend and let the Fairborn choose.

Blue

❧∴

Wallend is dead and I've destroyed all the bottles that were in the dome. No one has come to investigate the noise; the doors are thick and we're at the top of the building, away from everyone else.

I go invisible as I leave Wallend's office, and the corridor is as silent and empty as before.

Now for Soul.

I make my way toward the ground floor and the main Council Chamber where I used to have my Assessments. Behind that is a series of private offices and small meeting rooms. Soul's office is there; I have to hope that he is too. From what Wallend said, Soul knows I'm coming and the Hunters must be here to protect against an attack.

I've come down the main staircase now and I stop in the foyer. The Hunters are still here. I see Gabriel. He's perfect in his disguise as a brutish Hunter. I watch him for a few seconds. He holds his head up and looks around but not at me.

I head to the Council Chamber and am soon in a series of corridors like the ones I remember from my Assessment days, with stone walls and stone floors and many doors off to the left and right. I stand tight against the wall as two

Hunters patrol past, then turn left, then first right, and here is the corridor and the bench where I used to sit and wait with Gran.

It seems strange to see it now. I sat there every year, humiliated and afraid. The last time I was here, I sat there cuffed and Annalise came through the far door with her father. That must have been one of the days she was brought in for questioning. I'm sure it wasn't an accident, that they came this way and reminded her that I was still alive and a danger to society. Or was it all a setup? Was she a spy even then?

Now everything feels different. There's a Hunter near me and another one at the far end of the corridor. Two women come out of the Council Chamber, smiling, and sit on the bench, my bench. The women are talking about their children.

The door to the Council Chamber is open and, just like at my Assessments, a guard is standing inside the door. I move into the room and still it manages to make me feel small as it always did, although the room is laid out differently from when I've been here before. The large table is where it always was, but adjoined to it are three other tables, making a sort of square. Most of the seats are empty, including the three that look like thrones, the three that were occupied for all my Assessments and which I now am sure will be occupied by Soul and Jessica and possibly Wallend, though of course he won't be coming.

I need to get on. Soul isn't here and I need to find him,

preferably in a place a bit more private than this.

As I make my way back to the door, I see a man I recognize. I've only seen him once before, only for a few seconds, but the memory is clear in my mind. Annalise's father. He looks older and much more tired than when I last saw him. Is that how you look when your daughter is a prisoner or a spy? Or maybe it's how you look when two of your sons are dead. I'm not sure what I want to do about him, but I can't do anything at the moment. I've got to find Soul.

Back in the corridor, the women are still talking. One says, "I heard he's going to demonstrate the blue."

The other woman lowers her voice and replies, "Yes, but on whom?"

I turn right down the corridor, to the door at the far end. I can't risk opening it with a Hunter right there. I have to wait for someone to come out and it's a few minutes before that happens. But then the door opens and I manage to slide through without touching anyone.

I walk fast now, round the corner, right and right again, to Soul's private office, and it's all exactly as in the mock-up. There's a guard at this end of the corridor and another outside the door.

I've prepared for these guards, just as Celia told me to. The guards look bored but they also look to be the biggest men I've ever seen. Still, I'm invisible and invincible. I walk slowly and silently past the first, take hold of the doorknob and turn it slowly. The nearest guard might not notice the knob turning but he will notice the door moving. I open it and slide through, leaving the door ajar.

And now I face my enemy.

He's sitting behind his desk, pen in hand. He looks up at the door and it seems as if he's looking at me. The desk, a huge mahogany thing, has some papers on it and also a large glass bowl containing a turquoise blue liquid, and over the top of the bowl is a sheet of glass.

Soul frowns. The guard appears in the doorway behind me.

"Yes?" Soul asks. "Did you want something?"

"No, sir. I . . . I didn't open the door."

Soul shouts, "Get reinforcements!" But I'm already letting the Fairborn thrust itself into the guard's neck. Soul stands, whipping the glass sheet off the bowl and throwing it at me. It slices sharply through the air, and I send a blast of lightning that hits the glass sheet and another that hits Soul. The other guard appears in the doorway and I blast him with lightning too.

It's silent and still again. Shattered glass is strewn across the room, smoke coming from the jacket of the second guard.

I wait a few seconds, expecting someone to come running, but nothing happens except that Soul rolls on the floor by his desk and groans. I walk over and check he hasn't got a gun. I know he can't hurt me with it but I don't want any more sound.

The first guard fell sideways into the room but I have to drag the second in and out of sight from the corridor. It's ridiculously difficult because he's the weight of a small buffalo. I'm using all my strength and can barely budge him, but slowly and with a lot of effort I get him far enough into the office so that I can shut the door.

Soul is stirring. The man who has killed so many, ruined so many lives, tortured so many of his own people, as well as many Black Witches and Half Bloods and me, is at my feet. The Fairborn in my hand is slavering at the sense of blood close by.

Soul doesn't move but I see his eyes open just a little. It's a movement I recognize. The movement of someone used to being careful, to being watched, wanting to know who is watching him, someone whose brain is working hard, on full alert, when it looks like it's only half awake.

I nudge him with the toe of my boot and then feel annoyed with myself for being weak and soft with him and kick him hard.

He doesn't grimace and I think he must be healing straightaway as he turns his face to look at me. Yes, he's healing; I can see a look in his eyes, that thrill, his eyes sparkling brightly for a split second.

"Nathan! What a lovely surprise."

"Is it?"

Soul smiles. "Well, of course it's not so lovely to be lying here on the floor, but I have been looking forward to meeting you again." He raises his head and body further, saying, "Are you alone, Nathan? I don't hear shooting. I don't hear screams. Is this an attack?"

"Where's Jessica?"

"Your sister? *Half*-sister, I should say. She really doesn't like to be called your sister."

"Where is she?"

"I'm really not sure."

"Is she here in the building?"

"She comes and goes . . ."

I kick him again. "Let's try something else then. Where's Annalise?"

Soul looks at me and smiles, then raises himself further to rest on his elbows. He looks at the guards then back to me.

"It seems that you have more than one Gift. You can become invisible. And throw lightning. Gifts that you have obtained from your father. You ate his heart. That must have been difficult. Annalise told me what happened."

"Where is she?"

"Are you here to rescue her or kill her?"

"None of your business. Where is she?"

"Somewhere safe. But it won't be so safe if I tell you, will it?" Soul shuffles up a little further to rest on his hands rather than his elbows.

I put my boot on his chest and push him back down. "If you're not going to answer my questions, there's no point in you being alive."

"If I tell you, what will you do?"

"Talk to her."

"I meant what will you do to me?"

"I'm thinking about that." But I'm not. I realize now I'm not thinking about much at all. There's a smell in the room that reminds me of something. The scent of the forest maybe, but more than that. And then I know: it's the smell of Annalise when we were together, her jumper, and I see her and we're sitting together on the outcrop and she's catching the leaf and I want to stop her leaning over the edge.

I step back from Soul and look toward his desk and the bowl of blue liquid sitting on it. "What is that?" I ask, and move round to look at it a little closer.

Soul doesn't answer and I sense that the blue liquid is giving off fumes that are affecting my concentration, but surely they'll affect Soul as well.

"What does it do?" I ask, and I look around the room for something to cover the bowl with.

"Ah, my new potion. It's rather special and been a long time in production—Mr. Wallend does take his time over things but, then again, perfection can't be rushed. It's rather beautiful to look at, don't you think?" And Soul's now sitting up, I realize, but still he can't harm me. "It's called blue, for obvious reasons."

"What does it do?"

"It has several uses. It can . . . change your mood, bring memories, things like that."

"How?"

"How? Well, how does any potion work? But I think what you're really asking is how is it affecting you now?"

And is it? Affecting me? I remember I was looking for something to cover the bowl with. I walk around the room and from the bookshelf take a large thin book and approach the bowl. The blue liquid seems alive, swirling round and round and drawing me down. I shake my head and look away. Walk around the room again. I need to do something but I'm not sure what. I stop at the door and listen but hear nothing. I've got a book in my hand but I don't know why.

Soul says, "Do you remember that I wanted to give you three gifts on your seventeenth birthday?"

"Yes." I never really understood why.

"I wanted to do that very much. I saw great potential in you, Nathan, and I still do. You are the son of a powerful Black Witch but you are also the son of a powerful White Witch. I know many people ignore that and only see the Black half, but I see both, and I see that the White part of you is good and can be brought to dominate the Black. As it should. If a White Witch became a powerful and significant part of your life, perhaps the White part might rise further in your soul."

"My father gave me three gifts. It didn't make me any Blacker."

"No? Are you being completely honest with me, Nathan? Are you sure it didn't change you?"

And even though a huge part of my brain is saying it's a trick question and I shouldn't even enter into this conversation, another part of me feels I have to answer.

"Maybe it did."

"Maybe it did. But I can see that there's still a lot of White Witch in you. You are battling with yourself even now. Your father would have killed me in a second. But you have not. Even with his influence on you, your White side is strong, fighting back. It's good to see, Nathan. You are, or at least you can be, a good person. You do want to be good, don't you, Nathan?"

"I don't know what I want." And I don't know why I'm saying that. I ask, "The blue . . . is it in the air?"

"Why, yes it is. Quite strong, I should think now; though, of course, I'm immune to it. Or perhaps I should say that I control it and those who breathe it in. Look how it's swirling around, giving off its fumes. Step closer, Nathan, and look."

And I know that's a bad idea but I find I'm moving toward the desk and looking into the potion and watching how it swirls.

"You really are a good person, Nathan. And you could become a truly great witch. I have always seen you as someone with great power. Someone who could help me. And I'd like to help you. The Alliance doesn't care about you, Nathan, but I do. I want very much to see you realize your full potential. Working for me you could do that."

"I don't want to work for you."

"In time you'll come round to my way of thinking. Already you are, Nathan. Already you see how easy it is. How good it feels."

And he's so right. It feels good.

The Beginning of the End

..⋆

I feel relaxed. I've been too tense for too long—my whole
life it seems. It's good to feel the tension ebbing away. I roll
my head and loosen my shoulders. Soul is watching me. I
know I shouldn't trust him, can't trust him, but I can relax;
I'm invulnerable after all. He can't hurt me.

We're standing in front of Soul's desk. I realize he's
taken my arm and I think he's guided me here.

"Give me the book, Nathan."

I look at the book in my hand. I was going to put that
over the bowl to stop the fumes. I remember that.

"Give me the book," Soul says again.

I shouldn't do as he says. I look to the bowl and watch
the liquid move slowly around.

"Thank you," Soul says, and I see that he's holding the
book.

Soul puts the book on the table and reaches for a glass
tumbler. He passes it to me, saying, "Fill this with the blue."

My hand reaches for the tumbler but I don't think I
should do it. I don't want to do it. It's confusing how it's
happening. I'm confused. But doing what Soul tells me feels
good.

The tumbler is in my hand now and dipping into the

blue. The blue laps over my fingers. It's not cold like I was expecting but warm.

"Now drink it, Nathan."

I lift the glass and sip it. It tastes sweet: sweet, warm water. And I expect it to be hard to drink but it's easy. I'm surprised I've swallowed it all down. And the warm feeling spreads down my chest into my stomach and then down my legs and arms and up to my neck and my head. I roll my head again. I'm so relaxed. So warm. Not dizzy, not ill, not out of control, just very relaxed, and yet now I look around the room everything seems very sharp. Colors are brighter and sounds clearer.

"I must say, Nathan, you are cooperating so well."

I look at Soul. He's evil and my enemy but . . . I know I can deal with him later, when I need to.

"Nathan, shall we have a little test? I'd like you to give me the Fairborn."

I look at the knife. My knife. It's still in my right hand. There's no way that I'm giving it to Soul. And I have a strange feeling that I should kill Soul with the Fairborn, but that doesn't seem right anymore. The Fairborn feels odd in my hand now. I don't want it.

"Thank you, Nathan." And Soul is holding the Fairborn. He puts it on the desk. "Now, I'd like you to tell me why you're here."

"To kill you."

"Are you alone?"

And now I think of Gabriel and I know I mustn't tell

Soul about him. I must keep quiet. Not tell him anything. But it almost hurts not to answer his questions.

Soul says, "Answer me, Nathan. Tell me what the Alliance is planning."

"An attack." I know I shouldn't tell him that but thoughts become words and I hear myself say, "They're going to come when . . ." When Gabriel gives the signal but I will not tell him about Gabriel. But it hurts not to say.

Soul asks, "When are they coming, Nathan?"

I shake my head.

"Nathan, I know it's difficult for you. This is a big change for you to deal with. But it's the right thing to do. Tell me what you know."

I look at the Fairborn and I know I should kill Soul with it. I say to Soul, "I'm here to kill you."

"I think you're fighting the blue, Nathan. But I assure you that you'll feel so much better when you surrender to it. We're on the same side now, you and I. I'd like to show you that. Let's go into the next room. Let me show you what's in there."

He walks to the first dead guard and takes his gun, then with his other hand he takes my arm and guides me to the door behind his desk, which he unlocks.

The door swings open and somehow I'm not surprised to see who's in here.

She stands, looking scared, which is good. She's in a cage, which is better. She's wearing a prisoner's yellow overalls and she's chained by her wrists and ankles to the bars on the far side of the cage.

Annalise looks from me to Soul and to the gun in Soul's hand, which sort of makes me want to laugh. The gun is the least of her worries. I send a bolt of lightning to her feet and she screams and jumps back to the far side of the cage, shouting, "Nathan! Please! I never meant—"

I send another bolt of lightning to her feet and again she screams. I send another.

"Nathan, enough," Soul says, and I do as he says and that feels better. Doing what he tells me feels so good and I feel the warmth inside myself. But then I end up looking at Annalise again. She looks terrified.

I tell her, "It's good to see you, Annalise. Good to see you chained up in a cage. Not so good to see you alive but maybe I can do something about that."

And again Soul's voice is in my head, saying, "No, Nathan, not yet. Do as I say."

Annalise tries again. "Nathan, I know I hurt you. I shouldn't have done what I did. I'm sorry. I'm so sorry for what I did to you and to Marcus. I wasn't thinking straight."

"Well, of course she would say that, wouldn't she?" Soul mutters to me, "You can't trust anything Annalise says. But I'll let you decide her fate. She's yours to deal with—when you prove your loyalty to me, Nathan."

"Nathan," Annalise shouts. "Soul used the potion, the blue, on me. I know how it feels—"

"I don't care what he's done to you."

"But he'll use it against you, Nathan. You have to fight it."

I send lightning at her and she screams and jumps back again. "Don't tell me what to do!"

"But that's what Soul is doing, Nathan. Don't let him tell you what to do either."

Soul *is* telling me what to do but it feels good.

Soul touches my arm and says, "Annalise is as full of lies and deception as ever, Nathan. And she is too distracting, I think. I know you'd love to catch up on old times and I promise you can do that later. I'll keep her safe here for you." He takes my arm and guides me to the door, saying, "Come with me, Nathan."

Annalise shouts, "He's telling you what to do, Nathan. Don't take orders from him!"

And I stop. Soul is pulling at my arm. I don't know what to do. Annalise is standing close to the bars, as close as her chains will allow. "Nathan. You don't have to do as I say or as anyone says. Don't do what the blue says is right. Do what you know is right. Deep down."

"Come with me, Nathan." And Soul has me by the arm and is guiding me away. And resisting him hurts my head. I look back to Annalise and she's shouting at me, "Nathan, please! Fight the blue! Hate it! Hate it as much as you hate me!"

I hate her, but I remember I hate Soul too. It's all too complicated.

Annalise shouts. "If you betray the Alliance, you betray

all your friends. They'll all die. Gabriel will die too."

I turn back to her again.

"Don't even say his name!"

Soul touches my arm but I brush him off and growl at him. "No!"

Annalise shouts again. "If you do as Soul says, Gabriel will die. They'll torture him and kill him. Soul wants that. He wants to kill Gabriel."

And I'm so confused. I don't know what to do. But the blue is warm and comforting and I don't know how to fight against it. I can't trust my own body. And there's only one thing I can do, what I should have done from the start. I ask my other self for help.

And he comes.

the man, Soul, backs away. he shouts at us. he has a gun. there's a cage and a girl in it: Annalise. we advance on the man, Soul. our legs feel strong and our neck and back too. we stretch our jaws, getting the feel of them, snapping our teeth together. there's a warmth in our body that we don't like. the man, Soul, is talking. we don't understand his words. he moves to the side, edging away from us. he has a key and he opens the door to the cage. he wants us to go in.

the girl, Annalise, has moved. she's talking too. she's talking quietly, gently. we don't understand her words. she isn't a threat. she doesn't want us in the cage.

the man, Soul, is holding the door open. we move toward it. he's pointing the gun at us.

we are not going in the cage.

Soul shouts again and we run at him and jump at his neck. the sound of gunfire and a scream hits us as we leap through the air, clamping tight on Soul's throat, tasting blood, hearing bone crack. Soul shoots again and again. we stay holding his throat, tasting his blood, his sweat. then he's limp and heavy in our jaws.

Soul's body drops to the floor, blood running out slowly. I'm already transformed back to the human me, and I'm holding the gun. Soul's eyes are fluttering open. He's still alive, just. I heal myself, ridding my system of the residual elements of the blue. I feel clear-headed now and buzzing with healing.

Soul's eyes are on me, still full of silver shards. He's healing too. I point the gun at his temple and as I say "Die" I squeeze the trigger.

I know guards will be coming. They'll have heard the shots.

Annalise is talking to me.

"I'm sorry for what I did, Nathan. Truly."

I need to ignore her, but I can't. I raise the gun and point it at Annalise. She looks frightened, as she should, but she stands her ground. "Nathan, I'm sorry. I know I hurt you. I wish I could undo what I did. I've wished that a thousand times but I can't."

I keep the gun on her. "I don't forgive you, Annalise. My father is dead. Dead, Annalise. And many others from the Alliance are too. All because of you."

"And I have to live with that. But I never meant to hurt you, Nathan."

A Hunter bursts into the room. I'm not a great shot but I don't miss from this distance. Her partner runs in and shoots at me and I get her too.

I hear shouting. More are coming.

I tell Annalise, "Stay there and keep low and you might not get killed."

I go into Soul's office, shutting the door on Annalise. I haven't got the time to think about her now. I drop the gun and consider going invisible but I think it's time to fight openly. I want them to see they can't hurt me. I want them to fear me. I want them to know it's not me who's going to die.

The first Hunters to reach Soul's office run in and I let them shoot. The room is full of noise. It takes them a while to realize that bullets don't work on me. I send lightning back. A couple of grenades roll to me and I pick one up and throw it back so it explodes by the Hunters; the other one explodes to my right and I'm rocked to the side by the force but remain on my feet. And when it begins to go quiet then I shoot out more lightning, filling the room with light and noise and burning electricity. I'm protected inside a cocoon of the amulet's protection. The lightning I produce is bigger and stronger than anything I've ever done before. And then I snap it off and walk out of Soul's office and down the corridor.

One Hunter ahead shoots at me. I send a bolt of lightning at her and she falls to the ground. I feel more power-ful than ever before. It's not the Essence that Ledger was talking about, but I've accessed my Gifts at a stronger level. I'm not sure why, except I know I'm free of Annalise, free of Soul, and all I need to do is kill those in my way. And the more they try to hurt me the stronger I get. I'm not losing my energy but gaining more.

I move to the Council Chamber. The Hunters I come across haven't yet learned that I can't be hurt. They shoot and throw grenades and I send lightning back and they learn to retreat and a path clears before me all the way to the Council Chamber. Here the Councilors have formed a defensive line behind the big table, which is on its side, and some have guns and others use their Gifts—one sends flames, another heavy objects. Soul's throne and the other chairs fly toward me and ricochet away from me at the last second. And I stand there and let it all come, let them see what happens. Let them see they can't stop me.

"Surrender!" I shout. "Surrender now."

And Celia arrives with five of the trainees, guns point-ing. "On your knees," she shouts.

"Soul's dead," I say to Celia and she repeats it as a shout for the whole room to hear. And then arms go up. The sur-render begins and spreads quickly. I see Annalise's father with his hands in the air and I know I could kill him in a second. I go to him and spit at his feet, then turn from him. Celia will deal with him and all the other Council members. I need to concentrate on Jessica and the Hunters.

There's shooting and explosions from other rooms. I must clear the ground floor of Hunters to make sure the Alliance members aren't hurt. And I have to use my lightning carefully now, to ensure I don't hit any of our own fighters. I move from room to room, down each corridor. It's a huge building, lots of rooms, and lots of shooting and smoke and bodies. The Hunters still want to fight.

I've not seen Gabriel and that's bothering me. I know he'd come to me. He's dressed as a Hunter and in all the confusion he could be taken for one of them.

Greatorex and three trainees join me and we clear out the rooms, checking the interlinking passages. And we check as we go that the Hunters we kill really are dead. It takes time until we're satisfied that the ground floor is clear. Two of the trainees have been hit, one killed and one wounded. I tell Greatorex that they should keep back and let me lead.

The first floor is easier. It's a smaller area and the layout is simple. I move through it room by room and by the end of it another ten Hunters are dead. Greatorex and the trainees check the bodies and all the hiding places. I still haven't seen Gabriel but I try not to think about that. I'm in the furthest room when I hear more shooting and I head back along the corridor and catch a glimpse of three Hunters in a room and one of them sees me too.

Jessica!

She shouts at me and points her gun. "You!"

Jessica shoots and I send lightning to her but she's gone. These rooms are all linked and I run along the corridor to the next room expecting to see her but there's no one there. Is there another exit we don't know about?

More shots, and I run back to the corridor. Another of our trainees lies on the floor, close to the stairs. Greatorex and the others have taken cover in the next room.

From up the stairs I hear a Hunter shouting, "Keep back. Don't come after us or more of you will die. We have hostages."

And again I wonder where Gabriel is but I know I shouldn't think about that now.

I tell Greatorex, "I have to go up there."

"They can't hurt you but they can hurt the hostages."

"You have a better idea?"

She shakes her head.

"I think there's some of them in these rooms too," I tell her. "Jessica and two others. Check them out."

I go invisible and move up the stairs.

There's a group of Hunters just inside the first room. I can't see how many but they have their hostage standing in the doorway. It's not Gabriel. It's Adele. There are two guns pointed at her head and there's a thin rope round her neck. I see the skin on her neck is shiny and metallic where the rope is digging in.

But even invisible I can't rescue her without her being shot.

I need to talk to them.

I become visible and the shooting and shouting starts

again but I stay standing at the top of the stairs and wait. Eventually the shooting stops and it's quiet again.

I shout at them, "You can't hurt me. The building is full of Alliance soldiers. Your best option is to surrender. If you kill the hostage I'll kill you all. The only person who will live through this will be me."

I feel a bullet tap my forehead and another my chest. "Soul's dead, and Wallend. I've destroyed the witch's bottles so you can't go invisible, but I guess you've worked that out already. Now you need to accept that you've lost."

Another bullet taps my forehead.

"That's annoying but it's never going to hurt me. Surrender. Now. Let the hostage go."

"We're not surrendering. We're leaving. Let us go and we won't kill this one or the other one. You attack us, any of us, and they die."

And they push the other hostage to the front with Adele. He's dressed in Hunter black, but he looks like himself now, his hair hanging forward, part covering his face, blood from his ear running down his cheek. A gun is rammed up hard against the side of his head and a noose of thin rope is round his neck. The Hunter behind him is half holding him up. He looks at me and I know I'll do anything to get him free. If it's him.

"Speak to me, Gabriel," I say. "Prove it's you."

He leans back against the Hunter behind him and looks at me and his voice is choked and I can hardly hear him as he says, "You've been away a long time. Were you lost?" He sounds lost himself, half strangled and fighting to stay conscious.

"Wounded, not lost," I tell him, but I do feel lost.

One of the Hunters shouts, "We're going through a cut. Try anything, hurt any one of us, and we'll shoot the hostages. We're all going through the cut and we're taking the hostages. Follow and we'll kill them."

The Hunters move into the corridor; there's eight of them. They keep the hostages closest to me as they back away.

And I'm helpless to do anything. The gun is hard against Gabriel's skull. A jolt on the Hunter's finger and he'll be dead. I need to stop time. Then I can pick the Hunters off safely.

I have to concentrate. Rub my hands in a circle, concentrate on stillness, but all I see is Gabriel and the gun against his head. And the Hunters are shouting, "He's doing something! What's he doing?" And now they've backed into the last room on the corridor and I can't concentrate enough to stop time but I can go invisible and race along the corridor. They're in the room, at the far wall covered in bookshelves. And already two of the Hunters are disappearing through the cut. I try again to concentrate, rub my hands and think of stillness, but my eyes are on the Hunters too. Another pair of Hunters at the rear go through the cut. There's just two Hunters: one holding Gabriel and one holding Adele.

I rub my hands. Think of stillness, stillness. Calm, breathe out and hold. But it's not working. I know I'm not concentrating. I can't do it like this.

The Hunter holding Gabriel is reaching down for the cut. I have to risk it. I'm invisible and I run at the Hunter and snap her gun up and away from Gabriel. The gun goes off and I stab the Hunter in the neck with the Fairborn while shooting lightning at the one who has hold of Adele. Gabriel has collapsed to the floor. He's alive. I cut the rope round his neck and he gasps with relief. I look over to Adele. She's unconscious and so is the Hunter who held her.

Gabriel's neck is red raw from the rope. "You OK?" I ask him.

"Shot," he says.

"What?" I rip open his jacket. There's blood on his shirt. "Can you heal?" I ask him.

"I'm trying."

"Greatorex, I need Arran!" I shout. I'm not sure she can hear me but I don't want to leave Gabriel for a second. "Greatorex!" I shout again. "Get Arran!" I turn back to Gabriel and peel open his shirt. There's a lot of blood but the wound doesn't look so bad. It's a long but shallow cut along his side, but the bullet is not in him.

"You'll be OK. It's a flesh wound. The bullet's not in you. Just a bit of Hunter poison."

"So I'll live?"

"Definitely." And I'm shaking with relief. He still needs help, but the poison won't kill him.

"Greatorex! Get Arran up here! Now!" I shout again at the top of my voice.

There's no reply. I listen and am about to shout again when I hear more shooting from down the corridor.

Adele is getting up now, though she's staggering a little. The shooting has stopped.

Gabriel tries to sit up. He says, "I'm not that bad."

I tell him, "Adele can go and find Arran in a minute. Just lie back. If Greatorex doesn't come I'll send her."

"Did you shout for me?" It's Arran. I have my back to the doorway and turn as he comes to us. His eyes meet mine and they're full of concern but then I realize he's wearing Hunter black and he pulls his hand out from behind his back and moving behind Adele he shoots at me.

Jessica!

I send lightning at Jessica but Adele is in the way. Adele turns and shoots as she rolls to the left. Two more Hunters run into the room, shooting and sprinting, going for the cut. I'm trying to cover Gabriel and send out lightning to Jessica again. She's fallen to the floor. As one of the other Hunters goes through the cut, another—the last one—grabs her boot and they both disappear. Jessica is on the ground and I send more lightning at her but still she shoots at me. I feel pressure on my chest and I move to protect Gabriel as I send lightning back and she shoots again and I feel another tap on my shoulder, and another. Jessica is burning now, smoke coming from her clothes and her hair, and then her appearance changes from Arran to herself, and she's still.

Adele is standing now. She's OK.

"Nathan." Gabriel says my name softly and I turn to him.

He's lying on the floor, looking up at me. His eyes meet mine but then I see that I haven't protected him at all. Blood is pouring out of him. Jessica's bullets have deflected off me and hit him in the chest. I'm calling for Arran, the real Arran, and telling Gabriel to heal. He has to heal until Arran can get here. If Arran hurries, Gabriel will be all right. And Gabriel's eyes are open and staring at me and I bend over him and tell him that he'll be all right and Arran will be here any second and he says, "I can't . . ." And I say that he can heal and he must do it and Arran will be here and I see his eyes are not focusing on me now and the blood is pooling around his stomach and I tell him he mustn't leave me, that I couldn't bear it and he knows that. And I interlock my fingers in his and hold them so tight but he doesn't hold me back. His eyes are open and there are still glints of gold spinning in them. Spinning slowly. And I'm shouting for Arran again, screaming for him, and then Arran's with us and Gabriel's chest is sopping with blood and Arran's saying he has to get the bullets out and I'm telling Gabriel that it won't be long and he'll be OK and Arran cuts into Gabriel's chest and digs his fingers in and Gabriel doesn't even flinch but the glints in his eyes move slower and I'm screaming at him not to dare die on me and I'm screaming louder and louder and Arran pulls out a bullet and cuts again and this time Gabriel makes a noise and it's barely there and I know he's just said my name and he looks at me and the golden lights in his eyes twist slower and slower and Arran is saying he can't find the bullet and he thinks there's still another after that.

I have to stop time. If I can stop it, Arran can get the bullet out. I rub my hands and think of stillness but nothing happens and I know it's not working. I try again. Think of nothing, think of stillness. I've got to do this. I've got to be calm and do it. And I move my hands and think of stillness and then it's silent. All is still. But Arran is still too. I don't know how to stop him from falling under the spell and I don't know how to get the bullet out. And I look at Gabriel's eyes and there are two glints left in them, faint but there. And I tell him I love him and I need him and I hold him to me and kiss him but I know I can't keep time still for much longer so I kiss him once more and then time starts and Gabriel looks at me and the glints in his eyes fade until the last one disappears.

Diving off the Cliff

We're in Wales. Arran's with us too. He spends most of his time making potions and the rest of the time trying to make me drink them. They're to keep me calm and make me sleep, but all I want to do is be with Gabriel. When I'm with Gabriel I am calm and I don't need to sleep. Gabriel spends his time swimming and climbing and if I'm sleeping I can't be with him. Today it's sunny and I'm sitting in the sun on the grass by the small lake I told Gabriel about. Gabriel's swimming. He loves it here. It's a good place. Still not hot, but spring's arrived. We've been here two nights, Arran, me, and Gabriel. Arran sleeps in a tent. I've built a den like my father did, getting the brambles to grow up and around us. Me and Gabriel have a fire and some sheepskins. It's good. Not as poor as it looks, as my father said. I can make the brambles grow faster than ever now. I made the den in a few minutes. I know I can use all my father's Gifts easily if I want to, but I don't ever want to use the lightning again. Or even the flames. I light the fire with matches and take my time about it. Gabriel smiles at that. He always smiles.

I sit on the grass and watch Gabriel. There's a rock wall at the side of the lake and he climbs out of the water and up the rock. He's showing off a bit, I think. I like watching him.

I keep my eyes on Gabriel and start to shiver. I put my hands in my pockets and feel a stone. I take it out: it's the white stone for Annalise.

After months of thinking about what I wanted to do to her, how I wanted to punish her, nothing was right. I know my father would have killed her but I think he would understand why I couldn't. I love him and loathe her but still I couldn't kill her.

Celia and Bob have got the truth from Clay and from Annalise. She wasn't ever a spy. Though they tried to use her, she refused. Clay found the Geneva apartment through a Half Blood called Oscar and a Hunter who can detect cuts and a bit of luck. Annalise had nothing to do with it.

Gabriel is almost at the top of the cliff. There's a small overhang that he loves climbing.

I take the white stone out of my pocket, pull my arm back and throw it as far as I can, watching it splash into the water.

Gabriel is at the top. He waves at me and I wave back. He peers over the edge and pretends he's lost his balance and is falling but then turns his fall into a beautiful dive into the water. Definitely showing off. I don't want to take my eyes off him. He's swimming back to the cliff and going to do it again I think.

Arran says, "Someone's coming." But I can't think who it might be or what they'd want and I'm not sure if we should run or get Gabriel or what. Arran moves close to me. "Don't panic. It's fine. I think it's Adele and someone else with her." And he touches my arm and I look at him and then round behind me. There's a long view down into the valley and they're still a way off.

"It's Ledger," I tell Arran, and I can't see anyone else apart from him and Adele.

By the time they get to us I'm breathing normally again and Gabriel is sitting near me.

Arran stands when they get close but I stay sitting with Gabriel. They talk but I don't bother to listen and then Ledger joins us on the grass. He looks the same as when I first met him: that same boy.

He says, "I'm sorry about Gabriel."

And I shake my head because that's not right. I say, "That's not right." And Arran is beside me again, shushing me and saying, "Try to keep calm, Nathan."

"He always wants me to be calm," I tell Ledger.

And I look to Gabriel but he's gone and I say, "Where's Gabriel gone?" And Arran gives me potion to drink and I don't want it so I pour it on the ground. I just want to find Gabriel but I know I have to keep calm or Arran will make me drink it again and I just get tired then and don't see Gabriel at all when I have the potion.

So I try to look normal and meet Arran's eyes.

Ledger says, "I wanted to see you again, Nathan. I've destroyed the bottle. I have your finger. I said I'd return it to you."

And Arran says, "Good."

And I try my best not to look around for Gabriel. But I have a feeling he's gone back for another swim. And Arran and Ledger keep talking about my finger. Then Adele says, "I've seen Celia. She's trying to get things in order. They're setting up a Truth and Reconciliation Council."

Arran says that's a good thing, though I've no idea what it is.

"She says that there are a few Hunters still at large, but most of them have come under her control. She'll lead the Council until the new systems are running properly. Greatorex is leading the new Hunter Alliance. It'll be small and work as a police force like it was originally meant to. They're going to let Black Witches and Half Bloods join."

Adele adds, "Celia suggests you move. She's found a place for Nathan. Wales isn't a good place for him to be. There are still some who might try to harm him. It's too easy to find him here."

"We'll go," Arran says. "Soon."

Ledger kneels down close to me and says, "I came to see you, Nathan, to perhaps persuade you to come with me."

I can't really think of anything to say. Of course I'm not going with him.

Arran says, "It's something to think about, Nathan."

I don't want to think about it.

"Now isn't the time," says Ledger. "I see that, but I wanted to tell you that you will always be welcome."

Arran says, "Thank you."

Ledger reaches out and holds my hand. His is cool. He says, "Nathan, if you need it, the earth will help."

But I'm not listening anymore. I've spotted Gabriel back at the base of the cliff, climbing out of the water, and I know he's going to do another dive and it'll be beautiful.

We leave Wales the next day. We get a train to France and then somewhere else. Gabriel says we should visit Nesbitt in Australia and I tell Arran that and he takes my hand and says, "Gabriel's dead, Nathan. You have to accept that." But that makes no sense to me at all. And Gabriel is sitting on the other side of me, stroking the back of my hand with his fingertips.

The End

I live here now. Alone. I'm a lot better. At least that's what
Arran says, but I'm not so sure. Gabriel is by the river,
twenty meters up from the bank at the edge of the trees and
the beginning of the meadow. He'd like it there. It's facing
south and is sheltered. I dug the grave and took time over
it, making it deep. He was heavy and yet not as tall as I'd
expected. I worked out how to get him in carefully, but still
I had to drag him. He shouldn't be dragged. He shouldn't
be in a hole. He still wears the ring I gave him. He'll have it
forever.

I sit with him quite a bit and tell him what's happening.
I don't really talk out loud much; it sounds odd, noisy and
unnatural. Thinking about it, I haven't spoken out loud for
a while, months I suppose. My voice is hoarse when I try
it. Anyway, I tell him through my thoughts about what's
happening, which is mainly stuff about how blue or gray the
sky is and how the river is flowing faster than the day before
and clearer, and the noise it makes is cleaner too somehow,
and that I saw a water vole and a family of otters. I try not to
tell him about me too much—he knows anyway. He always
has known me better than anyone.

And I miss that, him knowing me. I miss everything

about him. The way he looked at me, the way he looked at others, the way he smiled, laughed, walked, stood. The way he teased me and mocked me. The way he read poetry. The way he spoke. And I'll never again see him look up as I approach or see him smile when he sees me and never again hear him ask if I'm OK and never again touch him and never again have him hold me and kiss me or talk to me or make me laugh. And the thought of that is too much and I turn animal. At least then I forget Gabriel, forget human stuff, and just live and eat and breathe. And yet I want to be human; I want to be thinking of him because then I feel he is alive somewhere, if only in my head.

The nightmares are back. Mainly I dream of Jessica. She points her gun at me and then turns it on Gabriel and shoots him while I'm screaming not to and then I wake up. Even though Gabriel is already dead I still dream of him dying. It shocks me every time.

I don't tell Gabriel about all that. I tell him about being an animal, an eagle. That's the best. I can be a fish too, which is weird and I've only done it twice. The second time was to prove to myself I wasn't too chicken to be a fish, but perhaps I am, 'cause I'm not doing it again. I've never been a chicken.

I've been here a long time now. Gabriel's grave is thick with grass. I think it would be good to have a tree growing by it. An oak, or perhaps a hazel.

Once, in the early days of the Alliance when we were

training, Greatorex and I hid in a stand of close-knit hazel trees. The trainees were supposed to track us down and attack us. They were taking ages about it. Greatorex and I stood there and listened and waited and while we waited a pair of squirrels ran around us up and down the trees.

At last one of the trainees found our trail. We could hear them approaching. They weren't much good, those trainees. And when they were nearly on us and we were ready to attack them, Greatorex was looking at me as if to say "Ready?" and at that moment one of the squirrels ran up my leg and my body, over my shoulder and head, pulling on my hair before he jumped onto a tree. Greatorex started to laugh. She almost gave us away. We still beat the trainees, of course. On the way back to camp she asked me if I could disguise myself as a tree. She was joking, saying, "You're a natural at it."

I didn't reply straightaway.

"You're thinking about it," she asked. "Could you become a tree?"

"I turn into animals; you know that."

"But they're alive like animals. So . . . maybe?"

I lie by Gabriel's grave at night, most of the day too, when I'm not hunting. And I wonder if trees are happy and I think about their roots going deep into the earth and all the elements of earth and life and I think perhaps trees are the happiest of us all and maybe I could be happy too if my roots could find their way to him and somehow his body would find its way into me and some life, some elements, something of him could be in me. And I think of the stake in the earth that went through my heart and Gabriel's hand and for those few moments that we were bound together all was perfect.

I have visitors: Arran and Adele. They bring me things. Food: jam, peanut butter, and fruit. And some clothes: two pairs of jeans, two T-shirts, and a jacket. The jacket's a bit big but it's OK.

Arran looks good, more handsome than ever, I think. And still so gentle and kind. They arrive and Arran does one of his smiles and steps up to me like he wants to hug me, and I feel a panic and I'm not sure why. I shouldn't panic when he's here. I don't know why I do that. I keep thinking about when Gabriel died and the potion Arran gave me. I didn't want it; I wanted Gabriel. And I realize I've got my hand on the Fairborn and Arran stops and Adele looks confused. I would never hurt them; it's just a reaction. I know I have to calm down and I am calm most of the time.

Arran asks me where I live. He asked me that last time he came. I think he's just worried about me.

I have my den, close to Gabriel's grave. It's in a tangle of brambles that are so thick the rain and wind don't get through. If it's wet I sleep in the den and have a fire in there, but I sleep outside most nights. The fire is by the second entrance to the den. I've got three escape tunnels, one short and two very long, and the main wider entrance.

"Can you tell us, Nathan, where you live?" Arran asks again.

"No." I hope that's that subject finished with. I wonder if they'll go soon. But they don't move and they keep on talking, telling me about what's happening in their world. The new Joint Witch Council is a mix of Black Witches, Whites, and Half Bloods. The new Hunter Alliance is a much smaller group, working like a police force, and they have to report on their activities to the Council. It's open to Black Witches but so far none have joined. Arran says someone will eventually. There are three Half Bloods in it. Greatorex is leading the new Hunters. Bob is in the south of France, painting again. Nesbitt is married. I don't ask about that, about anything or anyone; they just tell me.

Then there is a long silence and I'm remembering the time I got angry at Nesbitt, and Gabriel stepped between us. I had the Fairborn in my hand and Gabriel told Nesbitt to leave. I'm not sure where that was. A small castle. It was before Gabriel got his Gift back. Before I'd managed to control my Gift. I had blood and stuff in my hair. Gabriel leaned forward and touched my hair.

Arran says, "We've got news about Annalise too."

I'd almost forgotten her. I wait and look at the trees and see how they move in the wind and collect the sun's warmth.

"She's getting married."

I look at Arran to check he isn't joking. "His name's Ben. He's a fain."

I wonder how long she's known him. But I'm not sure how long I've been here now. How long it is since Gabriel died. I look at my hands and think how old they look but Arran doesn't look much older.

"He's American. They met in New York. Annalise moved there once she'd served her sentence. She served a year in prison." Arran pauses. I know he's wondering what I think of that, but I don't care about it at all, about her at all. He continues. "Annalise told us they're getting married next September. None of us are going; it's a fain ceremony, no witches."

I look back at the trees and the stream and remember lying on the outcrop back at home and waiting for her to come by after school and how I dreamed of marrying her, of living the rest of my life with her. How I knew it was impossible but it made me happy to imagine it and I thought we'd live in a place like this, a beautiful place by a river and we'd live happily ever after. And now she's living in New York with a fain.

I tell Arran, "I've been to New York. I went with Gabriel. We walked to the train station." And I remember Gabriel pulling me into a side street and holding me, kissing me. And we sat in the train station and he told me about his family and I shredded the bags of sugar and I was nervous, really nervous of meeting Ledger, and Gabriel knew that and if I'm quiet now I can almost feel his hand on mine.

Arran pulls out a piece of paper from his jeans pocket. "Annalise sent me this letter telling me about her wedding and I need to tell you about something else."

I look at Arran and tell him, "I went to New York with Gabriel. We caught the train."

"Yes, I know, Nathan, but I need to talk to you about something else." Arran leans closer to me and I can tell he wants to reach over to hold my hand or something, but I don't move. I say, "I think you should go. It'll be dark soon."

"Nathan. I have to tell you about Annalise."

"You should go now. It'll be dark soon. You're slow. You won't find your way in the dark."

"She's had a baby. A son."

"You should go."

"You're his father."

"Arran, please."

"He's called Edge."

I shake my head. Edge is my father's family name, but it's also the name of the hill where Annalise and I used to meet.

Arran continues. "She wasn't allowed to see him while she was in prison, but she has him back now. She says that she's going to tell her son about you. She wants him to know about you."

And I know it's true and I know he'll be better off not knowing about me. But if I was him I would want to know about my father.

I say, "She can tell him about me. She can tell him about

all the people I've killed and hurt. She can tell him who is dead because of me. But she must also tell him that his grandfather is dead because of her. That I had to kill him because of her. She should tell him exactly what I had to do because of her."

Arran nods and we sit for a bit longer and then Arran says, "We'll come again in six months. I miss you, Nathan. I've always missed you."

And he comes and hugs me then and I let him. I don't want to think about Annalise or anything to do with her, but I do want to remember that time in New York at the railway station and Gabriel's fingertips caressing my hand. And I remember how gentle he was and when I open my eyes it's getting dark and Arran and Adele are gone. I follow their tracks. It's a long way to the road but I soon see them. They walk slowly, holding hands, and I keep well back, out of sight, but making sure they find their way OK.

Arran and Adele come twice a year to see me. Spring and autumn. They've been six times so far. They bring me little gifts of food, clothes, and drawing materials. And they bring news of how the new Joint Witch Council is working and how many more Blacks are working in it and how there are problems but each one is dealt with. And they bring news of my son. Annalise writes to Arran and sends photos, which he gives me. My son, Edge, looks like me I think— the same black hair and olive skin, though his eyes don't seem so black. He smiles in the pictures and looks happy. And somehow I know if he ever met me that smile would go. I think of Marcus and how much I wanted to see him when I was a child, and then I remember having to eat his heart and all the terrible things I've done. I don't want my son to ever feel like I do.

I like to see Arran and Adele, and I talk to them OK, I think. Arran says he can tell I'm much better but mostly I don't feel it. I miss Gabriel desperately every day. But I remember what Gabriel told me: that I should use my Gift. So that's what I do and it helps. I transform a lot. I spent a couple of months as a wild dog and felt better for it. Now I go animal for a day or so at a time. I hunt and eat like that. But still every day is agony without Gabriel. And I remember what Ledger told me too. Ledger said the earth would help. I know that's true. I know that I can access the Essence and it's in the earth and in me too. I know what I've got to do, but not yet.

A couple of weeks after Arran's latest visit I have a new visitor. Only she doesn't really visit me; she just turns up and starts building a bloody log cabin. Straightaway I can tell what she's up to: chopping down trees and hauling them around using this great big horse that she's arrived on. It needs to be a big horse to carry her.

I watch from a distance, wondering if she knows I'm watching. She probably sensed it from the first second, knowing her. She still moves the same way: light, almost like a dancer, despite her size.

She makes good progress on the cabin over the next month. It won't be big but there is only her. Two rooms, I think. She cooks out front every evening. She's brought lots of tinned and packaged stuff, but I guess that making a cabin is enough work to do without having to bother about hunting and fishing too.

I've not spoken to her yet, not gone to see her. I'll take her a rabbit or two tomorrow.

I Read to Him

Out beyond ideas of wrongdoing and rightdoing,
there is a field. I'll meet you there.

When the soul lies down in that grass,
the world is too full to talk about.
Ideas, language, even the phrase *each other*
does not make any sense.

Jelaluddin Rumi

I never had children. I never wanted them, and Nathan isn't
my son but I feel a responsibility for him. I'll always feel that,
perhaps even more than if he was my son. I will always be
his teacher and guardian. I saw him up close a few days after
I got here from London, after I handed over all my responsi-
bilities to the new Council Leader. I hadn't seen him in three
years. He'd changed. Older obviously, but wilder and more
distant. I still remember the first time I saw him and the little
runt of a boy he was then. His eyes never changed, though:
dark and strange.

He brought two rabbits on his first visit here. As he

walked up he held them out to me for a second, not so much offering as showing, and I said they'd be more use cooked. Then he let them drop to the ground, got the fire going, and sat in front of the half-built cabin and skinned the rabbits. He made a stew with some vegetables I had stored—onions, carrots—and he picked some wild garlic and thyme. It was good. I remembered the bread he used to make, back when I used to keep him in the cage—he was good at that too.

His sleeves were rolled up as he worked. I'd almost forgotten how bad his scars were. Terrible scars and the ugly black tattoos. While the stew was cooking he watched me work and then we ate and later he left. He didn't speak at all.

That was spring last year. It's late summer now. The cabin is finished and I've added a range and a bed. Every month I go for provisions and one time Nathan asked me to get him paper and pencils. He said Arran had brought him some but he wanted more. He drew me and the cabin and the chickens, doing several pictures a day, almost like a record of life here. He asked me to look after the drawings and at first I thought he meant to keep them indoors, out of the rain, but he didn't mean that. He said, "They're for my son, for Edge."

He'd never spoken about his son before. I tried asking once if he wanted to see him but he just said, "I can't." He started doing portraits then. He did me first, and of course he did Gabriel too, looking as handsome as he ever was.

And then he did all his family: Arran, Deborah, his grand-mother, and even Jessica. On each one he wrote as carefully and neatly as he could the name of the person, and in the bottom corner: "For Edge. From Nathan."

I've got so many portraits now: Van, Nesbitt, Pilot, Bob, Ellen, Greatorex, Adele, even Mercury, and many more. All from memory and all excellent. Finally he drew Marcus, looking very much like an older version of Nathan, but he never drew himself. One day I suggested that he do a self-portrait but he drew a landscape instead. His land-scapes always used to be weaker, but this was beautiful: the river here and the hills beyond, the meadow in the fore-ground and a small gnarled tree standing alone.

I'd seen where he lived from a distance but had never been close. I knew he didn't want me there. I took some eggs one day when I'd got the chickens and I thought maybe I'd be allowed nearer, but he just stood there as if he was protecting his home, and the way he stood I knew I wasn't welcome, not on his territory. I shouted, "Eggs!" And put them on the ground. I wasn't sure what to do and so I saluted, in the old style, like we did when we qualified as Hunters. I haven't done that for years. He didn't salute back; Nathan wouldn't ever do that, but he raised his hand. I think that gesture said more than all the words he'd spo-ken to me since I arrived.

On Midsummer Day he came over. That's his birthday. We had a chicken. He killed and plucked it, all as efficiently as ever. We ate and talked about the chickens and the eggs and my new pigs, two small Gloucesters. I'll slaughter one before winter. He suggested keeping bees, which I was thinking of doing, but it'll have to be next year now. I'll look into getting a couple of hives.

I wasn't sure he knew what day it was, so after the meal I poured us out a tea and was thinking what to say. He spoke, though. He said, "It's the longest day today: my birthday."

"Yes," I said.

"I'm twenty-two." He sipped his tea and then said, "Sometimes I feel like fifty-two."

I think he was joking. He seemed much happier than I'd seen him and as fit and healthy as ever, more than ever. Lean and muscular and lethal.

I said, "I'm fifty-two and feel like twenty-two." Though perhaps I'm feeling more like forty-two, a good forty-two.

He did that look of his, wanting to laugh but going completely blank. He said, "Don't get too excited; you look like sixty-two." Then he did give me one of his sarcastic smiles and said, "And as usual I'm being overly kind."

He got up to leave, saying, "You should do some exercise, go for a run, do some press-ups. You'd enjoy it."

"So should you."

He started to walk away and then he stopped and said, "Ledger told me he thought the Essence was in the earth, and he's right, but it's in us as well and when we connect the two then we can access it, and anyone who's connected to it." Then he said something else, very quietly, something like, "Wounded, not lost."

The next morning I didn't see him, or that night or the next day. He was apt to disappear for days at a time so I didn't think much of it. But after a week I thought I'd check it out, just in case; I'm not sure in case of what. I went up the grass slope close behind his den. I'd never been there before. The view is perfect. The river bends and the hills are gentle, the shades of green numerous and the sound of the river and trees and birds are clear. It's the exact place in the drawing he made. And then I saw the tree and I realized what he'd done.

I go up there every day now, to read. I read aloud to him like I used to do, mostly poetry these days. I sit on the grass by the hazel tree that's in the meadow. It's different from the other trees and apart from them; it's not so old, not so tall, but horribly scarred.

Acknowledgments

I can hardly believe that I'm writing these words at the end of *Half Lost*, the final book in the Half Bad trilogy. When I started writing *Half Bad*, the possibility of being a published writer seemed so unattainable that it was too ridiculous to even mention to most of my family and friends, and now here I am (it seems like no time later) with a third book about to go to the printers. There are so many people to thank and I will endeavor to do it in person where possible, as here I can only mention a few people who have helped me along the way. Help comes in many forms, from critical editorial advice to an encouraging tweet, and I really do appreciate it all.

Throughout my Half Bad experience, I've had support, encouragement, and advice from a great team of people. Thanks to Claire Wilson of RCW (always so cool and calm); Ben Horslen, my (perfectly tactful) editor, and all the team at Penguin Random House UK; Ken Wright and Leila Sales, my US editors; and all at Viking in the US. Thanks also to all the editors, translators, and publishers around the world.

Special thanks to all the designers who have created the gorgeous covers in the series and especially for the cover of *Half Lost*—Tim Green from Faceout Studio, Deborah Kaplan, Dani Calotta, and Jacqui McDonough.

Thanks to all Half Bad fans around the world; it's great to hear of your love for the Half Bad world. Damien Glynn, @damog7 on Twitter, suggested that Adele's Gift be the ability to turn her skin metal-hard temporarily. Thanks, Damien, and everyone else for their suggestions.

And last but definitely not least: my thanks to Indy for putting up with me when I'm on the computer AGAIN!!!

* * *

The poem "Out beyond ideas of wrongdoing and right-doing" by Jelaluddin Rumi is from *The Essential Rumi*, translated by Coleman Barks.

Ledger's words "There's no truth, only perspective" seems to be a quote from Flaubert, though I misquoted Nietzsche's "There's no truth, only perception" and found I preferred it.

The quote "The only thing necessary for the triumph of evil is that good men do nothing" is most often attributed to Edmund Burke.

* * *

And finally, I've loved writing about the world of Half Bad, Nathan has been a huge part of my life for four years and he probably always will be—but for now I'm going to write about something else.

TURN THE PAGE FOR AN EXCERPT FROM
THE BOOK THAT STARTED IT ALL:

The Trick

•·•·•

There's these two kids, boys, sitting close together, squished in by the big arms of an old chair. You're the one on the left.

The other boy's warm to lean close to, and he moves his gaze from the telly to you sort of in slow motion.

"You enjoying it?" he asks.

You nod. He puts his arm round you and turns back to the screen.

Afterward you both want to try the thing in the film. You sneak the big box of matches from the kitchen drawer and run with them to the woods.

You go first. You light the match and hold it between your thumb and forefinger, letting it burn right down until it goes out. Your fingers are burnt, but they hold the blackened match.

The trick works.

The other boy tries it too. Only he doesn't do it. He drops the match.

Then you wake up and remember where you are.

The Cage

•˙•˙•˙

The trick is to not mind. Not mind about it hurting, not mind about anything.

The trick of not minding is key; it's the only trick in town. Only this is not a town; it's a cage beside a cottage, surrounded by a load of hills and trees and sky.

It's a one-trick cage.

Push-ups

•.•••

The routine is okay.

Waking up to sky and air is okay. Waking up to the cage and the shackles is what it is. You can't let the cage get to you. The shackles rub but healing is quick and easy, so what's to mind?

The cage is loads better now that the sheepskins are in. Even when they're damp they're warm. The tarpaulin over the north end was a big improvement too. There's shelter from the worst of the wind and rain. And a bit of shade if it's hot and sunny. Joke! You've got to keep your sense of humor.

So the routine is to wake up as the sky lightens before dawn. You don't have to move a muscle, don't even have to open your eyes to know it's getting light; you can just lie there and take it all in.

The best bit of the day.

There aren't many birds around, a few, not many. It would be good to know all their names, but you know their different calls. There are no seagulls, which is something to think about, and there are no vapor trails either. The wind is usually quiet in the predawn calm, and somehow the air feels warmer already as it begins to get light.

You can open your eyes now and there are a few minutes to savor the sunrise, which today is a thin pink line stretching along the top of a narrow ribbon of cloud draped over the smudged green hills. And you've still got a minute, maybe even two, to get your head together before she appears.

You've got to have a plan, though, and the best idea is to have it all worked out the night before so you can slip straight into it without a thought. Mostly the plan is to do what you're told, but not every day, and not today.

You wait until she appears and throws you the keys. You catch the keys, unlock your ankles, rub them to emphasize the pain she is inflicting, unlock your left manacle, unlock your right, stand, unlock the cage door, toss the keys back to her, open the cage door, step out—keeping your head down, never look her in the eyes (unless that's part of some other plan)—rub your back and maybe groan a bit, walk to the vegetable bed, piss.

Sometimes she tries to mess with your head, of course, by changing the routine. Sometimes she wants chores before exercises but most days it's push-ups first. You'll know which while still zipping up.

"Fifty."

She says it quietly. She knows you're listening.

You take your time as usual. That's always part of the plan.

Make her wait.

Rub your right arm. The metal wristband cuts into it when the shackle is on. You heal it and get a faint buzz.

You roll your head, your shoulders, your head again and then stand there, just stand there for another second or two, pushing her to her limit, before you drop to the ground.

one	Not minding
two	is the trick.
three	The only
four	trick.
five	But there are
six	loads of
seven	tactics.
eight	Loads.
nine	On the look-out
ten	all the time.
eleven	All the time.
twelve	And it's
thirteen	easy.
fourteen	'Cause there ain't
fifteen	nothing else
sixteen	to do.
seventeen	Look out for what?
eighteen	Something.
nineteen	Anything.
twenty	N
twenty-one	E
twenty-two	thing.
twenty-three	A mistake.
twenty-four	A chance.

twenty-five	An oversight.
twenty-six	The
twenty-seven	tiniest
twenty-eight	error
twenty-nine	by the
thirty	White
thirty-one	Witch
thirty-two	from
thirty-three	Hell.
thirty-four	'Cause she makes
thirty-five	mistakes.
thirty-six	Oh yes.
thirty-seven	And if that mistake
thirty-eight	comes to
thirty-nine	nothing
forty	you wait
forty-one	for the next one
forty-two	and the next one
forty-three	and the next one.
forty-four	Until
forty-five	you
forty-six	succeed.
forty-seven	Until
forty-eight	you're
forty-nine	free.

You get up. She will have been counting, but never letting up is another tactic.

She doesn't say anything but steps toward you and back-hands you across the face.

fifty   "Fifty."

After push-ups it's just standing and waiting. Best look at the ground. You're by the cage on the path. The path's muddy, but you won't be sweeping it, not today, not with this plan. It's rained a lot in the last few days. Autumn's coming on fast. Still, today it's not raining; already it's going well.

"Do the outer circuit." Again she's quiet. No need to raise her voice.

And off you jog . . . but not yet. You've got to keep her thinking you're being your usual difficult-yet-basically-compliant self and so you knock mud off your boots, left boot-heel on right toe followed by right boot-heel on left toe. You raise a hand and look up and around as if you're assessing the wind direction, spit on the potato plants, look left and right like you're waiting for a gap in the traffic and . . . let the bus go past . . . and then you're off.

You take the drystone wall with a leap to the top and over, then across the moorland, heading to the trees.

Freedom.

As if!

But you've got the plan, and you've learned a lot in four months. The fastest that you've done the outer circuit for her is forty-five minutes. You can do it in less than that, forty maybe, 'cause you stop by the stream at the far end and rest and drink and listen and look, and one time you managed to get to the ridge and see over to more hills, more trees and a loch (it might be a lake but something about the heather and the length of summer days says you're in Scotland).

Today the plan is to speed up when you're out of sight. That's easy. Easy. The diet you're on is great. You have to give her some credit, 'cause you are super healthy, super fit. Meat, veg, more meat, more veg, and don't forget plenty of fresh air. Oh this is the life.

You're doing okay. Keeping up a good pace. Your top pace.

And you're buzzing, self-healing from her little slap; it's giving you a little buzz, buzz, buzz.

You're already at the far end, where you could cut back to do the inner circuit which is really half the outer circuit. But she didn't want the inner circuit and you were going to do the outer whatever she said.

That's got to be the fastest yet.

Then up to the ridge.

And let gravity take you down in long strides to the stream that leads to the loch.

Now it gets tricky. Now you are just outside the area of the circuit and soon you will be well outside it. She won't know that you've gone until you're late. That gives you twenty-five minutes from leaving the circuit—maybe thirty, maybe thirty-five, but call it twenty-five before she's after you.

But she's not the problem; the wristband is the problem. It will break open when you go too far. How it works, witchcraft or science or both, you don't know, but it will break open. She told you that on Day One and she told you the wristband contains a liquid, an acid. The liquid will be released if you stray too far and this liquid will burn right through your wrist.

"It'll take your hand off," was how she put it.

Going downhill now. There's a click . . . and the burning starts.

But you've got the plan.

You stop and submerge your wrist in the stream. The stream hisses. The water helps, although it's a strange sort of gloopy, sticky potion and won't wash away easily. And more will come out. And you have to keep going.

You pad the band out with wet moss and peat. Dunk it under again. Stuff more padding in. It's taking too long. Get going.

Downhill.

Follow the stream.

The trick is not to mind about your wrist. Your legs feel fine. Covering lots of ground.

And anyway losing a hand isn't that bad. You can replace it with something good . . . a hook . . . or a three-pronged claw like the guy in *Enter the Dragon* . . . or maybe something with blades that can be retracted, but, when you fight, out they come, *ker-ching* . . . or flames even . . . no way are you going to have a fake hand, that's for sure . . . no way.

Your head's dizzy. Buzzing too, though. Your body is trying to heal your wrist. You never know, you might get out of this with two hands. Still, the trick is not to mind. Either way, you're out.

Got to stop. Douse it in the stream again, put some new peat in and get going.

Nearly at the loch.

Nearly.

Oh yes. Bloody cold.

You're too slow. Wading is slow but it's good to keep your arm in the water.

Just keep going.

Keep going.

It's a bloody big loch. But that's okay. The bigger the better. Means your hand will be in water longer.

Feeling sick . . . ughhh . . .

Shit, that hand looks a mess. But the acid has stopped coming out of the wristband. You're going to get out. You've beaten her. You can find Mercury. You will get three gifts.

But you've got to keep going.

You'll be at the end of the loch in a minute.

Doing well. Doing well.

Not far now.

Soon be able to see over into the valley, and—

The
HALF BAD TRILOGY
BY SALLY GREEN

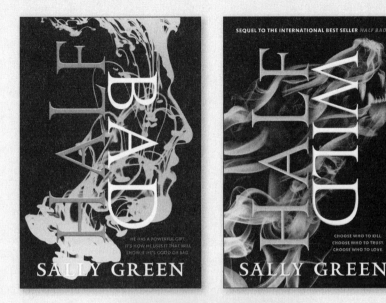

SALLY GREEN

HE HAS A POWERFUL GIFT.
IT'S HOW HE USES IT THAT WILL
SHOW IF HE'S GOOD OR BAD.

SEQUEL TO THE INTERNATIONAL BEST SELLER *HALF BAD*

SALLY GREEN

CHOOSE WHO TO KILL.
CHOOSE WHO TO TRUST.
CHOOSE WHO TO LOVE.

FINALE TO THE INTERNATIONAL BEST SELLING SERIES *HALF BAD*

SALLY GREEN

FIGHT FOR FREEDOM.
SURRENDER TO LOVE.